Incidents in the
Rue Laugier

by the same author

A START IN LIFE
PROVIDENCE
LOOK AT ME
HOTEL DU LAC
FAMILY AND FRIENDS
A MISALLIANCE
A FRIEND FROM ENGLAND
LATECOMERS
LEWIS PERCY
BRIEF LIVES
A CLOSED EYE
FRAUD
A FAMILY ROMANCE
A PRIVATE VIEW

Incidents in the Rue Laugier

Anita Brookner

JONATHAN CAPE
LONDON

First published in 1995

1 3 5 7 9 10 8 6 4 2

© Anita Brookner

Anita Brookner has asserted her right
under the Copyright, Designs and Patents Act 1988
to be identified as the author of this work

First published in the United Kingdom in 1995 by Jonathan Cape
Random House, 20 Vauxhall Bridge Road, London SW1V 2SA

Random House Australia (Pty) Limited
20 Alfred Street, Milsons Point, Sydney,
New South Wales 2061, Australia

Random House New Zealand Limited
18 Poland Road, Glenfield,
Auckland 10, New Zealand

Random House South Africa (Pty) Limited
PO Box 337, Bergvlei, 2012 South Africa

Random House UK Limited Reg. No. 954009

A CIP catalogue record for this book
is available from the British Library

Papers used by Random House UK Limited are natural,
recyclable products made from wood grown in sustainable forests.
The manufacturing processes conform to the environmental
regulations of the country of origin.

ISBN 0-224-04124-X

Printed and bound in Great Britain by
Mackays of Chatham PLC

I

My mother read a lot, sighed a lot, and went to bed early. She had been a Maud Gonthier, from Dijon, brought up to expect something better than the provincial restrictions which had stifled her as a girl. She never found it, at least not with my father. Boredom softened her slightly cross face into a contemplative frown, as if she were puzzled, as if she had mislaid something of considerable significance. My father, a disappointed man, left her to her own devices, thinking she had brought these troubles on herself. In fact he was jealous of her, of her silence, her composure; he even envied the melancholy, which conferred on her a distinction which nature had denied to him, although secretly he thought of himself as an unusual character, as we all do. He was a secondhand bookseller, with a small shop in Denbigh Street. My mother, who, as a girl, had hoped to marry into literary circles, had been agreeably alerted when told of this. When she saw the shop she felt an immense disappointment. *Ça fait prolo*, she thought, and hoped that her expression gave nothing away to the man she had somehow agreed to marry. He knew, of course, being sensitive to slights. Tiresome though it is to have to record this, he never quite forgave her. Theirs was an ordinary marriage, cemented by decorum, by custom, eventually by loyalty. My mother had a more mature attitude than my father, who never quite eliminated a certain edginess from his behaviour. He suppressed this as best he could, and in the end it could only be seen in the wolfishness of his smile. My mother read the classics and kept her own counsel.

Please accept me as an unreliable narrator. My parents died years ago, and I left home long before I lost them. When I was clearing my mother's flat (she survived my father by only four years) I found a notebook from which I have constructed the story which follows. What I found was not the diary, written in a faded hand, beloved by novelists. This was nothing more than a small spiral-bound pocket-book, of the sort to be found in any French stationers, with squared greyish paper and a shiny checked cover. In fact I did not find this for some time: I had put the suitcase containing my mother's few personal effects — her birth and marriage certificates, a few letters from myself, a rose pink silk kimono which I had not seen before — into the back of a cupboard, half meaning to leave it there, unwilling, for some reason, to disturb her shade, or the memory of her quietly reading. I only took it out again when I acquired more suitcases of my own and needed the space. The notebook was old, slightly bent at the corner, the pages stuck together. There were only a few notations, apparently written on the same day. '*Dames Blanches. La Gaillarderie. Place des Ternes. Sang. Edward.*' Further down the same page, and written with a different pen, a recipe for Sauce mousseline. Then a short list of book titles. Last of all Proust's opening line: '*Longtemps, je me suis couché de bonne heure.*' This I thought to be an adequate epitaph for a woman whom I remembered as infinitely reserved, and who, as far as I could judge, had left no very profound trace, apart from the usual memories, on my life.

But recently I have found myself repeating some of my mother's attitudes — reading, sighing, going to bed early — and I began to wish for clarification. It seemed to me impossible that a life could be covered by those so brief

2

notations, yet I was never in any doubt that it was in fact her life that was so covered. This muteness had a sort of elegance about it, unusual in these days when women have so much to say for themselves, and my mother was an elegant woman. It was entirely characteristic that she should not expand on what was little more than a code. Perhaps I regretted the fact that my mother never spoke of herself, or indeed spoke much at all unless she had something definite to impart. I found her dignified, admirable, but ultimately frustrating, at least to the adult I had become; when I was a child I seem to remember that we loved each other without restraint, but there were no confessions, no confidences, a fact I now find puzzling. What remained of her was somehow contained in those few words in the small notebook, written in her purposeful hand, with some deliberation, or so it seemed to me, at least collectedly, and indeed posthumously, for none of these words had any connection with the life I had known, and that she had presumably known as well. Only one did I recognise, but out of context. Something predated me, and I had no idea what it was.

Above all I was intrigued by the word 'Sang'. What had blood to do with my mother's distant and uncommunicative life? We had, as far as I could see, little in common: in fact I may even have removed myself deliberately from her infinite discretion, as did my father. Like my father I found her apparent serenity irritating, yet I have reached the age when a woman begins to perceive that she is growing into the person whom she least plans to resemble: her mother. When I thought of her in later life I habitually experienced a slight sinking of the heart, an involuntary lowering of the spirits, occasioned perhaps by a comparison between our two destinies, hers so fixed, so immutable, mine quite deliberately volatile. Something about her very immutability — there, on the sofa, in the drawing-room of our flat in Tedworth Square — commanded my respect, although the fate of women fifty years ago is something of a closed book to me. Marriage had seemed to be her destiny, as it still was for most women in those days, as it had no doubt been that of her own mother, whom of course I knew. It seems odd that she maintained a distance between herself and my father, although she was a faithful and diligent wife, observant in those matters which my own generation has learned to neglect.

I never discovered whether she had ever loved him; I rather thought not. Yet she was a moral woman, and I should have thought her a stranger to any form of calculation. He, on the other hand, was often quite harsh, and yet I am left with the impression that he loved her, not in any idealistic or worshipful sense, but with the raw force of his rather frustrated nature. They were on an uneasy footing. Only my mother's calm defused a potentially disturbing situation.

There were no arguments. There was no quarrel. And yet it always seemed to me that some gigantic quarrel must have taken place in the past, long before I knew either of them. All this is speculation, of course. Of my parents' secret life I am the only manifestation. Yet something went on before, something that created attitudes which I have inherited. The known part of a life is often misleading, a disguise. I now wish that my mother had been happier, or had had a memory of past happiness to sustain her. My impression is that she renounced her life long before it ended. Yet she kept the little notebook, with its inscrutable code, just as she kept the beautiful silk kimono, which she certainly never wore at home. I found to my surprise that as I contemplated this evidence my curiosity turned to sadness, for I realised that she was doomed to remain a stranger, had indeed elected to be a stranger, bequeathing me only little gestures, such as shading her eyes when she looked up from her book, as if the light of reality were too harsh, and those sighs, which I am told I utter without knowing.

I do not appear in the story that follows, or at least only

4

inadvertently. It is a fabrication, one of those by which each of us lives, and as such an enormity, nothing to do with the truth. But perhaps the truth we tell ourselves is worth any number of facts, verifiable or not. This unrecorded story — unrecorded for a very good reason — is a gesture only, a gesture towards my mother, whom I have come to resemble, and who told me nothing either of what had happened, or what had failed to happen, and how she came to live with us, so far from home.

At the time of her marriage Maud Gonthier had not been much interested in matters of class, ancestry, or status, believing herself to be above such matters, or if not above, untouched by them. She had known little of the world beyond Dijon, and little of her reduced family beyond her mother and the dimming memory of a young father, who, in the middle of playing with her, would be shaken by a cough and would have to sit down with a handkerchief to his lips.

Pierre-Yves Gonthier, who died of tuberculosis, had been a conscientious boy from a poor background, who, by dint of hard work, application, and family piety, had obtained a post at the Prefecture and in time fulfilled his mother's most cherished ambitions. He thus belonged to the most respected caste in France, the civil service, and although his work in the Bridges and Highways department was routine and undemanding he was always conscious of the dignity of office, as if he were the Prefect himself, was always impeccably turned out in a grey suit and a white shirt laundered by his mother, and was accepted by his colleagues with mild affection but with little interest. He was grateful to the authorities who had appointed him for a more personal reason: without this badge of respectability he would have been unable to marry Nadine Debureau, whose father, a doctor and a tyrant, was conscious of such distinctions and would not have countenanced a son-in-law who worked in his mother's shop, an unfortunately modest affair, far from the commercial centre of town, and doing a not very active trade in layettes and baby clothes.

Nadine, a handsome girl, longing to get away from her father, and from her elder sister, and resembling in fact her dead mother, was aware of Pierre-Yves's admiration and was eager to encourage it. She therefore attended all those functions at the Prefecture to which her father, as a local worthy, was invited. Within six months the young man had made his request and had seen it accepted. The father thought it better to acquiesce: his idea was to clear his house of daughters as soon as he could — he had an acquaintance ready to take the elder girl, Germaine, off his hands — so that he could settle down to a bachelor existence, could be looked after by a housekeeper, could play bridge twice a week at the Café Riche, and drink as much as he liked. This he would achieve to his eventual satisfaction, although along the way the rewards were not as fulfilling as he had envisaged. Germaine, once married to an army doctor with the rank of colonel, and satisfactorily removed to a small manor house in the Brie region, was seen only on rare visits; the younger girl, Nadine, continued to live in Dijon. The doctor failed to take his own advice and slowly turned purple with incipient apoplexy. He consoled himself by arranging for the proceeds of his house to be divided between the two girls after his death. This, he thought, absolved him from any accusation of selfishness.

The young couple set up house in a flat in the rue des Dames Blanches, a property which had belonged to Nadine's mother and which had been rented out by the doctor to an elderly woman of some means. Shortly before the wedding this woman had announced her intention of going to live with her daughter in the south, and the doctor could hardly refuse to hand it over to the bride and bridegroom, although he had vaguely intended to occupy it himself when he retired. The flat was not in good order, as the elderly tenant, in the way of old people, had thought it would serve its turn until she went south: the kitchen was gloomy, the bathroom rudimentary, but the salon, with its red striped walls, was rather grand, and its windows looked out onto the street, a short quiet grey street, with, in the distance, the imposing bulk of the Musée des Beaux Arts.

It took them five years to decorate and furnish the flat to their satisfaction, by which time there was a small child. Pierre-Yves, with the heightened sensibility of the tubercular, would gaze at the child with tears in his eyes: already he looked back with longing to the early days of his marriage, when he and Nadine, whom he called Didine, would walk arm-in-arm around the Place Darcy and down the rue de la Liberté, nodding to acquaintances, and deciding that there was nothing in the shops that they wanted beyond what they already had. He would look back on those days as if centuries had passed, as if he were an old man, although he was young, and did not know of his illness. The child was almost too much happiness to bear; he at least did not think that he could bear it. His joy turned to discomfort, and then to constriction; somehow he managed to conceal this from colleagues, being less disastrously stimulated during the daytime, among the Bridges and Highways, than at night, when he grew hot and restless. It was his superior who saw to it that he enter a sanatorium in the Haute-Savoie: the case was not uncommon, and there was a good chance of recovery. But he knew, as he waved goodbye to his wife and daughter, who saw him off at the station, that he would never see his home again, and from that moment slipped down quite rapidly towards his death.

At the funeral his mother and Nadine's father, who barely acknowledged one another, seemed to lay a burden of accusation on the widow. The mother clearly believed

8

that if he had not wasted himself in marital excess her son would be with her still; the father felt only contempt for a weakling with an impaired constitution. He himself was to die within the year, but succeeded in hiding from himself the undoubted dangers of his chosen way of life. The little gathering dispersed, leaving the cemetery to the sun and shadows of an ironically brilliant October day. There was little conversation.

In the rue des Dames Blanches wine was served, but no meal: there was disaffection in the air, and Nadine would have none of it. She had loved her husband, somewhat to her surprise, and although she resented his tragedy she was marked by it. In the curious excitement of his illness he had loved her more passionately than she had ever imagined possible, and she knew that she would never be loved like that again. 'Not in this life anyway,' she told herself bleakly, begrudging God His monopoly of the next. She was impressed by this love, although not altogether grateful for it: apart from the child, Maud, she had little enough to show for it, no money, apart from her husband's pension, and the prospect of a year's mourning. It was not until her father died, and she received her share of the proceeds from the sale of his property, that she was able to contemplate her life. As matters turned out she was in a position to give her daughter a first-class education at the most exclusive convent in town, and thus to ensure that she made useful friends. For the money would not last indefinitely, and before it ran out Maud would have to marry, and to marry well. She calculated that this might happen when Maud would be eighteen or nineteen. After that she would live on the pension, which would be enough for one, but not for two.

'Did you know the house was mortgaged?' asked Germaine on the telephone.

'No, of course not. You were closer to him than I was; he never confided in me.'

'Nor, apparently, in me. There will be less money than

9

we are entitled to expect. I believe there was a woman, too . . .'

'I don't want to hear any more.'

'Will you be able to manage?'

'I shall have to.'

'Of course, there are only two of you.'

Whereas you still have your husband, thought Nadine, although she did not envy her sister that particular husband, who was stout and heavy and over-confident and unsympathetic.

'Xavier is well?' she enquired. 'Robert is still in Germany, I suppose.'

'I am expecting him back next month. Yes, Xavier is very well. And Maud?'

'Maud is very well too.'

'You'll come to us in August?'

'We shall look forward to it.'

'You yourself are keeping well, I hope, Nadine?'

'Oh yes, I am perfectly fine.'

'You would let me know . . .'

'Of course. Don't worry, Germaine. And thank you. Goodbye.'

Although less favoured by their father, Nadine had always known that she was the prettier of the two sisters. But although she had married first she had not done so well for herself in material terms. This she had not previously regretted. Yet there had been a note of patronage in that telephone conversation, and she knew that if illness struck or if she were to have any sort of accident she would have to rely on her sister's generosity. This had never been much in evidence, but might seek now to advertise itself. Compressing her thin lips even more firmly, Nadine resolved never to have recourse to this particular form of charity. She would work in a shop, if necessary, she thought. But this of course was not a serious proposition. She had inherited her father's contempt for trade, had discerned something timid, self-effacing and servile about her mother-in-law on the few occasions when she had been obliged to meet her; she herself was more combative. At the same time she felt bleak with the knowledge that no one would come to her rescue. For the moment they could manage, and, more important, keep up appearances. That meant meat every day, if only a small cutlet, so as not to let the shopkeepers know that money was short. That meant the dressmaker every eighteen months, to add something well-made to the small but careful wardrobe. That meant the services of the concierge, Mme Fernandez, twice a week, so as to maintain her status in the building. That meant that Maud must always be in a position to do the same as her friends, to join school parties to places of artistic or cultural interest, to go skiing in the winter, to accept invitations to the flat in Paris or the villa in Corsica of her best friend Julie. This, however, although there had been only two such invitations, was more problematic. Perhaps she might ask Germaine if Maud could bring a friend, when they went to stay, as they usually did, in August?

'Oh, no,' said Maud. 'There is nothing to do there. Besides, they go to Corsica in the summer, and Julie wants me to go again.'

'I'm afraid that will not be possible,' said Nadine, compressing her lips once again. 'Your aunt would think it very rude.' And I am reduced to using her as an excuse, she thought, because I cannot offer hospitality. She tried to think with disdain of Julie's father, a vulgar cheerful man who owned the second-best restaurant in Dijon, and of his wife, equally vulgar, equally cheerful, and failed. They were kind: they offered nothing but kindness and wanted nothing in return. They thought that Julie should emulate Maud's natural hauteur, which was modelled on that of her mother, but they did not envy Maud's way of life or her circumstances, which they saw through with a clarity which was perhaps denied to the butcher, the dressmaker and the concierge. All of which Nadine knew.

It stiffened her spine and merely added a further dignity to her deportment.

In the years following her husband's death Nadine, no longer Didine, assumed an outward appearance of confidence and also of an austerity which was not becoming in a woman who was still young but who lacked admirers, perhaps because any man who was likely to approach her was also likely to be chilled by her unsmiling seriousness. She had always looked older than her age; now, at thirty-eight, conscious of her precarious situation and of the lack of anyone who might come to her rescue, she intimidated those who might have had rescue in mind. She could no longer regard any man objectively, seeing him only in terms of situation, wondering only whether he were sufficiently well placed to provide an answer to her problem. The problem became more acute as she grew older. This became known, without anything being said, among the few men of her acquaintance. And yet she was a good-looking woman, with her well-cut if severe features, her upright carriage, her dark golden hair and fine skin. She was beginning to put on weight, to become matronly; this was the only sign that her body was quiescent, that she was without a man. There was something unrelenting in her steady progress down a street, her wariness, her consciousness of the dangers of her life. If only she would relax, said these men, who eyed her from a safe distance: there might be something there. She needs waking up. Some man could do it, they did not doubt. Yet none of them volunteered. Their wives felt sorry for her, not without a certain satisfaction, for she was still very handsome. In public they praised her courage. There is no more effective way of precluding a softer approach.

But in fact her hauteur, which was entirely genuine, masked a cold fear that her daughter might have inherited some trace, for the moment dormant, of her father's illness. To this end Maud was closely supervised and denied many innocent entertainments, was surreptitiously examined for a cough, for a heightened flush, was adjured to go to bed early, which she did without unwonted protestations since she was fond of reading and in any event appreciated the night hours, with the light shining in from the street and the silence broken only by the striking of the hour by the bells of Dijon's many churches. This regime served two purposes: it ensured that Maud would not attend late evening parties, of the kind given by the parents of her friends and to which Nadine had no hope of reciprocating, and it preserved Maud's health, which gave no cause for concern, and her good looks, which were considerable. She had a slight but well-formed figure, and a profile which showed to its best advantage when she gazed straight ahead, as she walked with her mother through the Sunday streets, her mother greeting acquaintances who were returning from Mass, which they rarely attended, Maud serious and intent on the horizon, as if she were in a dream of her own. Even the mothers of Maud's schoolfriends acknowledged that Maud would be a beauty, but she was not the sort of beauty then admired. In the late 1950s, when these events were taking place, the taste was for arched eyebrows and emphatically outlined and coloured lips, for exaggerated eyes and a gamine air, whereas Maud's golden face was innocent of colour, her Roman nose was naturally matte, and her dark eyes, between long golden lashes, were untouched by cosmetics. She looked too stern for a girl; she had no flirtatious mannerisms, yet one or two of the fathers eyed her speculatively, as though she might be worth considering in a few years' time. As she entered her eighteenth year Maud, once a replica of her mother, began to eclipse that mother, so that Nadine, in her widowhood, sensed a falling away of interest in herself, and only her rigid sense of honour, and her fierce protectiveness towards her daughter, preserved her from an acknowledgment of defeat.

Yet there were no immediate worries. To all intents and purposes they were in good health. As a doctor's daughter

Nadine had always been expected to be in good health; indeed the doctor's patients were not acknowledged to be ill unless they were dying, or, to add a note of proof to the matter, dead. A resounding confidence — or was it indifference? — had served Dr Debureau well in his profession. He often quoted Voltaire, to the effect that the duty of the physician is to keep the patient amused until such time as nature shall effect a cure. His patients, grateful for a dictum with which they secretly concurred, were only too happy to trust him. Some died, of course, but then the doctor would take the grieving relative on one side, and tell him, in suitably lowered tones, that there had been no hope, but that he had not wanted to spoil the patient's last days with bad news. He had always known the outcome, he implied, but saw no need of tests, painful interventions, verifiable diagnoses. The patients died at home, which was what they wanted: he attended quite regularly, but was content to let nature effect a cure, or indeed the opposite, a cure in its way, as he was quick to point out. His wife, however, had died in hospital, attended by nuns. Puerperal fever, then irreversible, took her off, after a third child, a boy, was stillborn. Thereafter the doctor had avoided illness as much as possible. As long as his daughters presented themselves at the dinner table in a reasonable condition he made no further enquiries as to their health. If they remained well, as they had done, it was because they were largely ignorant of the mechanics of illness. In Nadine's case this ignorance had been shattered by her husband's decline, to be replaced by a watchfulness which never left her. This, finally, was what remained to her of her marriage, together with her daughter, who, so far, had not inherited her mother's cares. It was to Nadine's credit that she bore the weight of them herself, desiring for Maud a life dramatically different from her own. This too she kept to herself.

Occasionally the weight of her responsibilities brought on a bout of acute fatigue, yet the only time she was able to acknowledge this, and to rest, was when Maud was on an exchange visit to her friend Jean Bell in London. Knowing that both girls were sensible, were chaperoned, and were unlikely to be carried away by inappropriate excitement, knowing that they would be taken to the theatre by Jean's parents, and driven to the country and back in Jean's parents' car, she allowed herself, for the space of a fortnight, to get up half an hour later in the morning, to spend the afternoon sitting in the garden of the Château d'Eau, reading the obituaries in that morning's *Figaro*, and reflecting that when the time came Maud would be able to insert an equally dignified tribute to her mother, and every year would ask for a prayer and a thought on the anniversary of her death. Thus religion would be served, though they paid little enough attention to it in this life, restricting themselves to Midnight Mass in the cathedral at Christmas and the Good Friday vigil at Easter, always a bitter time, with the wind scouring the streets, their feet numb from the long inactivity, and only the thought of the summer to come — and not perhaps the Resurrection — as a sign of hope. This latent paganism, not otherwise in evidence in their modest and prudent lives, was the secret that Nadine and Maud kept to themselves, and, as a matter of respect, from each other.

A further advantage presented by Jean Bell was that when Maud brought her back to Dijon, for her part of the exchange, the visit was always a success. Jean Bell was a most appreciative guest, and even Nadine relaxed in her company, relieved that her hospitality was judged to be adequate. It was judged to be adequate for a quite proximate reason: Jean Bell was about to embark on a course in the History of Art, and Dijon, with its abundance of mediaeval and Renaissance buildings, was all the entertainment she required. Dijon, to Jean Bell, was the *Puits de Moïse*, that minatory wellhead in the grounds of the local lunatic asylum, was the weeping figures on the tombs in the Musée des Beaux Arts, was the façades of the houses in the rue Babeuf and the rue Vannerie. Nadine accompanied the girls on their afternoon expeditions, and permitted herself, in the course of these perambulations, a small smile of reminiscence.

'My husband and I used to take these walks,' she explained to the visitor. 'He knew a great deal about architecture. In an amateur way, of course. In fact there are some books of his at home, Jean, that you might like to look through. And you are very welcome to keep any that may be useful to you.'

And sending the girls off to photograph the portals of Saint Bénigne she called at the pastry shop on her way home and bought a cherry tart for their tea.

'Your mother has been so good to me,' said Jean Bell, vigorously brushing her short hair in Maud's bedroom later that evening. 'I really admire her.'

'Everybody admires my mother,' said Maud.

Her tone was neutral. It may have been that she had perceived the distance her mother kept from others. It may have been an inkling of her mother's loneliness. It may have been the burden of the responsibility her mother had wordlessly laid upon her to marry well and to marry early. But over and above all of this was a fierce loyalty, a longing to please, to delight, to gratify, which she was careful not to show. Any sign of weakness would, she knew, be frowned upon. A certain impassivity was favoured as a mark of breeding. Thus Maud's more instinctive feelings were rather hidden from view. It was unclear when, if ever, they would surface.

Secretly, and no doubt fruitlessly, Nadine placed all her hopes for Maud's future in Xavier, her sister Germaine's brilliant son, and the meetings between the cousins that took place every summer, in August, at La Gaillarderie, the house near Meaux, where Germaine lived with her frequently absent husband, both of them fairly pleased to be out of each other's way for a good part of the year. That was why the annual visit to La Gaillarderie was so important, although in many ways she would have been pleased to stay at home in the rapidly emptying city and spend drowsy afternoons with *Le Figaro* in the garden of the Château d'Eau. But Maud was eighteen; she had left school, and, apart from her intention to take a diploma in English studies at the university, there was little for her to do, her friends had dispersed, and her future must in some fashion be assured. La Gaillarderie signified various forms of exquisite discomfort, not all of them physical. Although the house looked large from the outside, there were only eight bedrooms, two of which, on the attic floor, were occupied by servants. Nadine and Maud were always asked to share a room, although the absent Robert's room was empty: a subtle caste system was in operation and it was unthinkable that the master bedroom should be occupied by a widowed sister who had no claims on Germaine de Bretteville's affections save those of convention. 'My poor sister,' she was in the habit of saying to her friends. 'The least I can do is give her a month of good food and country air. And she does so appreciate it.' Gritting her teeth, Nadine appreciated it, although she was all too aware of her daughter being prevailed upon to run to the post or to perform small tasks about the house, such as going to the kitchen to remind Marie, the cook, about a change in the evening menu. At least this way she would learn how to run an establishment, thought Nadine, fully conscious of the fact that Germaine found Maud far too pretty, and what was worse, far too unappreciative of her immense good fortune in being able to enjoy this invitation to be entirely acceptable.

All this they could endure, or rather Nadine could, for the sake of Xavier, the tall, courteous and brilliant son of the house. There could of course be no marriage between the cousins, although why not? Nadine would have sacrificed any number of grandchildren to know that Maud had an enviable future, even if that future included

17

Germaine as a mother-in-law, for she would never leave that house . . .

In bleaker moments, which these days came with debilitating frequency, she knew that she was fantasising, and worse, that she was prepared to sacrifice her daughter's future to her own peace of mind. She ached to cease her vigilance, to take her ease, to be responsible for no one but herself. Even her tiny permitted pleasures — that extra half-hour to herself in the mornings which she enjoyed when Maud was in London with Jean Bell — appeared to her in the guise of a promise. She was tired, and she knew that she had been denied the life of a real woman. Even her husband rarely figured in her thoughts these days; she was anxious to expel him and his memory from her consciousness; she had been relieved when Jean Bell had taken some of his books. Xavier, she realised somewhat shamefacedly, would have been sacrificed as well, and without compunction; she would have denied him children, and would have made him the guardian of a wife who might yet fall ill with her father's disease. Besides, Germaine would never allow it. But, she thought, desperation making her ingenious, Xavier was bound to have friends.

'Are you having a houseful?' she asked on the telephone, in her meekest voice.

'No doubt, no doubt,' said Germaine. 'You won't mind doubling up as usual? We shall be rather crowded. And I'm sure you'll understand if we say a fortnight rather than a month this year — the girls will be coming to play tennis, I dare say, and Xavier, well, Xavier has his own plans. You know what young men are like. In fact I have great hopes that he and Marie-Paule — you met her last summer — might be interested in each other. Such a charming girl . . .'

'Tennis?' enquired Nadine delicately.

'Oh, I'm sure Xavier will provide partners. He has so many friends.'

Maternal relish deepened her voice. Nadine recognised

the proprietorial spirit that had so alienated her from her sister when they were both young. Then it had been their father who had been so appropriated, but he had been sacrificed without a murmur. Now, however, she must be careful not to overstep the bounds that had been assigned to her: widow, unfortunate, no money, no man, a recipient of charity which must be gratefully and admiringly received. Nevertheless she had the information she wanted, and she replaced the receiver with a very slight feeling of reassurance. Maud was, after all, a very good-looking girl.

Maud's wishes, however, were not quite the same as those of her mother. Maud simply wanted to live in Paris, with or without a husband, preferably without. While careful not to let her thoughts show on her severe and slightly disdainful golden face, Maud had a secret desire to escape all forms of control. That was her abiding wish. The future was unclear to her, but she knew that it did not contain her mother, or her mother's plans, of which she was fully aware. Rigidly supervised as she was, she longed for freedom. She would escape, she would get a job — any job, looking after children if need be — and when she had saved enough money she would get a room of her own. In Paris. That room would of necessity be modest, but she was used to modesty. Quite simply, she wanted to live her life without constraints. What she would do without constraints was quite unclear to her, but the prospect enabled her to wait, composed, contained, for the time being. Therefore, when her mother said, 'You had better have two new dresses. I will make an appointment with Mlle Zughetta,' she merely replied, 'Two? Do I need two? And Mlle Zughetta? They have quite good things at Monoprix . . . ' And when her mother replied, 'These things are always noted. I will telephone tomorrow,' she acquiesced, without much interest, looking forward to the day when she would no longer be overruled.

3

Edward Harrison felt replete at the ending of the day, no matter how unsatisfactory the day had been. The simple actions of preparing for the night seemed to banish the very slight melancholy of the long light evenings, which conferred on him a lassitude that had nothing to do with fatigue. Besides, he was never tired; he was determined never to feel tired, as adults did, without due cause, or so it seemed to him. He embraced an ideal of rigour, which he thought would predispose him to a life of wandering, a life large enough to accommodate adventurous impulses. This predisposition, which he cultivated, pleased him as if it were a genuine attribute, handed down from Stoic ancestors, whereas his own ancestors, principally his mother and father, for he knew no others, were all gentle confusion, redeemed by an immense indulgence which still enveloped him at privileged moments, such as the moment when he shut his book and moved into his bedroom and there began the ritual of embarking on his night's journey. If he were lucky he would dream of a past which he thought of as aboriginal, though it was not far distant, brief ravishing dreams which, once he was awake, he would acknowledge with gladness, with gratitude. At times like these he was convinced of the poetry of life, of its unending circularity. He would glide through the dark hours on a raft of archaic remembrance, restored to the innocence of simple wondrous passivity. By the time morning came he felt himself to be renewed, returned to what he deemed the puzzling obligations of adulthood, which, as he was still young, too often caught him unawares. His ideal was a simple prolongation of immaturity, the immaturity of the artist. For this he had a plan.

His dreams encouraged him in this quest. For how could other nights have yielded up such treasures as had come to him in the mysterious depths to which he surrendered with such ease? No one he knew would have thought these dreams remarkable, but he realised that they were remarkable because they contained not a trace of the anxiety that dominated classic dreams, textbook dreams, dreams of trains, of examinations, of perilous flight. In this he knew himself to be singular. Rather he was restored to an eternal sunny afternoon, in a garden, with the scent of syringa wafting over a hedge. He was young, no more than eight, he thought, and he was looking after his little sister, Deborah, known in the family as Bibi, since this was his first attempt to approach the baby with whom his parents had presented him. She in her turn had christened him Noddy, a well kept secret, since only she was allowed to call him by this name. His attempt to live this down involved him in minor willed deceptions; he was Edward to his friends, Eddie, or too often Neddy, to his parents. These alterations were the currency of his days, whereas the nights were given over to authenticity. In dreams he inhabited a long Sunday afternoon; sometimes a brief shower sparkled on the long grass in the reviving June heat. Soon he would be called in to tea, and they would sit at the table, the four of them, mother, father, sister, himself, filled with the contentment of the long unchanging day.

This brilliance contrasted favourably, more than favourably, with his terrible inheritance, which had fallen on him without warning, just as he was leaving Cambridge, and about to set out, as he thought, on a series of journeys

21

which would continue until he was old enough to find another garden, like that first one, where he would be content to sit in the sun. His greatest need, he thought, was for solitude, for self-communion. He felt no desire for friends, though he made friends easily, and throughout his student years had been an amicable partner to various girls who had been attracted by his lean dark face and neat spare frame. His face, he thought, gave the wrong impression, in particular the two strong incisors that gleamed when he smiled and the straight dark hair that fell over his forehead. He looked romantic; in fact his emotions were elusive, always bent on some distance, either in the past or in the beckoning future, which would continue the past, its innocence, its promise of happiness. It was a future which he courted in his thoughts, far removed from everyday reality and its obligations. Practical considerations were entirely absent from what was not quite a fantasy. He was strong, he thought himself durable, he would not be averse to celibacy. Thus he would spend his life travelling, picking up employment as and when he could. He would take passage on the first ship out of Southampton, and work his way round the world. Sometimes it seemed to him that the promise of such a life was enough in itself; the sun, always the sun, would dispel the murky light of London, where he found himself stranded, this rainy day in July, his plans apparently negated by a malign stroke of fate.

He had inherited this shop, this hated shop, from an old friend of his parents, whom they had addressed as Ted, but whom he continued to think of as Mr Sheed, and after whom he had been named. A godfather of sorts, though not one in whom he had the slightest interest. Mr Sheed, a bachelor, apparently without a family, had departed from his Pimlico home on certain well heralded Sunday afternoons to take tea with the Harrisons in their small house on the outskirts of Eastbourne. His faithfulness in this matter was somehow taken for granted, although no one could quite remember how the association had started. It was supposed that he had known Arthur Harrison in the war; this was in fact the case, though they had only known each other briefly; by now they assumed that they were old friends by virtue of the fact that they had certain topics in common and also by virtue of a certain languor which was native to their characters. In their placid way native the Harrisons accepted him without much question. A more binding tie was commerce, since Harrison *père* was the owner of a menswear shop in the town. Perhaps for this reason he deferred to Mr Sheed, or Ted, who was after all a bookseller, in London, in Denbigh Street, near enough to the centre of things to evoke a certain respect. Mr Sheed had little to say for himself, apart from, 'You're looking well, Polly,' or 'How's it going then?' before settling down to a substantial tea, which on those days took place without the children, who were exiled to the kitchen. They were incurious about Mr Sheed, whose complacent and undemanding presence imposed no social duties upon them. There was something both mysterious and immemorial about this man who seemed not to age by a single day and who took his place at the table, once a month, while Edward grew up, went to school, went to university, came home for his last long vacation, greeted Mr Sheed, went up to his room to write to his current girlfriend, came down again, answered Mr Sheed's permanent question — 'And what are you going to do with yourself, young man?' — with his permanent answer — 'I haven't decided yet. I'd like to travel first' — and then, a month later, learned to his stupefaction that Mr Sheed had died and left him the shop, the flat above the shop, and a certain amount of money.

Initially he regarded this as a blow to all his hopes. He had been planning to spend the summer in Paris, in a flat lent to him by a Cambridge friend, Tyler, whose parents were friends of the owners. The owners would be away until the end of September and were under the impression that Tyler himself would be in residence. In fact Tyler would be accepting various invitations around France; the arrangement was that if Tyler decided for some reason to come to Paris, Harrison would move up to the maid's room on the sixth floor, leaving Tyler to pursue his inevitable liaisons in the flat below. Instead of this he had to go regularly to London, in humid dull weather, to be instructed by solicitors and to view with horror the dusty rooms above the shop which had once been the home of Mr Sheed and which now belonged to him. His parents, of course, were delighted with the bequest, which they thought typical of 'Poor Ted'. His father was on the point of selling his business to a chain, from which he had received an advantageous offer, and was thinking in terms of winter holidays, in Florida or Jamaica. His parents' eyes, bright with timid anticipation of pleasure, smiled their complete confidence that Edward would acquiesce in their wishes for him. He had not the heart to disappoint them, although he was determined somehow to implement his own wishes, even if he had to wait to put them into effect. With a heavy heart he had asked the solicitor to find him a tenant for the rooms above the shop. This was accomplished without difficulty. He himself, in a burst of gritted-teeth activity, rented a furnished flat in a purpose-built block behind the King's Road. He had disliked it on sight, but by that stage was so desperate to get to France that once he had transferred his belongings from Eastbourne he slammed the door behind him and fled.

But his steps led him inevitably back to the shop, for which he felt an increasingly exasperated distaste. The sight of the dull green façade, embellished with the single word 'Sheed', did nothing to encourage him. Who came here? Who would visit a secondhand bookshop in an ordinary, rather downmarket street in Pimlico? During the hour and a half he spent there on that first afternoon not a soul came near. Furious, he examined the stock, which was meagre, and seemed to be devoted to Latin and German textbooks and popular novels of the Thirties and Forties.

Who now read Harrison Ainsworth or Hugh Walpole, Warwick Deeping or Jeffrey Farnol? How did this stuff sell? And yet it must have done, for Mr Sheed had left him a quite useful sum of money, and so embarrassing was this generosity from a man whom he had neither liked nor disliked but in whom he had never had the slightest interest that he felt, with a groan, that he was bound to be the custodian of Mr Sheed's enterprise until such time as he could pass it on and get on with his real life. This would take place abroad, in circumstances which were not quite clear to him but which were surrounded by a great deal of very fine weather, either very hot or very cold, and in both cases very picturesque, in comparison with which the lightless street outside the dusty window appeared unendurable, not to be endured.

It occurred to him, on that first afternoon, that Mr Sheed must have sold pornography, but he could discover nothing of a questionable nature in the boxes under the counter, merely more Beatrice Kean Seymour and Rafael Sabatini. Who bought this stuff? Obviously, there must be collectors, of a simple-minded nature, but he could find no list of subscribers. He could find nothing in the drawers of the old-fashioned roll-top desk which would give him a clue as to the real nature of Mr Sheed. Who was this man who had placidly sat down to tea in his parents' home on innumerable Sundays, and whose presence, surely rather odd, had been just as placidly accepted? To begin with, one did not sit in a train on a Sunday just for the sake of a cup of tea. Was he in love with Polly Harrison, and was this fidelity to a situation long laid to rest behaviour of the highest chivalry? Or did he have a mistress in Eastbourne whom he saw on irregular weekends and whom he took to lunch at the Grand before topping off his stay with an innocuous cup of tea *chez* Harrison? Edward inclined to both theories, although he found them both unappealing. They had all, his parents and Mr Sheed, seemed to him so very virtuous, cheerful and right-minded and equable, conversing rather than chattering, and even enjoying peaceful silences, until Mr Sheed looked at his watch and hauled himself out of his chair. 'I'll walk down with you, Ted,' Harrison's father had invariably remarked at this point, and 'Children! Come and say goodbye!' he had called through the French windows. Growing older, Edward had tended to ignore him, out of distaste for his bulk and general unmanoeuvrability, or rather had continued to ignore him, only to discover in time that the thread had been there, that some residual feeling — a shy man's feeling — had been there all along, and thus his present and unwanted ownership of the shop was proof that he had, in some sense, been cherished. The alternative idea — that Mr Sheed had been hurt by his indifference and had wanted to clip his wings — was too awful to contemplate. Yet contemplate it he did.

Time was the problem, he decided, as he sat at the roll-top desk on that rainy July afternoon, time which would change him from an eager, unknowing and hedonistic boy into the resigned figure, who, if he did not take immense and immediate pains, would spend his life in this shop, which he would inevitably (he knew this somehow) transform into something profitable. And yet he still dreamed of his now remote childhood, when all who surrounded him were kind, kinder than he was ever likely to be. Perhaps he had fallen from grace, into this dull room, this poor adumbration of a disappointing future. He knew himself to be disastrously unqualified for any other career; his only positive thoughts were of evasion. His Cambridge degree was undistinguished. He had no ambitions, save those of flight. His parents would be massively disappointed if he turned his back on what they considered to be in the nature of an endowment, one which they could not have provided themselves, one, moreover, which left them relatively free. Once Bibi had left university she could live at home, until she married. The house was long paid for; they were relatively comfortable, now more than ever. The boy, in their view, was taken care of. And indeed he felt most disagreeably taken care of, as one might be taken care of in an institution.

That lost interval, as he thought of it, that Empty Quarter that remained unvisited, stayed with him like the tormenting fragment of a dream which his inopportune waking had disturbed. The essence of the condition was dreamlike, since the adventure had not taken place, but might have taken place. He was robust enough to know that his childhood was immutable, and could no longer be recaptured; nor could it yield more than it already had done. Yet what he retained of it was the idea of happiness, plenitude, and it was this that he made it his plan to recapture. For he had no doubt that he could recapture it, somewhere along the way, and to be deprived of the chance to do so was like the door to the future being shut in his face. His surroundings he thought of as a temporary aberration, from which, in time, he would stealthily depart. He would not die in England, he thought, although he loved the country in a brooding, almost shamefaced way, loved it for the very boredom which delayed him on this rainy afternoon. As he sat at Mr Sheed's desk he could hear a lorry discharging beer barrels into the cellar of the pub on the corner, and a blast of music when the door of the neighbouring hairdresser's swung open. He was surrounded by commercial transactions of a humble nature; the district was humble, and he did not despise it. He felt a mild frustrated love for the people in the street, all unknowing and, it seemed to him, innocent. At the same time he remembered the blind man and his guide dog whom he had passed outside Victoria station: the man cautious, questing, his sightless head turning from side to side, the dog obedient but straining, full of power, aching to fulfil his destiny as an animal. The sight had chilled him, its symbolism too apparent.

In the course of one tormenting afternoon he had become resistant to anything that suggested confinement, and this extended to the bars on the back window and the sight of scaffolding on the building opposite. He thought uneasily of the sheet of plastic that had detached itself from that same building and had bowled along the road, waiting to trap him by the ankles. Even the memory, the image, caused alarm. It was as if he had to keep his life inconclusive, until such time as his real life should be ready to unfold. This real life, as it continued to beckon from an ever more distant future, had to do with the feeling of plenitude which he knew from his dreams and which he knew to be the essence of his authentic, his desired reality. Not to know that reality would be an impossibility, more, an outrage, an act of ungenerosity towards life itself. Yet here he was, stranded in an alien room, almost a prisoner, surveying a rainy street through smeared windows, and apparently forbidden to journey abroad and to abandon this terrible place to its fate, which was surely extinction. He could shut it up, of course, go to Paris, forget it, and after a suitable interval put it on the market. The trouble was that no one would buy it, would pay to sit here surrounded by shelves full of Dornford Yates. He had a brief insight into the way in which Mr Sheed had spent his days. As he had no financial need to sell the books, always supposing that they were remotely saleable, he must have sat here and read them. That was the clue, of course, to Mr Sheed's somnolent and wordless existence, his pale affections, his nostalgia for the simple life of his Sundays in Eastbourne, when he could evolve among like-minded adults who would do him no harm, adults so genuine and undemanding that they seemed like children. And in the background the voices of children . . . A shy man, nourished by romance, comforted by a fictional flourish, consoled by a neat ending. Harrison grinned suddenly, relaxed his tense shoulders, felt a flicker of affection himself; this, however, was soon dowsed by the dusty chirrup of the telephone, all the more startling since nobody knew he was here. A feeling of being harassed settled on him, although he had spent the interminable afternoon quite undisturbed.

'Harrison,' he said sombrely.

'Gillian here. I've got Mr Viner for you.'

'Put him on.'

'Mr Harrison? Viner. You've settled in, then?'

'No, I just looked in.'

'Just as well I caught you, then. Some rather tiresome news, I'm afraid. Your tenant has decided against taking the upstairs flat.'

There was a pause.

'Any particular reason?' Harrison said finally. He could hardly keep his mind on what was being said to him. He glimpsed endless arguments with this fussy solicitor, as soon as he attempted to put his plans to work for him.

'He seemed to think it was rather dilapidated. He rather expected you to do a bit of decorating.'

'I rather expected him to do that.'

'A first impression, you know . . . Not too favourable. Perhaps if you were to clean the windows . . . '

'I'm afraid I have no time to do that,' he said firmly. 'I'm off to France at the end of this week.'

An enormous exhilaration swept through him as he said these words. He was not aware of having made up his mind. Clearly his mind was making itself up. His destiny was in control.

'You're not thinking of leaving it empty, I hope? Empty property is an open invitation to thieves, particularly in your area. The proximity of the station, you know.'

'In that case I'll put in a caretaker.'

'Oh. Yes, that might be a good idea. But you won't leave it empty for too long, will you? Will you want me to keep the spare keys? Until you take possession?'

'No, I think I'll collect them from you. I'm not sure of my plans.'

'Very well. Gillian will keep them here for you to collect. Was there anything else? You'll get in touch as soon as you return from France? How long do you think you'll be away?'

'I'm not sure.'

There was a sigh at the other end. 'Do be careful, Mr Harrison. You have a considerable asset there. Don't let it go to waste. The site alone – '

'Thank you, Mr Viner. I'll be in touch.'

He put down the telephone, thought for a moment, picked up the receiver and dialled a number in distant Worcestershire. He imagined the call travelling through misty shires, wolds, woodlands, coppices, demesnes, until it reached the home of Tyler, which he saw as palatial, a fit setting for the splendid presence of Tyler himself, whose actual physical embodiment Harrison saw as somewhat threatening. This he put down to the effort of looking up at Tyler's great height, and marvelling despite himself at Tyler's austere good looks, in comparison with which his own pleasant appearance shrank to anonymity. Also, Tyler was rich, and careless with it; his father was some sort of industrial magnate, and at the same time a gentleman. The contrast with his own modest background could not have been more marked. And yet for some reason he had been favoured by this prestigious creature, who broke the hearts not only of girls but of women too; there had been rumours, of which he had not taken much notice, but of which he could not help but be aware. Occasionally, in Tyler's company, Harrison felt like some sort of page, striding along manfully beside his liege lord. This feeling was not uncommon among Tyler's acquaintances. And yet he liked the man, without trusting him. Flattery came into it, and emulation too. Fortunately they had never had the same girlfriend.

'Tyler? Harrison here.'

'Ah. Noddy.'

Harrison winced. That was what was wrong with Tyler; he took unfair advantage. There had been an ill-judged invitation to Eastbourne one weekend, in the course of

30

which Tyler had become privy to various family myths and legends. Bibi, in particular, had been fascinated. Tyler, it could be said, had behaved well; at least the Harrison parents had been charmed, particularly Harrison's father who was unused to so much interest being shown in the menswear business. Tyler, apparently, was desirous of knowing how the shop was run. With a little encouragement Mr Harrison would have jumped in the car and taken Tyler into town to examine the premises. Grinding his teeth silently, Harrison had put a stop to that. In the kitchen, pink-cheeked, his mother was making a cake. 'Lemon sponge,' she confided to him. 'Will he like that, do you think?' Gracefully Tyler had thanked them for a very pleasant day. He had had the decency to make no further reference to it but to send good wishes to the Harrison parents. 'I still remember that cake of your mother's,' he was apt to say. Sometimes, Harrison thought, he said it too often.

'I just called to check whether it's all right if I go to the flat this weekend.'

'I thought you had inherited the mantle of commerce.'

'I can still go to Paris, can't I? If it's still all right.'

'Perfectly all right. The key is with the concierge. She has been told to expect me. You can stand in for me.'

'You will be coming, then?'

'Doubt it. I've been invited here and there. If I do turn up you'll have to move upstairs, of course.'

'Couldn't we share? Surely the flat is big enough?'

'Dear fellow, I shouldn't be alone, should I?'

'Oh. Oh, quite. Well, you'd give me warning, I suppose.'

'Don't worry about that. Well, enjoy yourself. What will you do there?'

'I hadn't thought. Go for walks, look at buildings, that kind of thing.'

'If I don't see you, leave the key with the concierge when you go. And do let me know how you get on. I'll look in on you, one of these days.'

And he would, Harrison reckoned. He would make the journey and survey the premises, and even offer some kind of support. Tyler displayed odd moments of kindness which, in the sight of many, compensated for his ruthlessness. Harrison, who never considered himself in the same league, maintained a worried friendship on that count alone. He had no desire to prevail upon Tyler, but appreciated his moments of favour with fervent loyalty. This never failed to surprise him; he was not, as far as he knew, given to hero-worship. At the same time, he knew that he and Tyler had very little in common; indeed, everything, except Cambridge, separated them. Tyler was not lazy, did not have consoling fantasies of flight. Tyler was very much of the moment, of the here and now. He was a master of situations.

When the receiver was once more replaced, Harrison felt a wave of exhilaration. He left the shop, now gloomier than ever in the sultry haze, locked the door behind him, and made for Victoria Street to collect the spare keys. At the top of Vauxhall Bridge Road, where Italian cafés shared space with shops selling kitchen equipment and bicycle spare parts, there was, he knew, an employment agency. The prospect of Paris at the end of the week made him bold.

'A youngish man,' he told the woman behind the desk. 'Not too young. To live on the premises — I can supply a flat. All he has to do while I'm away is clean the place up. The flat *and* the shop. You'll take up references, I suppose?'

'I've got just the person for you,' she said, surprisingly. 'He said he'd look back this afternoon. I could send him round to you.'

'What's his name?'

She consulted a card. 'Thomas Cook.'

It was an omen. He sped up to Victoria Street, and sped back again, to await the arrival of Thomas Cook. To give himself something to do, he typed a notice saying 'Closed

32

for Stocktaking'. He then sat tensely, waiting for the agent of his deliverance to appear.

At five o'clock, when he was almost ready to forget the whole business, when Thomas Cook, if he existed, seemed quite possibly a further figment of his imagination, the door opened and a fragile-looking youth of about his own age entered, with an air of being immediately at home. He wore jeans and a T-shirt, and appeared to have no possessions: at least his hands hung idly by his sides. His expression was amiable, if slightly witless: he might have been the character in the fairytale who is sent out on a long and hazardous journey, to return only after some years to claim his reward. Harrison looked at him with some perplexity. Cook seemed singularly unfitted for work of any kind. However, he had turned up; that was something. And now impatience took over; he could not bear to prolong this process any longer.

'Do you think you could take care of this place for a couple of months? Clear up, and so on? There's a flat upstairs — did they mention that at the agency?'

'Yes. That's what decided me, really. I've only just arrived in London, you see.'

'Where from?'

'The Isle of Wight. My parents live there.'

He had parents, to whom he was willing to refer. That, surely, was a good sign.

'I may have to engage someone permanently, of course.'

He felt that this was the kind of pompous remark he was expected to make.

'That's OK.'

'I'll be gone for a month or two,' he said daringly. 'You can move in straight away, if you like. Just tidy up as best you can. A lot of these books can go in the basement. You'll need cardboard boxes from somewhere. Leave the shelves free — I'll decide what to do with the books when I come back. Familiarise yourself with the layout. I'll pay you in cash, if you like.'

33

'I'd prefer a cheque,' was the prim reply.

'Really? Are you sure?'

'I'm saving up for a car.'

'Whichever you prefer. I'll leave a float for supplies, soap, etc. Tea,' he added.

Cook listened to Harrison's by now febrile plans without due enthusiasm, but seemed unsurprised by them. At the same time his large eyes ranged round the shop. Fleetingly he gave an impression of competence.

'This will be my number in Paris,' said Harrison, writing it down. 'Do you think you'll be able to manage?'

'Can't see why not.'

'Buy whatever you need,' Harrison cried, edging his way out of the door. If he hurried he could just manage to buy his ticket for France at Victoria. He was aware of obeying his destiny. If Thomas Cook decided to burn the place down he would accept the fact calmly, and without blaming himself. On the other hand if, with the assistance of Thomas Cook, he managed to transform the shop into something relatively viable he might be prepared to address the problem of making it pay. He would be a shopkeeper, but first he would be liberated. The late afternoon air was humid, hazy. Inhaling it deeply he set his face towards Victoria, and France.

4

Situated in a hollow between Meaux and Melun, the house presented an unassuming façade of rosy brick which belied its age. Originally built in the seventeenth century, La Gaillarderie had once formed three sides of a square, with a small private chapel raising its pointed roof in one corner. Most of this had been done away with in 1793 by insurgents from Meaux, who suspected the owners, quite rightly, of royalist sympathies. Now all that remained was the original *corps de logis*: both the wings and the chapel had left no trace, although architectural historians still occasionally came from Paris to study the foundations. What was left was a pleasant rather low-built single pavilion of two main storeys, an attic floor, and a pitched roof punctuated by mansard windows. It was not without distinction, though not essentially different from many other country houses of the same period. Only the quality and colour of the brick, and the clean-cut creamy quoins and window surrounds, indicated a past of far greater splendour than that enjoyed by its present owners, Robert and Germaine de Bretteville. Robert had inherited the house from his father, who had in his turn purchased it from the previous owner, a lawyer who worked in Paris, spent his weekends in the country, and found the situation in the valley rather damp.

This dampness — undeniable, and rather a problem in the winter months — in summer conferred upon the house a not unpleasant smell, redolent of apples and of fading pot-pourri. This, however, was noticeable only on the upper floors. In other respects the house was more than satisfactory. The interior was as unpretentious yet as dignified as what remained of the façade. A black and white tiled hall led from the front entrance to the garden side, where two drawing-rooms, a dining-room and a morning-room enjoyed the view through double doors which opened directly on to a broad terrace: from here one descended directly to lawns which led to distant trees, for most of the grounds were coppiced, although, as the lawyer had discovered, the shooting was poor. Robert de Bretteville, when he was at home, occasionally went out with a gun and shot a rabbit: throughout his childhood Xavier had endured cold November mornings standing quite still in an attempt to avoid his father's bluff admonitions to beat the not inconsiderable undergrowth, in order to dislodge whatever wildlife was thought to be available. Inhaling the rank smell of damp fern, in which he stood nearly up to his knees, Xavier would send his obedient mind back to what he could remember of his Greek and Latin texts and ignore his father completely. Robert in his turn, aware of his increasing girth, his ears crimson in the damp depths of the wood, would blame his studious son for being so unsuited to country life, and for preferring to spend the bleak but beautiful autumn days reading in his room. Xavier could, had he made a more enlightened choice, have accompanied his father on a round of neighbouring houses and farms, where the men, guns at the ready, were only too willing to turn out for a day's prospecting, from which they would return in the late afternoon, their breath smelling of *marc*, and at that moment most faithfully resembling the hobbledehoy aristocrats their remote ancestors might have been.

Xavier's room overlooked the terrace, as did the other four main bedrooms, his parents' room, with double doors, forming a right angle at the bottom of the corridor. All the rooms had fireplaces and fairly exiguous *cabinets de toilette*: at the end of the corridor, facing the parents' bedroom, was a bathroom, only occasionally used, mostly by guests, who had to accustom themselves to a staccato stream of rusty water before this ceased altogether, without warning. Thereafter the guest, or visitor, learned to use the washbasin in the cupboard off his bedroom, as, he supposed, did his host and hostess, who certainly had never struck him as less than immaculate. This matter of washing, however, created a note of uncertainty, which nothing in the manners of the house did much to disperse. His host, for example, decamped from time to time from the bedroom he shared with his wife and occupied another, seemingly at random. His hostess, her voice hoarse with feigned enthusiasm which she was at pains to maintain, almost gave the impression that she wished the house were empty, not only of guests but of her husband as well. If she longed for a different life from the one she had once so eagerly embraced she gave no hint. Only her wildly rolling eyes, as her husband embarked on yet another anecdote at the dinner table, betrayed an impatience which had neatly translated itself into pathological states: rheumatism, headaches, the peculiar hoarseness of her voice. Only by commiserating with those less fortunate than herself did she maintain her equilibrium, and indeed maintain the upper hand which was such a comfort to her.

It was somehow allowed that her husband should enjoy the favours of a mistress, in a room which he rented for purposes of business, in the rue de la Pompe in Paris, just as it was somehow allowed that Charles, the manservant, was permitted to avail himself of both Marie, the cook, and her daughter, Suzanne, the maid of all work. From time to time one of the women would absent herself from the room she shared with the other, go to Charles's room, return after an hour, and resume her place without a word being said. The visitor soon got used to this activity on the floor above his head, and understood that he should forbear to comment on any nocturnal disturbance. He realised that deprived of their habitual privileges the servants would leave, that it would be difficult to engage others, and impossible to persuade them to stay. By the same token he grew used to the slightly sinister intrusion of Charles into his bedroom in the morning, and the stealthy noise of the fire being built up, the windows having remained tightly shut all night, as recommended by his hostess. His shoes would disappear with Charles and, while he was waiting for them to be returned, a clatter of hooves might give him a pretext to open the window and to lean out, taking a great gulp of the forbidden air, and to give a wave to Xavier, who sometimes went out for a solitary canter before breakfast. This — coffee and bread only — the guest was able to enjoy in the morning-room, the other members of the household having got up earlier and dispersed. He would not see them again until lunch, and then again at dinner, at which Charles officiated in a slightly grubby white jacket and a pair of frayed cotton gloves. Under those cotton gloves the guest could imagine the hands that had handled the sticks and paper in his fireplace that morning, and may even still have been unwashed. He would hastily persuade himself that the bathing facilities on the attic floor were none of his concern, although it might occur to him that the hands which had provided the food he was now eating were not above suspicion. But the food was generally so excellent that the guest soon abandoned his finicky city preoccupations and settled down to an appreciation of country life.

When the sun came through the windows onto the same black and white tiled floor of the upper storey, Maud, on previous visits, had lingered, out of range of her aunt's commands, of her mother's ambitions, of her cousin Xavier's courteous questions, of the visitors' unexpected entrances and exits, and for a few minutes had stood quite still and perfectly quiet, enjoying the fall of the light onto the grey walls, on to a small Louis XVI table, which some ancient vandal had cheerfully painted white without lessening its charm, onto the glass of a picture whose subject was hidden from her by the dazzle of the afternoon glare, in this, the hottest month of the year, which she was always condemned to spend in the isolation of the countryside, in the company of people whom she knew too well and who would always remain the same. Even the guests, for the most part friends of Xavier's, failed to interest her, for they were usually absent for most of the day, and were only encountered over the dinner table. Lunch was one course, was eaten without ceremony, was not always fully attended, and was over well within an hour. This was to allow the servants, whose voices could be heard from the kitchen quarters, to have the afternoon off. In the afternoons her mother and aunt would take a siesta, Xavier and his friend or friends would disappear somewhere in the car, and she would be left to her own devices. It was assumed that she would go into the garden, or sit on the terrace with a book, but as often as not she lingered in the upstairs corridor, redolent of heat and sleep, heavy adult sleep, or leaned her head against the glass of a sunstruck window, and wished that she were in Paris.

This year promised to be no different from all those which had preceded it. They had been met at the station by Xavier, who had murmured, 'Aunt,' and 'Maud,' while kissing them on both cheeks. They had arrived during the siesta hour and had the impression that they had put everyone out. Nevertheless Germaine was waiting for them on the terrace, her fractious smile in place, her eyes darting from side to side in an attempt to deflect Xavier from disappearing. Maud, in one of her new tight-waisted full-skirted dresses, stepped forward obediently to present her face for her aunt's kisses: she thought she appeared to some advantage, and had prepared her entrance to impress whatever guests might be lurking in the hall, but, 'Good heavens, Maud,' said her aunt. 'This is the country. We don't dress up here. By all means change for dinner — we

39

all do that. And I'm sure you look very nice,' she added in a kindlier tone, seeing the girl recoil, her affront masked by apparent indifference. 'Did you bring something simpler? I think something simpler would be more suitable, don't you?' Aware that she had hurt them both, for she was not completely insensitive, she waved them gaily indoors. When Maud descended to the morning-room, where coffee was provided, half an hour later, she was complimented on her brown cotton skirt and white cotton blouse. Her only consolation was the knowledge that the blouse, short sleeved, open necked, and slightly too small, showed off her beautiful arms to advantage. Nevertheless she was mortified by the prospect of having to wear blouse and skirt for the rest of her stay, and resolved to keep out of the way as much as possible.

This was something she was used to do. She knew, as if it had been programmed in advance, that her cousin would ask her if she would like to take a walk, that they would indeed walk round the garden, always referred to as the park, that he would ask her how her English studies were progressing, and that she, finding this subject boring, and fearful of revealing too much of her impatience — for rigorous control would be demanded of both her mother and herself on this visit, which they both knew to be a form of charity — would quickly deflect the question and in her turn ask Xavier if he had written any new poems lately, and if so, whether he could bear to let her read them. He always did, and this was a further opportunity for her to express appreciation, for appreciation, she knew, was expected of them both, and in this way she could play her small part. Xavier was destined for his uncle's bank, the uncle being in fact a second cousin of his father, but he had confided to her that he would much rather devote himself to poetry. She sympathised, discerning in him a desire for independence, albeit weaker than her own, but he was obedient and would not disappoint his mother.

'If you are on the terrace later I could show them to

you,' he said. 'At least I could leave them with you. I have a friend coming to stay, and I shall have to collect him from the station. I know you'll take care of them. Perhaps we could have a proper talk in a day or two.'

'How long is your friend staying?' asked Maud.

'David? A couple of weeks, I think. He is English. I met him last year in Cambridge. I'm sure you'll like him.'

Of that he had no doubt: all the girls he had known, during that visit to Cambridge, made to perfect his English, which was already good, had seemed to like David. Yet, stealing an appreciative but experienced sidelong glance at Maud, Xavier thought she might be the exception to the rule. She was untouched, that was quite clear: her stern and remote expression, which she had inherited from her mother, made her seem older than her nineteen years. And he discerned in her, as well as her obstinacy, a certain fearfulness that had kept her at home and had inhibited whatever desires she had, or must have, in that rather splendid body. She was handsome, he could see that, but she was rigid, cautious: that stern expression on her golden face (the slight tan having been acquired during the afternoons she spent with her mother, sitting in the garden of the Château d'Eau) was not likely to appeal to his worldly friend, who had seemed, during that month in Cambridge, to appreciate easier, livelier girls, given to shrieking their delight, and willing to stay up all night, moving from one party to another. At least he hoped she would not appeal: he did not want an awkward situation on his hands, and he intended to keep his mother from expressing her disapproval. Of his aunt's reaction he was quite sure: he knew her to be a prude, was used to his mother's commiserations, and preferred to keep on purely formal terms with a woman who, he suspected, had designs on him. He did not intend to hand over his friend to her scrutiny.

Over and above these considerations, however, was a desire to keep that friend out of harm's way, and to detach him from the company that his mother was sure to provide,

in the shape of the two silly nieces of their nearest neighbours, the Dubuissons, or Du Buissons, as they preferred
to style themselves, and who would inevitably stroll over
with tennis racquets on the following afternoon. He half
wanted to pursue his own interest in David, who, during
that month in Cambridge, had inspired in him feelings he
had not hitherto suspected. When he had appeared in the
doorway of Xavier's lodgings in Selwyn College and asked
him if he had everything he wanted, and whether he knew
his way about, explaining that he himself was a recent
graduate who had taken on a summer job of showing these
students — most of them tourists, Americans for the most
part, tempted by the prospect of a month at a Cambridge
college, some of them even determined to do a little work
— around the university and the city and providing them
with such entertainment as might be covered by their fee.

'I have a list of the lectures,' Xavier had said; he was
one of those prepared to work hard. 'But it is very kind
of you.' He was charmed by the Englishness of this caller,
his height, his graceful body in a blue open-necked shirt
and cotton trousers, his abundant curling hair growing low
on his forehead, and his thin hawklike nose. He thought
him splendid-looking, and felt a glow of appreciation at
being included in this man's company, however briefly. He
allowed himself to be taken out to a pub, where he drank
a pint of powerful English beer, although he had been
planning a studious walk. The beer made him sleep
through the afternoon, so that he missed a lecture. When
he awoke he told himself that this must stop, but when
David looked in after dinner and announced that there
was some sort of party going on at a friend's flat, it seemed
natural to fall in with him. That had been the pattern of
the succeeding days and nights. Little work got done;
on the other hand his conversational English benefited
from the bewildering turnover of girlfriends who swam in
David's wake and who were willing to be temporarily
diverted by this charming if awkward Frenchman, with his

so careful blazer and tie. By the end of a week he had flirted with three girls and had slept with one of them, a procedure which he enjoyed less than anticipated. The talk with these girls was always of David, as if the girls regretted his absence, as if they were still alert to the sound of his name, even if they had to pronounce it themselves.

At the end of the second week it had seemed impossible to capture the attention of these girls for any length of time, nor, in truth, did he find them attractive, with their big feet and their noisy voices, certainly not as attractive as David, who emerged from various bedrooms, looking amused and restless, as if ever ready for the next partner. When he realised the extent of his friend's power over him, Xavier became very thoughtful, locked his door in the evenings, and resolved to return to France and to obey his mother, who wished him to marry someone suitable as soon as possible, so that he could begin his apprenticeship at the bank with a full panoply of honourable attributes. David, who was intelligent, had sensed this, had not pressed his advantages, and had invited Xavier not to any more louche parties but to his parents' lavish flat in Chelsea, and then, for two successive weekends, to their house in Worcestershire. In the presence of a wealth he had not suspected, Xavier felt impressed, unsure of himself, but the parents were offhandedly kind and asked him the sort of questions of which his own parents would have approved. At home David's sexuality disappeared as though it had never been. The absence of any kind of saturnalia, of any female company at all, reassured Xavier, who thought his earlier feelings must have been the effect of drunkenness. He was allowed to play a splendid piano in the Worcestershire drawing-room, and began, cautiously, to feel at ease with himself once more. When he issued his invitation to spend the following summer at La Gaillarderie the invitation was graciously accepted. A year later, it occurred to him that this may not have been such a good idea. His own feelings, now that he had gained some insight into them, were under control, but now there was Maud to be considered. He shrugged his shoulders. Maud was old enough to look after herself. Besides, there might be some antipathy between them, some mutual disapproval. David, he knew, did not take kindly to disapproval, and Maud had a scathing eye. He dismissed the knowledge that her scathing eye, together with her distant gaze and imperious expression, were summoned up to conceal a very real feeling of inadequacy. He had noted the inexpensive blouse and skirt. She was not only untouched, he told himself: she was disastrously unprepared.

Maud, sitting on the terrace with her mother and her aunt, and once more caressing her wide skirts — for they were all now changed for the evening — reflected that if she had risked upsetting her mother she could at this moment be with her friend Julie in the latter's villa in Corsica. In the end some residual affection, something like pity for that unrelenting mother, had made her drop the subject shortly after she had introduced it. She loved her mother, but tried to distance herself from that same mother's plans for her: she had been ashamed, on more than one occasion, of her mother's unforced enthusiasm whenever she invited Julie and Julie's brother Lucien to tea — and Lucien was not even an acceptable escort, in her mother's opinion. She was determined to conduct any flirtation that came her way out of her mother's sight, if that were possible. So far the matter had not arisen, nor had she seriously thought to thwart her mother's plans for her. Sadly, she realised that those plans were all too obvious, and felt a resentment that brought in its wake that unwanted pity. Only she knew how her mother looked forward to Sunday afternoons at the cinema, knew of her secret admiration for certain highly stylised actresses. Only she knew how much it cost her mother to spend two weeks under the humiliating patronage of her sister, for the pleasure of eating that sister's excellent food, even if it came with a full complement of unwanted advice. And

44

for the odd excursion by car, if Xavier were not too busy. And, always and above all, for the chance to meet Xavier's friends, to be in the front row, as it were, when he brought those friends home. In return for these various advantages Nadine played her part, was agreeable and self-effacing, and was pleased to see that Maud's good manners reflected her own.

It was the witching hour, 'between dog and wolf', as Germaine never failed to observe. On the terrace they sat momentarily silent, becalmed by the beauty of the summer evening. A golden light lay on the park; beyond the spacious lawns the trees of the little wood stood motionless. From the house they could hear the distant voices of the servants, who indeed seemed to talk all the time; it was agreeable for once, thought Maud, to know that they were being taken care of, or rather that her mother was being taken care of. She herself endured these summer visits much as she would have endured an enforced stay in some foreign country, in which, for reasons which were mysterious to her, she was detained against her will. Briefly, and almost tenderly, she thought of Dijon, and its monotonous but acceptable routines, in comparison with which this place was both more challenging and more abrasive. She felt no sense of affinity with her aunt, although she responded in a mild way to Xavier's courtesies. She was conscious of her lack of status, conscious too of a very real social inflexibility, which frequently mortified her. She could not laugh and joke and flirt, as other girls seemed to be able to do. In a way it suited her to sit silent on the terrace, at this late golden hour, Xavier absent, her mother and her aunt for once not exerting their formidable and conflicting wills.

She acknowledged the beauty of the setting, although she thought beauty an altogether extravagant term, whether it was applied to poetry or scenery or the harmonious features of an attractive face. She told herself that she had not yet encountered beauty, in its purest form.

What she meant by that was not quite clear to her; in the meantime she rejected what she thought of as imitations. She was aware of opposing a certain resistance to the world, yet all the time she was secretly prepared for that resistance to be overcome. She longed for a lover, one whom she did not know. She would, she was convinced, recognise that stranger, would appropriate him, away from watchful eyes. But this was her secret, the secret that kept her own eyes downcast and her fine lips pressed prudishly together. It would be managed eventually: it would have to be managed. For now her silence, as always, would be the best concealment.

Maud watched a solitary leaf fall to the grass, the first no doubt of the coming autumn, although the sky now held the whiteness of a late summer evening. She admired her foot in its narrow ballerina shoe and suppressed a yawn.

'Tomorrow there will be company for you, Maud,' said her aunt, who had seen the slight grimace but who was uncharacteristically well disposed at this time of day. 'The girls will be coming over. You remember Marie-Paule and Patricia, don't you?' Maud remembered them, without enthusiasm. 'They will want to play tennis with Xavier and his friend. Perhaps they will give you a game, Maud. Did you bring a racquet? No? Well, I'm sure Xavier can find a spare one. Or perhaps you would like to go into Meaux with your mother? Xavier might be able to drive you, although you'll have to take a taxi back. Ah! I think I can hear the car!' She got to her feet. 'Yes! It's Xavier back from the station with his friend. Good. I know dinner has been ready for a few minutes, and Marie gets so put out . . . Here they are.'

Maud and her mother stood up in honour of the epochal arrival of Xavier's friend, who now emerged from the car, rose to his full amazing height, and with every appearance of pleasure surveyed the house.

'Mother,' said Xavier, 'may I present my friend, David Tyler?'

'So good of you to invite me,' murmured the visitor. 'I wonder if I might have a quick bath before dinner? I seem to have been travelling for most of the day.'

Mme de Bretteville, who was not used to having her hand kissed by so handsome a stranger, and who was agreeably impressed by his manners — by his courtliness, in fact — said, in a voice which was only minimally flustered, 'By all means . . . Xavier will show you . . . And if there is anything you want . . . '

'So kind. I usually bathe in the evening, if that is all right with you. But of course you must tell me the house rules. I don't want to be a nuisance.'

When he reappeared they all — Maud, Xavier, Xavier's mother, Maud's mother — gazed at him as if he had successfully survived some initiation ceremony. Across the dinner table they inhaled the aroma of Yardley's lavender soap. The dinner was ruined, but seeing him eat with such good appetite they felt that this did not, for once, matter. Conversation, largely between Mme de Bretteville and the guest, was delicate, muted, almost flirtatious.

'And have you chosen a profession?' enquired Mme de Bretteville with a girlish smile.

'Advertising,' said the guest, manoeuvring a burnt and adhesive slice of apple fritter to his mouth.

'Fascinating,' approved Mme de Bretteville, ardently. 'And such an enterprising choice.'

'Not really,' he said, gazing into her eyes. 'My father owns an agency.'

Maud, noting that this man was probably very wicked, suppressed a smile. At this stage the honour of her family, of her mother and herself, was uppermost in her mind. She was by no means averse to her aunt being made to look a fool. In herself she registered nothing more portentous than an agreeable lightening of the spirits. This holiday might, with a bit of luck, be a little more entertaining than the others.

5

From the rue Laugier one can take one of three main walks. One can turn left into the Avenue de Wagram and go due north until one hears the shunting of the trains in the goods yard beyond the rue de Tocqueville. Another, more promising, way leads one through the Place des Ternes, again along the shorter arm of the Avenue de Wagram to the Place de l'Etoile. The third, and most attractive, takes one to the Place des Ternes, then down the rue du Fauborg Saint-Honoré, which leads straight to the Place du Palais Royal and the centre.

By the end of his third day Harrison had taken all these routes, preferring the third, which released him from the oppression of all the commanding avenues and delivered him to a more recognisable Paris, the city he remembered from previous visits and which he flattered himself he knew quite well. But on those previous visits he had not been alone, had been with his parents, or with Bibi, had taken the Métro with an air of triumph at how easy it all was. Now he felt duty bound to walk, had in fact walked several miles, only to discover that crossing the wide streets was hazardous, even in this month of August, when Paris was supposed to be empty. His head buzzed with noise; he drank too much coffee, just for an excuse to sit down. He would have worried about the amount of money he was spending, had he not been aware of the fact that in the bank, at home — for he supposed that London was now home — was the comfortable sum left to him by Mr Sheed. Nevertheless it pleased him to think of himself as a poor student: indeed, for several reasons he felt a sense of genuine penury which for the moment he did nothing to dismiss. In this place, so large, larger than he remembered it, and so unexpectedly adult, the feeling of penury, of caution, even of suspicion, felt authentic, as if it had been dictated that he should be cut down to size. On more than one occasion the thought had struck him that he was not up to this. In view of his proposal to see the world, in the guise of an amused traveller, his present state of mind was disconcerting. Temporary, of course, but disconcerting nevertheless.

Much of his present dismay had to do with the manner of his arrival. It had been swelteringly hot when he emerged from the Gare du Nord, and his decision to take a bus, worked out well in advance, had disintegrated as soon as he saw the last taxi on the rank preparing to drive off. He had leapt forward and secured it, had bundled his bag on to the rear seat, had squeezed himself in beside it, and had spent the journey to the rue Laugier trying to avoid the hot acrid breath of the driver's dog, which kept a not too friendly eye on him and panted into his face. As the taxi jolted through the evening crowds he had briefly experienced the spirit of adventure which he had supposed would attend him as a familiar. 'I have arrived!' he told himself, dismissing a faint disappointment that there was no one to greet him. Fumbling with his money, also prepared in advance (but it was not enough), he had glanced up at the imposing grey stone building that was to be his home — for how long? He did not know. He had knocked on the glass door of the concierge's apartment, and had announced himself. 'Harrison,' he had said, aware of thirst, and of his shirt sticking to his back.

'There is no one of that name here,' said a small

secretive-looking woman. 'How did you get in? You should have rung the bell.'

'Someone was coming out,' he replied.

'But that was irregular. You should have rung the bell. Whom did you want?'

'Vermeulen,' he said.

'Monsieur and Madame Vermeulen are in Brittany. They are not expected back for another month. Nicole!' she called to someone in the room behind her, which he could not see, the door being open little more than an inch or two. 'The soup! I regret, Monsieur,' she said, making as if to close the door in his face.

'But I am expected,' he said. There was a pause. When the pause proved inconclusive he held out a ten franc note, which she took without acknowledgment, unless, 'Your name again?' was the acknowledgment he had been waiting for.

'Tyler,' he said firmly.

'Ah, yes.' The tone was now pensive, detached. He added another note. Had he been less tired and thirsty he would have been gratified by the predictable nature of this performance, particularly by the detail of the soup, prepared, he supposed, for the evening meal. From the scarcely open door a smell of leeks stole out into the echoing stone vault under which he seemed condemned to stand for ever. He had read about this sort of set-up in a hundred novels, but now found himself too impatient to appreciate it. The note was abstracted, again without acknowledgment. No change of expression was reflected on the woman's not unattractive face. Implacable, he thought; maybe it went with the job. The door silently closed. When it reopened the woman emerged, shutting and locking it behind her. In her hand she held a large key.

'Tyler, you said. You are staying for how long?'

'I don't know. I mean, I'm not sure.'

Unexpectedly, the flat was on the ground floor. The first impression Harrison received was of impenetrable darkness. When a light clicked on behind him, he found himself in a lobby surrounded by closed doors. Trying these he found them to be locked. Beyond the locked doors he imagined closed shutters. The concierge urged him forward. The one door that proved to be unlocked led into a small bedroom, obviously not much used by these Vermeulens, whom he had never met. Here too the shutters were closed, and the air stale and warm. The windows opened inwards, the shutters outwards: with enormous relief he let in air and light, which, since he was on the ground floor, was of a disappointing opacity. To his alarm he could hear footsteps outside the window, advancing and retreating. When he peered out to investigate he found that these footsteps led to a set of dustbins, aligned in a dusty courtyard. Not much of a view, he reflected: this room was obviously used to discourage visitors, who would take the hint and move to a hotel. He however would stay, he told himself, surveying the walnut bed covered with a dubious fur rug, the two armchairs upholstered in a dirt-defying brown material, the small table in *faux bambou*, the wallpaper with its design of autumn leaves, the mirror, again in a frame of *faux bambou*, and a reproduction of Millet's *Angelus*.

It was like the room of someone who had died, some elderly relative, piously taken in, and removed in due course to a hospice, the room kept unchanged as an earnest of good intentions. He wondered why these Vermeulens, whom he understood to be quite rich, preserved this sad room, unless it were destined for the more unfortunate members of their family, who would, in their declining years, or under the threat of some mysterious illness, accept it as appropriate. He himself felt a curious sympathy for it, although he could see that it would be more acceptable in winter than in late summer, when its suffocating brownness, colluding with the faint smell of dustbins from the courtyard, made him determine to be out of it as much as possible. The concierge, crossing the room on silent feet, opened another, unseen door, and revealed a small bathroom.

'I expect you will want the water turned on,' she said.

'Please.' This time he had a note ready. 'And the kitchen?'

'Madame Vermeulen was quite clear that there was to be no cooking. The kitchen therefore is closed. Not available. There is a café on the corner if you wish to take breakfast.'

He was a man who liked his cup of tea, who was used to his mother's cakes and pies, and who, at Cambridge, had achieved not bad results in the kitchen of the house into which he had moved in his third year, and which had won him considerable popularity among his friends. Now there was not even a gas ring, not even a kettle: well, he would just have to make the best of it.

'Thank you, Madame,' he said. He was damned if he was going to give her any more money.

'Be sure to lock up when you go out,' she said.

She was more prison governor than servant, he reflected; if he had been expecting a welcome of sorts, he had no more hopes or illusions on that score. Yet when she left he was momentarily disconcerted by the silence, a silence broken only by the occasional banging of a dustbin lid. He tried the other doors of the flat, which was now revealed as large, but with ramifications which supposed either an extended family or a set of ancillary sitting-rooms: all were locked. His room was clearly the last in a league table of possible rooms, the one that would lose nothing by being lent out to the son of a friend, whom one was obliged, by the terms of that very friendship, to accommodate. Harrison felt a qualm of unease; the arrangement with Tyler had been unofficial from all points of view. The Tyler parents knew nothing of it; certainly the Vermeulens, business associates of Tyler's father, believed that Tyler himself was occupying the room, and would not have offered it had they known it was to be appropriated by an acquaintance of Tyler's, or even a friend.

Why then was he here? He could be in a decent hotel, one which would serve him breakfast, for a sensible outlay which he could well afford. He did not have to stay in this brown prison — there were bars, he noticed, on the window — until Tyler arrived. Tyler was the key to all this. Tyler had suggested it for reasons of his own, or perhaps out of genuine altruism. Being rich, Tyler was not given to spending money unnecessarily. It was far more natural for Tyler to stay in a room like this for no cost than to spend money vulgarly on creature comforts. Compared with Tyler, Harrison felt like any *nouveau riche*, with his craven dependence on laundry and refreshments, and his longing — yes, that was what it was — for a courtesy, however unfairly acquired.

He supposed he must now stay here because Tyler had arranged it, and that he would have to wait for him in case he turned up. He berated himself for succumbing so easily to Tyler's offhand kindness. There had been no need. But with Tyler it was almost a case of *noblesse oblige*: that is to say, Tyler's nobility put everyone else under an obligation. There was a kind of flattery implied if Tyler spared one a thought. And somehow, if he were to move out now, as reason told him to, he would feel that he owed Tyler some sort of explanation, even apology. It would be unthinkable to reject this hospitality as being somehow not up to standard. Therefore he would have to stay here out of sheer embarrassment, reflecting that if he were Tyler, or someone of Tyler's stature, someone not tormented by ideas of cleanliness and simple bourgeois comfort, he would find this dire room quite acceptable. In Tyler's circle, he supposed, hotels were *infra dig*, refuges for conventionally minded people. Of whom I am one, he told himself. Nevertheless, after a wash he felt better. The presence of a telephone in the hall reassured him.

The following days were spent walking. Each morning he left his room with a sense of deliverance, vowing not to return there until he was so tired that all he had to do

53

was go to bed. The weather was still glorious; on the street people congratulated each other, as if responsible for this prolonged sunshine. He found the café the concierge had indicated, had his breakfast, and walked down to the Louvre, his collar open, his jacket over his arm. He found himself going to the Louvre every morning, mainly because he could not think of anything else to do; he was entirely free, and freedom was beginning to breed a certain anxiety. He found to his dismay that he was almost indifferent to the paintings, but liked to linger by the glass cases containing Egyptian scarabs, tiny secretive fetishes which bred in him a fellow feeling for smallness of any kind. Paris was too big, it seemed to him. Everything was too big; the buildings were too big, the streets too wide, the people too severe. The worldly Egyptian smile, encountered several galleries away, seemed to him strangely young, as if worn by a girl or a boy, sophisticated beyond his imagining. It was with a sense of relief that he left the huge building and took the bus across the river to the Luxembourg Gardens.

This was the best part of his day. He drank another cup of coffee in the Place Saint-Sulpice and thought about his future. At this distance the shop seemed not such a bad idea as it had done at first, the prospect of travelling the world alone, like the Flying Dutchman, having lost some of its charm. Sitting in the hot sun, with the taste of coffee in his mouth, it occurred to Harrison to wonder whether this was all that was to be vouchsafed to him in the way of pleasure and contentment, whether those so distant dreams of his childhood garden were merely Wordsworthian glimpses pointing to the glory that was lost rather than pointing forward to a joy that was to come. He was lonely, that was the truth of it. He had thought himself self-sufficient, and he had discovered that he was not. What mattered now, in the light of this revelation (for he had not felt this way before), was to create some sort of attachment for himself, not the spurious deferential attachment

54

that drove him to the likes of Tyler, but a life containing some sort of affection, of stability.

He thought of the furnished flat that he had rented so speedily, without really looking at it, such had been his haste to get away. It would have to do for the time being, he supposed, until he thought to acquire a permanent home. Home! It was a concept, not yet a place. Something else was needed to bring it to life. He thought of his parents' placid undemanding existence, undemanding because they demanded nothing beyond what they already possessed. He more than envied them; he respected them, although he had left them quite happily, thinking to prolong that precious and now legendary childhood by leaving lightheartedly, secure in the knowledge that he could always return. Now, for the first time, he felt cast out, expected to make his life as a man, divorced from the caprices and the velleities of childhood.

He would seek companions, he told himself, for he was newly aware of a coldness which made the heat of the day, the gleam of the sun on his watch, the heaviness of the summer trees little more than devices for throwing this new conviction into sharper relief. He would have to settle down, since he did not have the courage to do otherwise. He felt an access of grief that all his proposed adventures had reduced themselves to this brief interlude, in the hot sun of an exceptional summer, taking the place of those wider wanderings that he had always promised himself. Or had those wanderings been the illusion, the sea on which he had thought to embark and which had so swiftly proved to him his own inadequacies? He knew now that he was not a hero, and the knowledge shamed him. Here, on the Place Saint-Sulpice, he was visited by shame and sadness. It did not comfort him to know that he had done no wrong, that he was innocent. To be guilty — but to be guilty of extravagance, of accomplishment, of a certain grand carelessness — would have been a relief.

Perhaps later, he thought, when I have settled down,

55

made my way in life. That is the time to go away. Perhaps it was always a dream of maturity, of retirement even. Then I shall be fully justified, and surely more experienced, more courageous. Perhaps I am merely too young.

He paid for his coffee and took a taxi back to the rue Laugier. In the hall of the flat he switched on the light, consulted his diary, then telephoned the shop in Denbigh Street. He had no confidence that the call would be answered; for all he knew Thomas Cook had decamped as soon as his back was turned. The man's slightly effeminate voice, so at odds with his incurious face, came through quite clearly, making him jump: his nerves were decidedly on edge this morning.

'Cook? Harrison here. Everything all right?'

'Yes. I've moved in, if that's OK with you.'

'Of course, of course. I've just thought, don't get rid of any of those books. Someone must want them. I might do a catalogue when I get home.'

'When's that then?'

'Oh, I don't know. Soon. I'll let you know, of course. Have you managed to clean up at all?'

'It's looking OK. Wants a few coats of paint though. Navy'd be nice.'

'You're right. I'll have it refurbished when I get back. You could take a few days off if you wanted to. Just as long as you're in the flat. I don't particularly want the place to stand empty.'

'I don't mind. Perhaps I'll take a week when you get back. Having a good time?'

'Fine, thank you.' He was amazed how easy it was to communicate with this man, whom, after all, he hardly knew. But then, he had not done much communicating recently, he told himself. And maybe the book business would not be too bad after all. This afternoon he would take a look at the second-hand boxes by the Seine to see what was on offer and how it was priced. He had, when he thought about it, a great deal to learn, and the process might take him some time.

But in the event he went back to the Luxembourg Gardens, and merely sat in the sun, thinking back on the emotional changes that the last few days had brought about. Now that his future was, as he thought with a pang, more or less settled, he was in less of a hurry to move, to put himself out. It was as if his resolution, or his defeat (for he thought of it as a defeat), had afforded him a further interval of freedom. He would not go back to the Louvre, he thought; he would have a holiday. After more coffee in a nearby café he took an iron chair, sat down, folded his arms, and prepared to spend the afternoon in this manner. Almost immediately he felt restless. All this would be more than tolerable, he reflected, if he had a girlfriend with him. Or even a friend. The girls he had left at home now appeared to him distant and diminished, as if seen through the wrong end of a telescope, or in someone else's photographs. They had all been pleasant, those friends of his sister's, with whom he had grown up: agreeable, uncomplicated, polite to his mother, and more than willing to keep him company. He was thought to be attractive, with his slight but wiry frame, his hungry smile, but somehow it had been impossible to misbehave in such a setting, with so much goodwill being demonstrated around him, his mother bringing out a tray of lemonade into the garden, his father offering to run the girls home. And the garden, always that garden.

He had made up for lost time at Cambridge, but here again he had been lucky; his girlfriend, Sally, had been just as decent and friendly as the companions of his blameless adolescence. Therefore making love at last had involved no loss of innocence. It was not even a rite of passage, more an extension of play, with an unexpected conclusion. Guilt and anxiety were unimaginable, though now that he was on his own he knew both. He had been remarkably fortunate, he now reflected. He and Sally had kept each

57

other faithful company for three years, sleeping together but as often as not going on long walks or listening to music. Their liaison was regarded as a settled thing by their friends; they were neither challenged nor disturbed. It had been an interlude of almost miraculous harmony, of lack of tension. Yet perhaps for that very reason, at the end of three years they knew that they would part, and would part no less amicably than they had stayed together.

He would see her again, he thought, but vaguely, without urgency. He was ready now for something different, something that would fill his horizon and take the place of that pilgrimage he had promised himself to the end of the world and for which he had proved unready. It was not sex he wanted, for sex had never seemed to him to present any problems, to be readily available, to be enjoyed without impatience or anxiety, to be an extended form of friendship. He wanted someone to fill the void, to appease the sudden lack which afflicted him even now, sitting in the sun, watching the children being fed their afternoon snack by their mothers. These mothers smiled at him, which made him feel shy, unworthy. He did not quite know what to do with himself, although the day had passed somehow, and not unpleasantly. He supposed that he might spend a few more days in the same manner, just to prove to himself that he was having a holiday. Then, he thought, he would pack it in and go home.

If the days were tolerable the evenings were not. He seemed to be too early for the night's activities. He took his bath at six, glad to get rid of the dust of the afternoon, and then, refreshed, walked out to find a brasserie for his apéritif and dinner. Yet he seemed always to be the first customer, and was paying his bill just as others were arriving. Then began more wandering, although, tired by now, he did not move far from the Place des Ternes, and after a final cup of coffee, he would be back in the gloom of the rue Laugier by nine-thirty at the latest. Sleep was no problem; he could always count on sleep. But sleep seemed a poor substitute for the adventures he had planned. In bed, ruminating the day's emptiness, he reflected that although little had happened since his arrival a week ago, he had been bedevilled by thoughts, all of them, for no reason he could fathom, unwelcome.

When the telephone rang he nearly screamed. He must have been asleep, ambushed by one of those brief but steep descents which take the mind by surprise. He stumbled into the hall and picked up the receiver with a hand made nervous by surprise.

'Hello?' His voice sounded higher than usual.

'Noddy. *Comment ça va?*'

'Tyler! Where are you?'

'I'm staying in a rather agreeable house, not too far from Paris.'

There was a pause. There were many pauses in Tyler's telephone conversations, which served to disconcert the recipient. Harrison wondered if he had been too enthusiastic, whether he should have been nonchalant, and debonair, as debonair as Tyler. '*Quel bon vent?*' he should have said. But this was impossible: Tyler's qualities were a matter of caste. To emulate them would merely expose one to ridicule.

'You play tennis, don't you?'

To this apparent *non sequitur* he replied that he did, but that he had not played for ages.

'The thing is' (and here Tyler's voice mysteriously deepened) 'that tennis is being played here, at this house I'm staying in, and the girls are rather short of partners. In a word, you're invited for the weekend: they can lend you a racquet.'

'What girls?'

'Oh, just girls.' There was another pause. Voices could be heard in the background.

'How do I get there? Tyler? Are you still there?'

'You take the afternoon train to Meaux. I'll meet you there. Goodbye.'

'Tyler! Are you sure? I mean, I don't know these people. Who are they?'

'Bring a tie,' said Tyler, and the receiver was replaced, at Tyler's end.

Whatever went on in that place was evidently destined to remain opaque. But he was generally if diffusely keyed up by the prospect of going away, of seeing Tyler, of seeing anyone, although this invitation seemed to be Tyler's own. He did not even know the names of the people whose house this was. Yet he would go, since Tyler seemed to have the matter in hand. The house appeared to be in his gift, just as this flat was. It was impossible not to accept.

The following morning he retrieved his shirts from the laundry on the corner, packed his bag (surely there was no need to come back to this room?) and made his way to the station long before he needed to. It was stupefyingly hot. He had not reckoned on the French getting ready for their mid-August holiday, and found himself jostled and bumped on the station and was obliged to surrender his seat on the train to an elderly woman carrying nothing more than a string bag. When he emerged at Meaux the silence seemed almost palpable. He would have liked to linger on the station forecourt, so precious did this hot country silence seem to him after the dimness of the rue Laugier. Indeed, he was obliged to wait for some thirty minutes, during which no one met him. He wondered whether the whole thing had been a hoax, one of Tyler's jokes, whether he would not be obliged to go back to Paris on the next train, and was about to give up, heavy hearted and disappointed once again, when a car drew up in a spurt of dust, and Tyler emerged, long legs preceding him, blue shirt sleeves rolled up to reveal brown arms. He was accompanied by a girl of medium height, with dark blonde hair, a fine bosom, and a closed secretive face.

'There you are,' said Tyler. 'This is Maud, by the way. She speaks excellent English.'

The ensuing silence, as they travelled back in the car to

60

whatever house was apparently — by Tyler's decree — ready to receive him, might have made him nervous had he not been lulled by the heat, by the fixity of the sun, by the sheer relief of being in a car instead of on his feet, and by the undemanding presence of the girl, the back of whose brown neck he was obliged, out of a sort of courtesy, to contemplate. He assumed that she was the daughter of the house, wondered what social duties were expected of him. He thought it odd that she paid him no attention, for if she were indeed his hostess he might have been grateful for certain overtures. But on the whole he found the silence acceptable: clearly Tyler was in charge. Once again, as was usual in Tyler's company, he gave himself to the pleasure of being taken over, of being directed by a will superior to his own. In Tyler's company it was natural to contemplate Tyler's destiny, as if assisting at some pageant, in which the hero, recognisable by his physical splendour, performs some symbolic act of valour. To his knowledge Tyler had never performed such an act. Nevertheless, his contemporaries at Cambridge, particularly an envious chorus of women, discussed him as if he were indeed that hero, or perhaps as if they needed him to be. His intellect had not been outstanding, yet he was capable of random shafts of brilliance. It was his ease that they loved and envied; he himself was not immune to its spell. The girl, he noted, sat carefully not touching him. Tyler himself did not put out a hand to touch her. But then he had no need to. Harrison, with a certain grim amusement, had watched Tyler in action, or rather in inaction, before.

'Here we are,' said Tyler pleasantly, drawing up outside what seemed to be a rather imposing house. A tall man, the sun glinting on his glasses, came down the steps to greet them. 'Xavier de Bretteville,' he said. They shook hands.

'My mother will be delighted,' said Xavier. 'Dinner is at eight. Maud, I believe you are wanted.'

Harrison followed them inside, grateful for the coolness of the black and white tiled hall.

'Xavier is your brother?' he asked of the girl.

'My cousin,' she answered. Those were the first words he heard her speak, and, it seemed, the last, as she disappeared silently up the stairs. The organisation of this visit, he could see, was fated to remain mysterious. He turned to meet Tyler's lazy smile.

'You'll have your work cut out,' said Tyler, with exactly that mixture of menace and comprehension that he had come to expect.

6

Tyler was looked upon with favour at La Gaillarderie, particularly by the servants, to whom he offered gratuities as well as his laundry. With the exception of Xavier they addressed him as Tyler, as if they were all at school. He was treated with the respect accorded to a head prefect, but beneath that respect lurked thoughts of plunder, theirs, and, they hoped, his. He had only to appear in his white shirt and shorts (dazzling, thanks to the ministrations of Mme Besson, who came in every weekday to perform whatever tasks were allotted to her by Charles), his handsome head slightly tilted, for them all to feel invigorated, on their mettle, and also on their best behaviour, ready to be charming, but also to submit to his wishes, for Tyler was adept at organising the day's entertainments.

Soon Marie-Paule and Patricia were arriving earlier and earlier with their tennis racquets, and were sometimes obliged to spend an hour talking to Maud, while Tyler, Edward and Xavier went to Meaux in the car to buy the delicacies which Mme de Bretteville, in an excess of extravagance, decided that she needed for the evening meal, or simply lingered in the woods before returning to the girls, with their short skirts, their enthusiasm, and their all too transparent designs.

Even in these peregrinations Tyler took the lead, Xavier and Edward accompanying him loyally but in a subordinate manner, as if they had taken an oath of suzerainty, and were ready to follow him on his exploits and to carry back, like minstrels, the account of his prowess. In this, Xavier at least was wholehearted, gratified by the mere presence of his friend and the galvanising effect he seemed to have had on the entire household. Edward privately — but only privately — admitted to the occasional twinge of jealousy. Seeing Tyler's long lean body relaxing on the lawn it occurred to him to wonder whether perhaps, in middle age, that figure might not undergo the depredations common to middle-aged men, might not put on weight, become less lithe, perhaps look a little ridiculous in its pursuit of every woman in sight? Unfortunately there was as yet no sign of such a fall from grace. They were all in love with Tyler, it seemed, as much for what he represented — youth, health, beauty — as for what he was. They conferred on him the function of master of the revels. As each golden day succeeded the last they imagined that they saw in him the spirit of summer incarnate.

For it was, they agreed, an exceptional summer. Every morning the brilliant light poured in through open doors and windows; the lightest of dews evaporated from grass fast fading from green to yellow; the trees, weighted with heavy foliage, stood motionless, poised for a sign, which never came, that it was time to shed their leaves. They were all aware that they were living through a period of enchantment, so that ordinary occupations had no purchase on their minds. Even Germaine and Nadine spent mornings seated on the terrace, talking more intimately than they had ever talked before, but in fact drawn by the spectacle of the young people, to whom this summer seemed to belong.

They did not begrudge them their leisure, this interval of extended play. They followed with almost loving eyes their lightning dashes across the lawn, noting despite themselves that weightlessness that would be lost with the passing of the years, feeling in themselves an unsought-for stolidity which detracted from the honourable positions they had created for themselves, their assured status as wives or widows, their complacency as mothers. Nevertheless they felt that they had done well, had performed their allotted tasks as best they could, had no need to bluff or to dissemble, could meet the world more or less on equal terms, above all had no further need to compete. Yet perhaps because of the light, the great sun, some edge of regret came back to them, together with the sound of balls hitting racquets in the far distance, so that they turned to each other in something like consolation. Convention had brought them together; the image of their vanished youth made them, for a brief moment, intimate.

'You never thought of marrying again?' queried Germaine.

'I may have thought of it. No man ever did.'

'Were you unhappy?'

'I regretted much. I loved Pierre-Yves, but he was only with me for six years. After that I was left alone, although I was a young woman. But I had a child, you see, and so I was expected to behave like a nun. And I did.'

She compressed her lips, thinking back with bitterness on those years and on her poor compensations, her afternoons in the municipal gardens reading the obituaries in the *Figaro*, her visits to the Lux cinema where she would succumb with longing to the sight of glamorous women no younger than herself, that painfully gained and so precious half-hour in bed when Maud was visiting her friend in London.

'A woman's life is very short,' said Germaine. 'At least it is if you were brought up as we were brought up, with no mother, the house badly run, no relatives to speak of. It was natural that we should have married the first man who came near us. And then we were trapped.'

'Aren't you happy with your life?'

'Father bundled me off, you know. Robert was almost a stranger. And now I hardly ever see him. When he's not

65

on a tour of duty he's in Paris. I don't ask what he does there. It was the house I loved, to be honest with you. I wanted to make it my house. Now that it is I find it more restful when Robert is away. But that's what I mean — we gave up.'

'Or were given up,' said Nadine sombrely.

'Look at those girls, Marie-Paule and Patricia. They are charming, but they are certainly not intelligent. Yet they know exactly what they want. They want fun, they want a good time. They don't want to settle down — why should they?'

'They want men.'

'Oh, they want men all right. Why not?'

'Do you think they . . . ?'

'I shouldn't be surprised.'

There was a brief silence while they digested the implications of this remark.

'Perhaps they are right,' said Nadine. 'Yet they are very blatant about it. Don't they want to get married?'

'My dear Nadine, there's nothing to stop a girl like that getting married if she wants to. And often a marriage of that kind is very successful; the girl is experienced, and she has more partners to choose from. You're thinking of Maud, I know.' She shot a glance at her sister, wondering how far she might go. 'Maud is very beautifully brought up, and very charming. But so quiet, Nadine, almost prim. This morning I had to urge her to go out and join the others. I think she was prepared to spend the morning sitting indoors with a book.'

'She is a little frightened by those girls, I think.'

'Not by the boys?'

'Frankly, she finds the girls too loud, too forward. It is not pleasant for her to watch them flirting.'

'Then she should flirt a little herself.'

'Maud does not know how to flirt. And if she did she would be too proud to flirt in public. She has deep feelings,

66

I believe. And she is easily hurt. There is a lot of her father in her.'

'Not . . . '

'No, thank God. Not that.'

'Yet you want her to marry?'

Nadine sighed. 'I long for her to marry. If I knew that she were settled I could settle myself. My life, such as it is, would be easier. I love her, and she loves me, but we are no good for each other. We make each other lonely. I don't want her to stay with me. I'm not a good influence.'

'How strange that you should say that. I think my heart will break when Xavier marries. Yet marry he must, of course, and he will. He will make some girl very happy.'

'Yes. He is a gentle boy, too gentle for those girls you have saddled him with.'

'I thought they would bring him out, relax him.'

'You thought wrongly. They inhibit him. Xavier and Maud are quite alike in certain respects.'

'You are not thinking . . . ?'

'No, no.' She sighed. 'Xavier will be all right. His English friends will make a man of him. He is fascinated by them, particularly by Tyler. Both those girls are. I only wish that Maud were having a better time. Marie-Paule and Patricia are not very kind to her.'

'Girls like that are not kind to other girls.'

'You take it all very lightly. Maud deserves better. Perhaps she will be happier when she gets to England; she is going to stay with her friend Jean Bell next week. Jean Bell, frankly, is a better class of girl than those two. And Maud is nothing if not refined.'

'Quite,' said Germaine drily. She had a faint suspicion that her hospitality was being abused by the uncensored nature of these remarks. In the brief silence that followed, something of the sisters' old antagonism revived. Each judged it prudent to gaze abstractedly over the park to the wood which shielded the tennis court from their direct gaze. The sound of the game, and of the accompanying voices, had been in abeyance for some time before they became aware of the pause, or the interval, which in its turn gave rise to a certain tension.

'They will be very warm,' murmured Nadine.

'I will bring out the lemonade. They should be coming back soon. The girls are staying for lunch. Do persuade Maud to join in more, even if you think this is all a waste of time for her.' She was now combative. 'She could talk to Harrison. He seems quite pleasant.'

'She prefers Tyler. And Xavier, of course.'

'Tyler would not look at a girl like Maud. Tyler is a scoundrel,' she said appreciatively. 'I doubt if he would be interested in someone who makes so little effort.'

'And of course Maud would not look at Tyler.'

'Why ever not?'

'He is, as you say, a scoundrel. Maud has more sense.'

Maud, at that moment trailing dispiritedly across the lawn, did not look sensible. The rare moment of dismay was so profound that it had stripped her face of its normal expression of impervious calm, although she was careful to rearrange her features before approaching her mother and her aunt. At least the morning's humiliations were behind her, the humiliations she had come to expect since the arrival of the two Englishmen and their effect on Marie-Paule and Patricia. She had only to note their heightened colour, to become aware of their increased heat, to know that she would have to endure their shrieking excitement, to be followed by the portentous silence which ensued when they retired to the summer house, with Tyler, supposedly to smoke a cigarette, while Xavier and Edward played a desultory and embarrassed game of tennis and she bent her face studiously to her book (*Jane Eyre*) and attempted to summarise plot, characters, and style, as she had been taught to do.

The misery of these mornings was all but unendurable. Worst of all was her ignorance of quite what went on in the summer house. She had only to see the tennis racquets thrown down on to the grass, as if at a prearranged signal, to imagine scenes of lubricity which brought a colour to her normally matte cheeks. She longed to know exactly what went on; she longed to be included. But, more than to be included, she longed for exclusivity. In her mind she eliminated Marie-Paule and Patricia, for they were her intimate enemies. She did not distinguish between them, although Marie-Paule was marginally the more gentle of the two. To Maud they were grossly, obscenely physical, with the abundant rippling hair they tossed back from their necks and foreheads, the beading of perspiration on their upper lips, and their insistent odour of scent and sweat. Yet she found that their very grossness bred a kind of excitement. She imagined them ready for anything, like prostitutes, and allied in some terrible *camaraderie* in their desire to please Tyler. So naked was their intention that it had the grandeur of fearlessness, and this was very occasionally enough to tempt the other man, Harrison, to join them, while Xavier gallantly kept her company and asked her about her book. At such times she was tempted to get up and run into the shelter of the wood to hide her burning face.

She envied them, and yet how she despised them. They made her feel awkward, but they made her feel superior. 'Good book, Maud?' Patricia would ask, emerging from the summer house, and, picking up her racquet and striding away, she would not wait for an answer. Above all they made her feel lonely. In her fierce remoteness she sensed rather than observed Xavier's kindness, and the Englishman Harrison's humble curiosity. But most of all she was aware of Tyler and of what he was doing in the summer house. Or rather what was being done to him, for she imagined him being set upon, being tormented by those two Amazons, who, in their dreadful way, seemed unmoved by gratitude or love, but simply energised by victory. Tyler, when he emerged, would sit ruminatively on the steps of the summer house, sucking the stem of a blade of grass, equally unmoved. Did she detect, or did she simply want to detect, a very slight moodiness in his attitude, the head bent, the arms clasped round the knees, the expression absent? Could she have thought up anything to say at such moments she would have approached him. But nothing appropriate ever came to mind, and so the moments passed.

Walking under the trees, in an attempt to calm her furious disapproval, her unhappiness, she would sometimes encounter Harrison, with a disconcerted expression on his not unattractive face. Harrison too was unhappy but supposed it did not matter. He had not chosen to stay in this place; it had been chosen for him by Tyler. And out of a sense of how it behoved him to conduct himself, he modelled himself as best he could on Tyler, since Tyler appeared to be giving satisfaction all round. On one occasion he had allowed himself to be led into the summer house by Patricia, only to come upon the other two furiously engaged. To stay would have been unthinkable, to leave equally so: he stayed. This went so sharply against his instincts that he thought back almost with nostalgia to his quiet days in the rue Laugier, where at least no one outraged him. In his worst moments, the moments following the scene in the summer house, he saw himself pensive, his head bent to a glass case containing Egyptian scarabs, his mind on higher things. He discounted the loneliness. Loneliness, he felt, was sometimes the price one paid for integrity. Yet he felt uneasily that he was bound to stay here for as long as Tyler did, for he was in some sense Tyler's guest. And Tyler showed no desire to leave, although Harrison knew that at some abrupt and unheralded moment Tyler would decide the day of their departure. Then, he supposed, he would be free, free even to go home, although at this juncture he could hardly remember the shop, which he saw as some kind of fiction. He dismissed the part of his life that he knew would be lived in shadow, away from the light of this place, which he could see was beautiful, but with a beauty not entirely meant for him. When he came upon Maud, whose expression indicated that her thoughts were not dissimilar to his own, he felt a shock. Something inside him softened; at the same time he rejected the sense of failure that apparently united the two of them, or would have done, had they been more in sympathy.

'I'll walk back with you,' he said awkwardly. 'It must be nearly one o'clock.'

Neither made any reference to the events of the morning. Those events were experienced, in retrospect, as alien. Yet what shame they felt was not the shame of onlookers but of outsiders. Fate had ordained that they should be unclaimed, uninitiated. Harrison knew that Patricia had exhibited not kindness in leading him into the summer house, but a sly pleasure in his confusion. How these women liked to take the lead! He had a passing moment of compassion for Maud, the unqualified, until he remembered how disastrously unqualified he was himself.

On the terrace the heat was extravagant. A wasp settled on the sticky rim of Tyler's empty lemonade glass.

'It will be too hot for tennis this afternoon,' said Germaine. 'I dare say you will want a siesta.'

'Oh, no,' said Tyler abstractedly. 'I like the heat.'

'Ah, here are the others. Take my sister in, Tyler. She thinks she may have a touch of the sun.'

'It is cooler in Dijon,' Nadine explained, her hand to her forehead. 'I am not used to such sun.'

'Then no doubt you are looking forward to going back,' said Germaine tartly.

'Yes, perhaps we should think about that. Maud goes to London next Monday.'

Germaine, moved against her will by her sister's red face — how quickly she had lost her looks! — said, 'Then you could stay here for a few more days. Xavier will drive you to the station when you want to go. Perhaps we are both a bit tired. It has been a busy time.' She sighed. It was time the others went too, she thought. The girls would surely melt away as soon as the visitors left. She had thought her words to contain the most delicate of hints to Tyler, although at night, alone, she willed him to stay after the others had left. In the light of day she thought differently, and otherwise, longing to be left alone again, among more manageable sensations. Tyler, however, appeared not to have heard her.

At lunch they were more silent than usual. Germaine regretted that the roast veal with endives was too heavy a dish for so hot a day, although the young people ate mechanically but with good appetite. Marie-Paule and Patricia, like the healthy animals they were, wanted only to eat and to fall asleep. Maud and Harrison ate precisely, not looking at each other. Even Tyler seemed abstracted, while Nadine, her hand moving gingerly to her forehead, drank glass after glass of water. Nobody wanted cheese. Only Harrison and Maud ate a peach. It was almost with a sense of relief that they rose and moved away from each other.

'I will ask Marie to make you more lemonade,' said Germaine, tired now. 'Remember that the servants are not to be disturbed. They are going out anyway. The cinema, I believe. In this heat! But it is probably cooler in the dark. Come, Nadine. We will leave these young people to their own devices. But perhaps Marie-Paule and Patricia have something planned? Your aunt will not have seen much of you today.'

Harrison and Tyler saw the girls down the drive and across the road to the house inaptly named Le Colombier, where their aunt was lying down in the dark with a head-ache and desirous not to be disturbed. Harrison yawned, and quickly effaced the yawn with his hand. 'I think I'll go in,' he said. 'I don't feel up to much after that lunch. I'll see you later.' After they had watched him go back into the house Maud turned resolutely away, determined not to ascertain whether Tyler was following her. She made her way instinctively to the summer house, and sat on the steps, as she had seen Tyler do that morning. After a few minutes she registered the fact that she was entirely alone. She sighed and lifted her face to the sun, tired of the holiday, which was not a holiday, tired of the further politeness that would be demanded of her, and which she would offer, with her usual dignity, to Jean Bell's parents. It would be all art galleries and ancient buildings in London, she thought, and when Jean Bell returned with her it would be all questions about the date of the tombs in the Dijon museum.

She surrendered herself to the heat of the day, opening the collar of her blouse a little wider to allow the afternoon sun to reach her skin. The heat met some desire in her for expansion; she wanted to melt, to be absorbed. To be taken over! With this desire came a sorrow that she could not be more active, could not hold, or, it seemed, even attract attention like those girls had done this morning, could not in fact energise or convert the feelings that had so disconcerted her when Tyler had disappeared into the summer house and then reappeared alone, and had sat as she was now sitting, his back view expressing something new, solitariness, as if he were subject to ordinary human feeling, even as she was. But that was the difference between them, the insuperable barrier that would hinder any exchange, for while she was aware of her inadequacies, Tyler appeared to have none. Even the other man, Harrison, whom she had initially thought to be more interested in her, had given way to easier distractions. They were like some primitive species, she thought, like mayflies, or plants that bloomed only once, with the difference that their more evolved condition, their higher animality, enabled them to revive again and again, ready for further play in the humming summer air.

The grass was so dry that she did not hear his footfalls, and when she saw his feet approaching she lowered her eyes suddenly to the ground. The wooden steps creaked under his weight as he sat down beside her.

'Here you are,' he said absently. 'Aren't you too hot?'

'No,' she replied. 'I like the heat.'

Indeed she felt that the heat had given her some power, so that she did not immediately move away from him.

'I think you are not having a very good time, Maud.'

'No,' she heard herself say. 'Not very.'

'I expect you miss your own friends. Your boyfriend. You have a boyfriend?'

'Of course.'

This was not entirely untrue. The young instructor of her English course was plainly fond and had asked her out several times. When it came to inviting him to the house and introducing him to her mother she had decided that her mother's enthusiasm would be more than she could endure and had deduced from this that the man had no real fascination for her other than a mild liking and an opportunity to avoid the Sunday visit to the cinema. He would drive her out into the country: they would have lunch: they would kiss in a manner more consistent with friendship than with desire. Sometimes, on the return journey in the car, she would almost regret not having gone to the cinema with her mother. It was the cinema that now came to mind, images of other kisses, other bodies.

'You seem quite happy here,' she said with an effort.

'Oh, I'm not happy all the time.'

He picked a blade of grass and slid it between his lips. Inside the open collar of her blouse he could see her breast rising and falling. He stood up abruptly, but lingered. She waited, bracing herself for disappointment.

He held out a hand. 'Come on. I want to show you something.'

She took his hand, touching him for the first time. He led the way across the parched lawn, into the cool of the house, up the stairs and along the upper corridor. He took her to a door at the very end which was always kept locked, turned the key and pointed to another dustier staircase which she had not known existed. It was very dark. When he pushed open a door at the top the sudden glare confused her until her eyes adjusted to the light and she saw that they were under the roof. It was very hot, very silent. She walked to the dormer window and rested her head against the glass. She knew without looking that he stood behind her. Then he turned her round, put his hands on her waist, and laid her down gently on to the bare boards.

'I have never done this before,' she said.

'I know,' he replied. 'That's all right.'

It was over too soon. It was she who reached up to him and encouraged him to start again. When a distant clock chimed four she put out a hand and reached for her clothes. 'I love you, Tyler,' she said. He said nothing.

They locked the door at the bottom of the stairs behind them, stood for a moment looking at each other, then parted without a word. When she slipped into the room she shared with her mother she merely noted that her mother was asleep, then stretched out on her bed and fell asleep herself.

That evening, at dinner — stuffed peppers and pancakes — they were all in a better mood. All, it seemed, had slept and were refreshed. Nadine noted that her daughter looked better, had lost that air of haughty composure that occasionally made her look too old for her years, a fact apparently also noted by Harrison, who gazed at Maud with frank admiration. How simple he is, thought Nadine, who appreciated quite another kind of simplicity in men. Tyler was at his most charming, waiting on his hostess with the most delicate attentions, making her laugh, even teasing her. Germaine, her colour high, attempted to tease him back, without, it must be said, a great deal of success. Our generation is no good at this sort of thing, thought Nadine, who was not altogether unhappy to discover this. She is making herself look ridiculous, she thought; then, in an excess of sisterly solidarity, resolved to put a stop to it.

'Maud must think about leaving,' she said. 'She is expected in London next week. When did you tell Jean to meet you, Maud?'

'Next Monday. It will mean a very early start if I am to catch the train. Or perhaps I should leave here on Sunday and spend the night somewhere in Paris. I could ring up a friend . . . My friend Julie,' she explained. 'Julie is studying in Paris.'

'But will she be there?' enquired her mother. 'I think you said she will be in Corsica until September.'

'Well, it is nearly September,' said Maud calmly.

'I have a better idea,' said Tyler. 'Noddy and I must be going too. You have been too kind and we have had a marvellous time. I can't thank you enough. But we should be moving on. Maud can come with us tomorrow and spend some time at the Vermeulens'. I know they'd be delighted. Armand Vermeulen is a friend of my parents.'

'I don't think . . . ' said Germaine.

'Nothing to worry about. And then we'll put her on the train on Monday morning. That way she'll be taken care of.'

'What do you think, Nadine?'

'I think it's very kind of Tyler, and — what did you say your name was? What did he call you? Noddy?'

'Edward,' said Harrison firmly. 'My name is Edward.'

'Then that's settled.'

'You're sure, Nadine? After all, it means imposing on these friends of Tyler. Of Tyler's parents.'

'I am quite reassured to know that Maud will not be alone in Paris. After all, the times have been so unsettled.'

'But this is 1971, Madame. You need have no fears on that score.'

She smiled at him. 'And now I should like to offer an invitation. I should like to take us all out to dinner tomorrow night, to say thank you to Germaine, and to thank her not only for her hospitality but for a most enjoyable holiday. Where do you recommend, Germaine?'

76

'Well, they say the Anneau d'Or in Meaux is quite excellent, but really, Nadine, there is no need . . . '

'There is no need, but, I'm sure, every wish.'

She smiled triumphantly at her sister, surprised a smile on Maud's face, she who never smiled. Harrison — how simple he was, she thought again — smiled as happily as a boy. Tyler did not smile but stood behind his hostess's chair. When she stood up and turned round to thank him he took her hand and kissed it.

All went to bed quite happy that night.

7

Harrison did not immediately enquire how Tyler had prevailed upon the concierge to open all the doors in the flat, which was now revealed as agreeable and even welcoming, in sharp contrast to the archaic bedroom to which he had earlier been consigned. He particularly appreciated the salon, with its yellow walls and carpets, its two navy blue sofas, its glass coffee table, and its *faux-naif* pictures of cows in sunlit pastures on the walls — an interior decorator's touch, he deduced, and bethought himself fleetingly of the red brick building in which he had so hastily rented a flat. Instantly he decided to move from there, to put down roots, to exert his claim to pale walls and carpets, and to say goodbye for ever to makeshifts, to sharing, to discomfort.

He even looked forward to putting down roots in the rue Laugier now that he had been rescued from loneliness. He reckoned he might stay another two or three weeks, or until these Vermeulens let it be known, via the concierge, that they were about to return. He was, after all, owed something in the nature of a final holiday before taking up the burden of his adult life. Moreover there was something attractive in the prospect of spending days in the company of Tyler and Maud, three being a more propitious number than two for his immediate purpose, which was to drift in their wake, like a child with his parents, not having to speak or even to listen, but simply to stroll dreamily ten paces behind them, and thus free to enjoy the sights and sounds of Paris without that obligation to be constantly on the alert which destroys pleasure.

'Which room shall I have?' he asked, heaving his bag into the salon. It seemed, as always, natural to ask this of Tyler. Maud too, he noted, waited respectfully for him to pronounce.

Tyler ran his fingers through his black hair, which was growing rather long. He had caught the sun at La Gaillarderie and was now brown down to the opening of his shirt which he wore carelessly, as he wore all his clothes, but with an elegance which Harrison knew he could never master. He regretted his tie, his blazer, his lace-up shoes, all relics of an earlier life which should have been left behind long ago. He might ask Tyler to accompany him to the shops or perhaps advise him in some way: no, the idea was instantly repugnant. He would just have to keep a weather eye open for that exact colour of blue Oxford cloth, and that type of cream cotton trouser. In the meantime his blazer and flannels would have to do. Fortunately he had plenty of white shirts, but none so well cut as Tyler's, which, owing to his dramatic height, would have to have been custom made. This interlude in the flat would provide him with an ideal opportunity to study Tyler for his own purposes, to acquire from him by stealth pointers to successful living, to watch him at leisure and unobserved, while Tyler's attention was devoted to Maud, poor Maud, who would soon be eaten up and as easily digested as all the others who had gone before and who would certainly come after. Not that he was out of sympathy with Maud; he thought her very pretty and admirably quiet, but he pitied her for allowing herself to be beguiled by Tyler, particularly since she had already witnessed the tenor of his behaviour from his activities in the summer house.

If he thought of Maud and Tyler making love, as he not infrequently did, certain looks and tiny gestures on her part having been intercepted by him — or was he preter-

79

naturally alert? — it was with a kind of woeful excitement which was both pleasurable and dangerous. If he thought more of Tyler than of Maud in this connection, the fact did not strike him as unnatural. He had predicted this affair before it had even happened, simply by virtue of Tyler's being Tyler; he could not see that Maud had anything to offer him, attractive though he could observe her to be. She was, quite simply, not as glamorous as Tyler; Tyler outshone her, as he was programmed to do, probably for the rest of his life. Thus Tyler's success held the seeds of Tyler's downfall, for although he would constantly be loved, admired, appropriated, he would always be frustrated by the sameness of the pattern, and the quest for his true partner, who by the nature of things must be as prestigious as himself, would be unending.

It did not displease Harrison to think along these lines, while waiting for an answer to his question about the rooms. Tyler, however, stood silent, head lowered, contemplating the yellow carpet. Finally, with an air of resolution, he took a crumpled handful of money from his pocket, turned to Harrison, and said, 'We need supplies. Milk, bread, that sort of thing. Fresh stuff. I noted a shop on the corner. Could you be an angel? Maud and I will sort ourselves out here.'

'Oh, all right. Have you decided where we are to sleep?'

Tyler smiled. 'Not yet. Off you go,' he added gently. Take your time, was the implication. 'There's a string bag on the back of the kitchen door. Fruit,' he added, pushing Harrison into the hall. Maud looked at him silently, her colour rising. He felt a slight distaste for her urgency, thinking it at odds with her superior expression. At the same time he acknowledged a stab of fellow feeling for her obvious lack of self-mastery, of any kind of mastery, for how could someone so transparent subdue a character like Tyler? He had it in him to pity Maud for the imminent breakdown of her entire personality. That haughty air would not serve her for much longer, he thought, unless she were strong enough to resist the temptation to become Tyler's slave. He felt that he should warn her, should take her on one side, and tell her that as Tyler's friend he felt it his duty to offer some advice, unacceptable though it might be: her best plan might be to catch the next train to Dijon, or to London — but if she were going to London that meant staying here until next Monday, and it was only Thursday morning . . .

It also occurred to him that if Tyler turned ruthless, Maud might be in need of his protection. At the same time, he wanted not to be cast as the blameless character who would be called upon to defend a woman's honour. He would prefer, if given the choice, that odd sensation of being drawn on by them, of literally following them around, of observing their gestures, watching their progress. The idea excited him. He told himself that this did not necessarily constitute a misdemeanour. Indeed it was largely innocent, part of the pattern, now repeating itself, of a contented childhood spent loitering in the wake of the adults, while thinking his own thoughts, amusing himself mildly by imitating their walk, or simply kicking a pebble along, his mind reduced to animal level while others did his thinking for him. Hence the degree of self-absorption which no doubt accounted for his not very active sex life: he liked women, but had difficulty in divorcing them from their sisterly status. He even liked Maud, or was prepared to like her, although he could not perceive her as a sister. Her heightened colour, now functioning as an automatic signal, alerted him to the fact that she was a sexual being still in the process of discovering the depths of her sexual nature. It was her imperviousness to himself that nettled him. Only the truly inexperienced can afford to neglect their manners in this respect. He felt irritated with Maud on several counts, not the least of which was the nagging thought that at some point someone was going to have to take charge of her, to wrest her from temptation, to put her on some train or other. Only then could he get together with Tyler and discuss more normal matters.

He bought bread, milk, bananas, teabags, and, as an afterthought, a bottle of shampoo. When he got back to the flat he put his string bag down on the kitchen table without unpacking it and returned to Tyler in the salon, determined to discover where he was to spend the night. He was tired, somewhat disappointed to discover that he was not to be in anyone's confidence. The complicity of the other two was beginning to annoy him. He had time to notice that the flat already smelt of coffee and cigarettes, like a café.

'Where's Maud?' he asked.

'Having a bath,' said Tyler, lying full length on one of the navy blue sofas and easing several cushions under his head.

'I hope you know what you're doing, Tyler.'

'What an extraordinary remark. As far as I'm concerned we're all just staying here, enjoying the Vermeulens' hospitality.'

'They don't know we're here, do they?'

'Not exactly. Not in detail. But they did say I could use the flat while they were away, if I happened to be passing through Paris. Which is what I'm doing. Your room's upstairs, by the way, on the sixth floor.'

'With the other servants,' said Harrison bitterly.

'Oh, don't be such a bore. Here's the key. I found it just inside the kitchen door. And don't look like that. The room's perfectly all right. I went up and had a look.'

'Why can't I . . . ?'

'Don't even ask. Be your age, can't you? Now if you want to come out with us be down here in half an hour. Otherwise please yourself. I've hired a car, by the way. I thought we might go out somewhere this afternoon, perhaps go out and have lunch in the country.'

'Where were you thinking of?' asked Harrison, with what he hoped was heavy irony. 'A day trip to Versailles?'

'Why not? Versailles is perfectly possible if you don't go inside the building. What's wrong with Versailles? Or Fontainebleau, come to that. Ermenonville. The Vallée de Chevreuse. Are you going to be clever about all of them?'

'Deep down, Tyler, you are totally conventional.'

'Dear Noddy. To think it's taken you all this time to find out.'

The arrival of Maud, flushed from her bath, and wearing one of her wide-skirted, and, he could now appreciate, thoroughly old-fashioned dresses, put an end to this exchange. Disgusted, he traipsed up to the sixth floor, thrust his key into a gaping lock, and threw his bag down on to the flowered coverlet of an iron bedstead. He was back with the wallpaper again, he noted, this time of blue garlands on a white ground, an unsteady bedside table, and a small washbasin with an unframed mirror above it. It would do, he supposed; at least it was light and quiet. It might even serve as a retreat if those two got tiresome, as they seemed bound to do. And of course there was nothing to stop him going home.

Later that morning, in the back of the car, his temper cooled. He was in the company of adults, and it was enormously restful just to relax and let Paris take care of him. The sun was still strong enough to bring a prickle of sweat to the back of his neck, but now there was a brassy tinge to the light, as if it contained the threat of its own dissolution. Every now and then an edge of cloud approached the sun, not quite meeting it, and then dissolving, so that it was easy to believe that the fine days might last for a little while longer. For the moment the sun still produced a dazzle on the chrome of cars, but he noticed one woman carrying a precautionary umbrella. He lolled in the stuffy heat of the car and contemplated the two heads in front of him, Tyler's almost black, Maud's dark gold, the damp hair still curling from her bath. She was on her best behaviour, he noted, her hands in her lap, although he thought he could sense one longing to creep out to Tyler's thigh.

'We are going to Versailles,' announced Tyler. 'Only Harrison's such a snob he won't go inside the building.'

'Oh, don't keep on. I never said . . . '

'It's too hot, anyway. We'll have lunch and walk in the park. That satisfy you?'

He turned suddenly and flashed Harrison a white-toothed grin. Harrison thought he saw there an unsought-for but no less welcome complicity. This then was to be the tone: amiable bickering. He thought he could manage that. All he had to do was to keep on the right side of Tyler, whose favour it was always important to ensure. He breathed deeply, pleasurably, determined to declare a holiday, to ignore whatever manoeuvres the other two were up to. In this heat he could no more think of making love, of anyone making love, than of running a marathon. At the same time he could have kicked Maud for being so insistently there, though he had to admire her self-control. She might be any convent-educated girl out for the day with her brother. Except that to an expert eye he would be unerringly cast as the brother. With either one of them out of the way he might exercise his rights to full membership of the human race, instead of being slightly out of it, restful though the position promised to be. Without Maud he could get on to some kind of footing with Tyler. On the other hand, without Tyler he might aspire to Maud. Not that he felt anything for her, he assured himself, but she had a certain appeal; he had to confess to himself that she intrigued him. It is a natural wish to have a hand in humbling the proud. So far she had paid him no attention whatsoever. He sensed rather than saw in her a mixture of pleading and hauteur. And he all but felt her left hand twitch in its desire to touch Tyler.

At Versailles they ate lunch in an overblown tourist restaurant, which smelt faintly of urine from the swinging doors to the *toilettes*. Outside the plate-glass windows coaches shuddered to a halt in the parking space: ladies of a certain age adjusted cardigans and sunglasses; cameras even at this stage were readied. Maud excused herself for what seemed a long time. Tyler lit a cigarette and abstracted himself from any attempt at conversation. Harrison, enormously hungry, as he always seemed to be, ate bread, exhausting the supply on the table. 'Aha!' said Tyler, as the main dish was set before him, and Maud stole back into her seat. 'Tough, but not unpalatable,' he observed, his teeth sinking into his veal chop. Oil gleamed on his mouth. Maud was silent, eating daintily. Harrison thought he could observe the food sliding down her graceful throat. Even love could not disrupt a French girl's appetite, he thought.

For he had no doubt that she loved Tyler, although he had not so far fully acknowledged the fact. The thought struck a sudden chord of dismay which he did his best to analyse. He was to be, then, definitively on the sidelines, a position which he had once thought to cherish. He struggled to contain, even to suppress, a desire to be at the centre, to have something in his gift which another might cherish. Not to take it and pass on, as Tyler might, almost certainly would. Unless Tyler did the decent thing and succumbed to this pretty but enigmatic girl, with her prim expression and her juvenile clothes. He had something of an insight into her preparations for her holiday in her aunt's house, of her boredom, then her expectation. Finally, of her coming alive, and the havoc it would cause, when she went home to that grim mother of hers and was obliged to say nothing of her adventure. He doubted whether she had ever lied before, although she gave the impression of someone who could keep her own counsel. But to be silent about one's thoughts was a far more innocent procedure than to be silent about one's actions. Maud would now have to keep doubly silent to evade her mother's vigilance. Of that mother he had no great opinion. He saw a dangerous avidity there which might make Maud a victim. Between her mother and Tyler she would be entirely unprotected, was in fact entirely unprotected. He stole an uneasy look at her as she composedly drank her coffee. Tyler, tilting his chair back and lighting another cigarette, intercepted his look and smiled pleasantly.

'You'll get cancer,' Edward said, for something to say.

'You mean you wish I would,' said Tyler, still pleasantly.

They strolled out into the hot dusty street, past the coaches, past the ladies in cardigans, and the cameras, round the flank of the great portentous building, four-square to all comers, past the gesticulating stone gods of the Apollo fountain, and into the park, whose green depths drew them on. They were silent until they were past the two Trianons, then by wordless consent they sat down on a stone bench and surrendered to the full heat of the day. Maud closed her eyes and leaned her head back. Tyler unbuttoned his shirt. Again their hands rested in their laps, quiescent, blameless. Whatever tension was in the air seemed to be the property of the air itself, in which heat could be felt to be accumulating until it chose to be dispelled by a storm, a showdown, some sort of resolution. Harrison felt the beginning of a slight headache and wandered off into the shade of a regulated stand of trees, densely geometric, peremptory. He was relieved to be alone, wondered if he might not, on the following day, make for the Louvre and his old habits. Then he contemplated the general unacceptability of being absent, of re-entry and its embarrassments, contemplated the power of Tyler, and his natural ability to impose his will. He would go along with whatever was ordained, he thought soberly, and again felt a twist of the excitement of the voyeur. When he strolled back to the bench Tyler and Maud were holding hands. He felt a sudden stab of desire, but for whom he could not have said.

On the journey back his headache grew more insistent. He also felt slightly sick after the apple tart he had consumed with a further cup of coffee, the others waiting patiently until his appetite was assuaged. With this bodily discomfort went a more general malaise. Why was Tyler being so obvious? Why this trip to Versailles, why this holding of hands? Was this irony, or, more probably, mockery? Tyler was not averse to making fun of his victims, at least those to whom he was not entirely indifferent. Indifference suited him better, was most probably his most natural, his most reassuring state of mind. A breach in his defences, as seemed to be taking place here, resulted in a kind of willed unkindness, as if he resented having his emotional account overdrawn. Or, and this was a more puzzling alternative, was he genuinely affected by this very ordinary girl? If so, what was the nature of the hold she exerted over him? She was apparently unaware of his stage-managerial tendencies, which had decreed that they should be reduced to the status of tourists, like all the others who had tired themselves walking through the splendid formidable rooms or gasping at the complicated jets of water springing upwards into the hot heavy air. Why that ghastly restaurant, with its conflicting odours, and the food that was surely unsuitable in this weather? Even as Maud confidently placed her hand on Tyler's thigh, Tyler himself seemed to have lost heart, to have become morose. Little was said. Harrison leaned his aching head back until the posture became unbearable. In the face of Tyler's increasing broodiness, and his apparent incommunicability, Maud withdrew her hand.

In the flat they trooped languidly into the yellow salon and collapsed on to the navy blue sofas. Harrison surveyed his dust-covered shoes, eased his finger round inside his collar.

'Would you mind if I had a bath?' he asked.

Tyler shrugged. 'Help yourself.' He looked sulky, with less than his usual air of command.

Boredom, decided Harrison. Tyler's *Doppelgänger*.

He slid into the cool water as into a bed. And bed was what was now on his mind, not theirs but his own. He could not face the thought of going out again to eat; in any case food was the last thing he wanted. What he wanted now was a return to some kind of normality, to innocence, to a state of simple companionship, in which the three of them would be equal, and equally sexless. This was not impossible, he reasoned: he at least could hold to that position, which had in effect been his all the time. He banished from his mind that memory of the scene in the summer house, himself forced both to witness and to compete. And yet he was normal, he puzzled, or at least he thought he was. Fortuitous encounters were simply not to his taste. But he knew that in reality he feared them, feared to let the genie out of the bottle. If he were innocent — so far — his thoughts were not. Somewhere inside him bloomed a desire to assert himself, to take over. To take control. As this urge was at war with his desire for innocence his state was decidedly uncomfortable. This in its turn made his headache worse.

He opened the door of the bathroom to air it, smelt Tyler's cigarette smoke, heard him say, 'Hadn't you better contact that friend of yours? Tell her when to expect you?'

He lingered, heard Maud say, 'I already have. I telephoned her this morning, when you were buying cigarettes. She knows I'm not coming. And I managed to get her to postpone her visit to Dijon. So I can stay here with you. Are you pleased? Say you are pleased, Tyler.'

'What about your mother?'

'I doubt if I need tell my mother anything.'

'You mean?'

'I think she knows I'm with you.'

There was a silence, which Harrison, lurking inside the bathroom, could not bring himself to break.

'I hope your mother is not getting the wrong idea,' he heard.

'If she is she no doubt thinks, or hopes, it is the right idea. My mother is a romantic at heart.'

'So are you, my dear.'

The wryness of that last remark alerted Harrison to potential danger, so that with an elaborate clearing of the throat he was able to present himself in the doorway.

'I'll go upstairs, if you don't mind,' he said. 'I've got a bit of a headache. I'll see you in the morning, if that's all right.'

'We might do Fontainebleau some time,' said Tyler.

'Are you sure? It's still pretty hot. There'll be crowds of people . . . '

'Don't be so bloody ungrateful. I go to the trouble of hiring this car, I do all the driving, I don't expect you to do anything but be pleasant . . . '

'All right, all right.' Tyler's sudden changes of mood were well attested. He had once stormed out of a Cambridge party, at which Harrison had been present, when his hostess criticised something he had said or done, only to reappear half an hour later with his arm round another girl, who, to judge from her appearance, had definitely not been invited.

'I'll say goodnight, then.'

'Goodnight,' said Maud pleasantly.

He lingered. 'What will you do? Will you go out to dinner?'

'I dare say we shall manage to occupy ourselves,' said Tyler.

Harrison left the flat with something like relief, a feeling which increased once he was lying on his bed in the hot stillness under the roof. As he lay, welcoming the silence, and even the friendly stuffiness, this relief gradually became tinged with curiosity. What exactly was the nature of this love affair? To this he could provide no answer that made sense. He had always known Tyler as one of those romantic seducers who arouse more envy in men than loyalty in women, who greet former lovers lightly, thus challenging them to bear him ill will. Harrison was prepared to bet that Tyler had a million girlfriends, all of whom were glad to engage in scurrilous gossip about him as soon as they were deprived of his company. But that was only because he had an effortless way with women: all, however critical, however resentful, could see that he was meant for a larger scale of action, that he had actually to lower his sights to engage in seduction, regretting that he was not on some field of glory or subduing rebellions. What his friends and enemies recognised was leadership, yet paradoxically he was not to be trusted. He won forgiveness, time and time again, on account of his very great physical ease, his height, the strength of his limbs, his sombre and melancholy blue gaze, the dark dense curly hair growing low on his forehead. Thus, by a form of primitive reasoning, others felt bound to defer to him, to forgive him misdemeanours which, in the light of later experience, were seen to be not so very serious after all.

Harrison had seen him approach women, and shortly after that first encounter, appropriate them, only to express genuine surprise when in the course of time they reproached him with faithlessness. Yet, as far as he could make out, Tyler had saddled himself with this girl, Maud, for no other reason than that he was used to being accompanied by a submissive female presence. At least, they were always submissive until they became quarrelsome. Maud was certainly submissive, yet she had a certain dignity which raised her stakes in the game, if game it were. Harrison, in the fading light, imagined them abroad in the city, loping silently through the drifting crowds, Maud, in her soft little shoes, following in Tyler's wake, until night laid its spell on them and brought them home. They might linger for a last drink in the Place des Ternes, where he had somehow never managed to become part of that nighttime throng. Then they would return, and no doubt at last make love.

It was an ideal picture, and it affected him most painfully. His feelings came into sharper focus: he longed to be with them, and if possible to be part of them, not to make love, but to be one in a conspiracy of three. Whereas all that was allotted to him was a minor role, his duty, as Tyler had put it to him, to be pleasant and nothing more. Yet he was necessary to them, he knew. Without him their love affair would proceed too quickly to some sort of a conclusion: boredom would be experienced on the one hand, terror on the other, and all would end badly. Whereas his presence served to put some sort of a brake on things, confining Tyler to a semblance of conventional behaviour, allowing Maud to maintain a semblance of decorum. He was the duenna, he realised, a role not noted for its nobility. Yet inevitably he would say goodbye to these people when his stay in Paris came to an end, or when he began to think of going home: Tyler he would see again from time to time, Maud probably never. And since he would see Tyler, and since Tyler was somehow phenomenal, and therefore worth conserving, he would continue to play his part, with as much goodwill as he could muster, and no doubt continue to puzzle over his own behaviour, as well as that of the other two, as if the whole affair were subject to stricter than usual scrutiny, as if it might prove to be a test of some kind. As he turned over to sleep, feeling at last the delicious languor which had escaped him throughout the tiresome day, he resolved to cultivate a detachment, to be as pleasant as the situation demanded, but not to involve his feelings in any way, to eschew rage, pain, jealousy and compassion, all of which he had already experienced, with an intensity which he found was unwelcome. Not my affair, was his last conscious thought, as sleep overcame him.

He got up the following morning with his resolution intact, and found that he was able to greet Maud and Tyler with equanimity, and to eat breakfast with them, having, in an access of goodwill, gone out earlier to buy croissants. He was able to sustain this pleasant humour for several days, throughout the various elaborate excursions ordained by Tyler. Saint Germain-en-Laye he endured, Compiègne, Pierrefonds, Malmaison, Chatou, even, for some reason,

Saint-Denis, where Tyler was perversely delighted by its hideousness. It evaporated somewhere on the long car journey to Fontainebleau, which was unfortunate, since Tyler was in an uncertain mood and Maud was silent. One injudicious word on his part, he reckoned, and they would all be in trouble. All he could remember of Fontainebleau from previous visits was a horseshoe staircase, on which he had chased his infant sister until told to come down, and a hinterland of forest. He hoped that they could take the palace for granted and merely wander under the trees. It was again very hot, an unpleasant sweltering heat that would not break, with the occasional bruised-looking cloud drifting towards the sun. They all ate lightly, then made for the darkest patch of shade, looking for a hollow not obstructed by the strange prehistoric boulders that littered the forest floor, and when they found the ideal place instinctively prepared for sleep.

Harrison slept briefly and profoundly. When he awoke it was mid afternoon, and he was alone. He looked about him in a panic, wondering if the others had abandoned him and gone back to Paris. This was the sort of joke Tyler liked to play. He got up, brushing grass from the sleeves of his shirt, and blundered through the trees, not quite daring to call their names from a genuine fear of revealing himself as childish. At last he saw them: they had not been so very far away after all. Tyler was lying with his head in Maud's lap, and she was caressing his forehead. As Harrison came up to them Tyler shot him a glance, of warning, Harrison thought, and thought too of a picture of *Samson and Delilah* which he had seen on one of his solitary visits to the Louvre. Then, before he had time to digest the implications of this, Tyler was on his feet, throwing him the keys of the car.

'You can drive,' he said. 'Up you get, Maud.' His tone was rousing, artificially jolly. Maud got to her feet, puzzled by his change of mood. Harrison thought she moved awkwardly, for so graceful a girl.

'Chartres tomorrow,' pronounced Tyler from the back of the car, as Harrison drove slowly through the home-going traffic.

'Oh, God, Tyler, can't you stay put for a bit?'

'Why? What delights did you have in mind?'

'Well, I wouldn't mind going back to the Louvre.'

'What do you say, Maud?' Harrison could hear Tyler's hand descending rather heavily on to Maud's knee. 'Do you want to go to the Louvre?'

'You are hurting me, Tyler. Don't lean on me so heavily. I am quite happy to go to Chartres, if that is what you want.'

Nobody asked him what he wanted, Harrison noted, bringing the car to rest in the rue Laugier. He deduced further that his company was no longer required that evening. He decided that he was quite grateful for this reprieve. It had been an exhausting day, but an intriguing one. That couple of lovers, with their tensions so much in evidence that they reduced their audience — him — to silence, would intrigue anyone who had a taste for such things. He was newly aware, now that he was attuned to such matters, of some conflict in Tyler, of his temper slowly but inexorably moving towards the surface. He went to his room, washed his face, then crept down the stairs, unwilling to arouse their attention or to give Tyler a pretext for being annoyed with him. He ate his dinner in a nearby brasserie (early again), and once more enjoyed a peaceful and unbroken night's sleep.

'You know the way, I take it?' said Tyler on the following morning, handing over the keys of the car. 'Take care of Maud.'

'Why?' he said, startled. 'Aren't you coming?'

'I've got some calls to make. Get on with it, Noddy; don't stand there staring. Must I do everything around here?'

'I thought you wanted to go. To Chartres, I mean.'

'Just go, can't you?'

Maud, he noticed, looked frightened, sad. He took her by the arm, willing her not to cry. 'We'll see you later, then,' he called over his shoulder, and to Maud he said quietly, 'Take it easy. We're not going to Chartres, you know. We're going to sit in the Luxembourg Gardens. Then we are going to have a quiet lunch. Then we are going to take a gentle walk. And then you will feel much better. And incidentally so will I.'

His words amazed him, but he appeared to have said the right thing. Leaving the car keys in the hall had been an excellent idea. As they sat sedately on their iron chairs he heard himself talking on determinedly, telling her about himself, about his home in Eastbourne — the cliffs stood out sharply in his mind's eye, superimposed on this sultry greyish haze — about his parents, whom he loved, and finally about the shop. He was homesick, he reckoned: why had he not realised this before?

'I'm sorry to be talking so much,' he said. 'You must find this frightfully boring.'

'Not at all.' She smiled at him with what seemed like genuine friendship, 'I like to hear about your parents.'

'Do you miss your mother?'

Her face closed again. 'No. I love her, but I don't miss her.'

There was a silence.

'I must be going home soon,' he said. 'Back to England, I mean. Will you be all right?'

'Of course. But you have been very kind. Thank you.'

They drifted through the afternoon, drinking coffee, watching the children in the Parc Monceau, until, tired, they turned by mutual consent and made their way back to the flat.

'Tyler?' he called. 'We're back. He doesn't seem to be here,' he called to Maud through the open door.

She appeared from the bedroom, looking very pale. 'I found this note,' she said.

'Gone to visit friends in the Ardèche,' he read. 'Will telephone.'

He stared at her, at the tears springing from her eyes.

'Don't leave me, Harrison,' she said.

'Edward,' he replied. 'Call me Edward.'

8

It rained in the night, not rhetorically, with a cloudburst that would have satisfied everyone's taste for drama, but softly, insistently, and with a northern steadiness. In the Vermeulens' big bed Maud lay sleepless, listening to the faint hiss of the rain which filled the night with a kind of surreptitious activity, as if it were urging on a change of season and marking off the past from the present. At some point a disturbance was heard in the street outside; then it died away, leaving no echo. She held her breath, willing for someone to come, waiting for the dawn which she knew would be tardy, hazy, blurred by the damp, resolutely different from the brilliant days that had gone before.

She rose early, went to the bathroom, noted that her condition was unchanged, and ran a hot bath, rubbing the steam from the damp windows. She dressed in one of her wide-skirted dresses, which now bore a slight bloom of dust and was limp from her body and its secret tensions. Impulsively she discarded it for her white cotton blouse, which she had managed to wash but not to iron, and her brown cotton skirt, now marred by grass stains. Her baller-ina shoes, never meant for walking, were almost worn through. She brushed her short bronze hair, now curling from the damp, and inspected her fine skin, which was tanned and unmarked by the exhaustion she felt. She searched through Mme Vermeulen's wardrobe and found a light satiny raincoat with a prestigious label: this she put on, took the key, and prepared to leave the flat. Her intentions were vague; she only knew that she must walk until nightfall. At some point she must take the rest of her clothes to the dry-cleaners, for it would be important to greet Tyler, when he returned, looking pristine, as he had first seen her, on the terrace at La Gaillarderie, bored and disdainful as she had been, intact, her wilfulness successfully hidden. Since then she had experienced every form of dissolution, having been given an education which, she sensed, few women were allowed in so short a time. To give herself courage she reminded herself of Tyler's look of admiration, as he contemplated her, narrow eyed, as she lay coolly waiting for him, her rapid and visibly beating heart telling him all he wanted to know.

But was that indeed what he wanted? He always broke away from her afterwards, as if she had made unrestricted demands on him which he was not minded to satisfy. She had hidden her bewilderment, knowing, for all her lack of experience, that he was not a man who cared to explain himself, that integrity for him lay in a refusal to clarify his intentions. She did not much mind this, for she reasoned with herself that inscrutability was the characteristic most frequently displayed by romantic heroes. Indifferent to most men, she nourished a deep atavistic longing for the most commonplace of stereotypes. Her very genuine impassivity had made her insensible to the sort of experimental flirtations indulged in by her friend Julie and by others of their circle. She was not displeased to have retained her virginity, thinking it a small price to pay for the grand love affair that she had always had in her sights: one man, and one only, who would satisfy and consume her entirely. This economy of outlook had nothing to do with her mother's marriage plans for her, which she considered bourgeois, provincial. She knew, as if she had already experienced them, that those plans included a white dress from Pronuptia, and a wedding breakfast at the

Hôtel de la Cloche, at which her aunt Germaine would at last be an accessory rather than the main player, a guest and no longer a châtelaine. And she knew that her mother would regard this celebration, this signing of the contract, as marking the conclusion of her maternal obligations, after which there might even be a slight parting of the ways which would be acceptable on both sides.

Behind her façade of decorum, inculcated at her convent school, she had nourished other ideas. And even now she marvelled that she had had her own way, had met the mysterious stranger, had succumbed, had exulted, and in so doing had triumphed over her mother's vigilance, her mother's fantasies. She could now regard with genuine pity Julie's surprise parties, at which she had always been awkward and more often than not unpartnered, the young men thinking her disdainful, and not noticing, or if noticing rejecting, her loneliness. Her triumph was still absolute, for the memory of Tyler's lovemaking still had precedence over the fact that he was absent, and that his absence was unexplained. In fact she drew strength from the fact that it was unexplained, for it was like Tyler to act on impulse. He was a free man: she would not impede him. All she had to do was wait for him. He had taken a bag, but not all of his clothes. These she kept in view as confirmation of his return.

Except that without his urgent active presence there would be such a lot of time to kill, and she could think of nothing to do but walk, for if she did not get physically tired she would not be able to sleep, and if she did not sleep she would become plain and lose that golden burnish that was her greatest asset. She needed no cosmetics, was not tempted by adornments: these she left to her mother to plan. The rough, densely waved, and curled gold-brown hair, which fitted her head like a helmet, had never needed the ministrations of a hairdresser, and her dark eyebrows arched naturally and disdainfully over her slightly slanting brown eyes. She was grateful for her good figure, her full bosom, which now threatened to become fuller, for her small dry hands with the oval nails which she manicured so carefully. One memory of her mother would always be her instruction in that respect; when engaged with nail-file and orange stick in the dusk of a Sunday evening, after their visit to the cinema, they had been momentarily at one. Also the lessons on the importance of hairbrushing, of hygiene, of fastidious presentation: these were acknowledged, credit being given where credit was due. But it was due from a distance, as if the relationship were now at an end, as if Dijon were a place she had once visited and now need never visit again, except as a married woman. She would give her mother that satisfaction, she reckoned, but until then she would keep the satisfaction to herself. For despite a residual uneasiness, caused, she thought, by Tyler's absence, she was quite confident. Except that the Ardèche was a long way away, a day's journey from Paris. And he would need to stay two or three days, at least. And there was the day's journey back. So that he might be absent for four or five days, more if he were enjoying himself . . . But he would surely telephone, as he had promised, so that she really ought to stay in the flat as much as possible, so as not to miss his call. Alternatively, there was this equally pressing need for strenuous physical exercise, so that certain matters might naturally resolve themselves. Dejected, still wearing Mme Vermeulen's raincoat, she sank down on to the bed. That was another problem: the sheets would have to be taken to the laundry, and the flat put to rights. Even if she were to entrust matters to the concierge she had no money with which to pay her. In fact she had no money at all: her only asset was the return half of her ticket to Dijon. All the more pressing need, therefore, to await Tyler's return.

When the doorbell rang she caught her foot in the valance of the bed, stumbled, thought briefly that this might work to her advantage, and then ran effortfully down the corridor in her haste to welcome Tyler. She was not quite sufficiently aware of her change of expression when she opened the door to Harrison; in any event she was too indifferent to Harrison's presence to make the effort to be pleasant.

'I thought it was Tyler,' she explained, when at last she made sense of his disappointed face.

'Tyler would use the key, surely,' he said.

'No,' she replied. 'He didn't take the key. I found the key in the bedroom, where he usually leaves it.'

'Then it sounds as if he's not planning to come back.'

'That's ridiculous. He's left some of his things.' She indicated a discarded shirt and a tin of talcum powder. 'Anyway, he said he would telephone.'

'We need to discuss this, Maud. Perhaps you could make some coffee. Here, I brought you these.' He handed over his bag of croissants. 'I want to make a couple of telephone calls myself.'

She went to the kitchen and filled a kettle. She could hear him saying, 'Mother? How are you? How's Dad?' His voice sounded eager, enthusiastic. 'I'll be home at the end of the week,' she heard. 'Yes, really home. Then I'll make a start on the shop. Or at least decide what to do with it.' There was a silence, which she imagined to be filled with sage advice. Then, 'I know, I know. But I haven't really decided yet. I might try it out, I suppose. OK, we'll talk about it. Love to you both. Bibi still in Italy? Very good, yes, but I'm ready to leave now. See you at the weekend. 'Bye.'

How pleasant he sounded when he spoke to his mother, she thought, arranging cups on a tray. She felt his impatience to leave this place, whose point seemed suddenly lost. She was aware of the crumpled sheets on the bed, of the dust that had settled since their arrival, of the smell of Tyler's cigarettes in the salon. The smell of the coffee made her feel slightly sick, a feeling which she hastily ascribed to her all but sleepless night. In the hall

Harrison, who seemed newly energised by the thought of going home, was dialling other numbers.

'Cook? Harrison here. Just to let you know that I'll be with you next Friday. Everything all right? You have? That's great, thank you very much. Well, I'll see you on Friday and we'll decide how to proceed. Excellent, thanks, but the weather's broken. I'll be quite glad to get home. OK then, until next week. Goodbye.'

He shook his head in admiration as he took his cup from her. 'The willingness of that man to consider himself my employee never ceases to astound me. I guess it's because I'm young. He probably wouldn't work for anyone older, anyone with authority. He's satisfied himself that I won't presume. I'll have to start thinking what to do with him. Aren't you having one?' he asked, waving a croissant at her. She noticed his strong white teeth, his decisive way with food. When his upper lip lifted like that he looked quite different, she thought, less ingenuous. In time he might be quite an attractive man, but only if he did not have to stand comparison with other more prestigious men. Whatever looks and charm he possessed were perhaps on the modest side, but he seemed kindly; to judge from what she had heard of his telephone conversations he was straightforward. But then, she reminded herself, he only appears to his best advantage in the absence of Tyler. If Tyler were here he would instantly fade into the background, as he had done ever since they had come together.

' . . . think about going home,' she heard him say, though her thoughts were sad and her attention intermittent.

'I'm sorry?'

'I said you must think about going home. Don't you want to telephone your mother?'

'Later. I'll ring her later. When I know how long I'll be staying here.'

He stared at her. 'Maud, you can't be serious. You don't really think Tyler's coming back, do you?'

'Of course I do.'

'My dear girl. I hate to say this, but he may not. Tyler is quite unpredictable. At least he is to women. Men tend not to trust him anyway. I've seen him around women: they fall for him, and he treats them badly by way of return. I have to say they don't seem to mind. But it's usually a bad business all round . . . '

'You don't like him, do you?'

'I like him less than I did. I wonder now if I ever liked him. I was always impressed by him — who wouldn't be? But after three years in the same college I still didn't feel I knew him. After this holiday I feel I know him better. It's just that I don't find his exploits quite so amusing. He's a spoiler, you know.'

'You're jealous.'

He considered this. 'Yes, perhaps I am. But that doesn't alter the fact that I don't think much of the way he carries on. If you knew him as well — or as little — as I do, you might put less faith in his return.' He knew he was being unkind, and resented the fact that Tyler had left this task to him. But that was part of Tyler's mythical status, that he left the explanations of his behaviour to others, he reflected, and once again sighed with a mixture of admiration and resentment. To be so free of earthly ties! Again the shop loomed into his consciousness, only to be dismissed. Clearly he was not to be allowed to get on with his life until this tiresome girl had been dealt with.

'Tyler loves me, you know.'

'Has he said so?'

'Of course.'

'Well, that is the easy part. If he loves you he can follow you to Dijon, can't he?'

'I'm staying here. You can leave if you want to. Don't let me keep you,' she added politely.

'Forgive me for being blunt, but did he leave you any money?'

She turned away, but before she did he saw her sudden pallor.

'I'll stay with you, of course,' he said. 'But on one condition. If he's not back by the end of the week we'll both go home. And I'll see to it even if I have to put you on the train myself. Now, what would you like to do today?' he asked, more gently than he had intended.

'I'd like to walk.' Her head was high, her expression once more disdainful. 'You don't have to come with me.'

He was suddenly aware of her extreme youth, and of his own. But instead of panic came a certain wry sympathy, not only for the girl but for himself.

'I'll tell you what,' he said. 'We'll do as many districts of Paris as we've got time for. Just walk in a certain direction each day and explore. Until we get tired. Would you like that?'

'Thank you,' she said. It was as much as she could manage in the way of a concession. She strode past him to the door, her head held high. He caught a drift of alien perfume from her raincoat. He felt, in addition to his underlying annoyance, a twinge of pity. The perfume had done that. He began to see her as just one more in a line of fallible women, Tyler's women, all of whom seemed to progress, in a state of discontent, to the dubious pleasures of experience, once they had recovered from the fact of his dereliction. This one, he thought would be more diffi-cult. Yet if there were to be a contest of wills he was determined that his own should carry the day. With Tyler out of the way this seemed entirely possible.

For the next two days they followed the pattern they had set themselves, or that he had set for them. He brought the croissants for breakfast, she made the coffee; then she donned her raincoat, and they set out on an apparently aimless walk, during which each was absorbed in thought. They saw little of their surroundings, were aware only of late drops of rain falling from overhead leaves, and of the damp striking through the soles of their shoes. Harrison was acutely aware of Maud's shoes, which were now stained and shapeless. He felt under unwelcome duress, yet could not consider abandoning her. She strode along silently beside him; once he attempted to take her hand, but after a moment she withdrew it. She had nothing to say to him, although she was glad of his presence. She began to think seriously of her position, shying away yet again from its implications. When Tyler comes back, she thought, I will put it to him. Yet in the rue Saint-Antoine, at the very end of that main artery of Paris which they had traversed almost without noticing how far they had come, a cold fear settled on her, and would not be dispelled by her anticipation of Tyler's return. She allowed Harrison to pay for their meals. She knew that without him she would have to subsist on whatever she could find in the Vermeulens' kitchen. She felt alternatively sick and full as she swallowed hastily, anxious to eat as much as was allowed. Watching her, Harrison ate with less than his usual appetite.

On the third day they got no further than the Tuileries. The excursions seemed to have been halted, or come to an end. Around them the day was grey, inert. Tourists, of whom Edward had been one, had disappeared indoors, into the Louvre, where he had previously spent his time longing for company. Now he longed for solitude, and for home. He had no idea what to do with this girl, yet his eye was drawn to her, as she stood with her back to him, surrounded by a maze of unwaveringly geometrical flowerbeds. In her straight back he perceived a solitude far greater than he, perhaps mistakenly, aspired to, a revelation that was unwelcome to him. He watched as she slowly turned to face him, and in her downcast face at last had an intimation of what kept her here, a prisoner, apparently in his power.

'Maud,' he said, guiding her to a seat. 'Is there something you want to tell me?'

She shook her head.

'I mean, forgive me for asking, but you are on the Pill, aren't you?'

She shook her head again.

'But why ever not?'

'It would have meant going to the doctor. Our doctor is old, he looked after my father. He would never have dreamed . . . It's not easy in France, you see. And anyway, I didn't know . . . I hadn't met Tyler then, you see.'

'And now?'

'Well, of course when I tell him . . . '

There was a silence while he digested this. Then, 'How late are you?'

'Twelve days.'

'Does he know?'

'Of course not. And you mustn't say anything. I'll explain when he comes back. Promise me you won't say anything.'

'I doubt if I shall have an opportunity,' he said, as drily as he could manage. He felt rather then saw the afternoon darken around them, but in reality the darkness only presaged another shower of rain.

'He should have asked you,' he said.

'Oh, no. That would have spoilt everything.'

He understood her, understood her need to meet her lover unthinkingly, without calculation. Calculation would have made her another kind of woman, a practised practical sort of woman, rather than the dazzled girl she had turned out to be. Behind her haughty face swarmed the usual fantasies, in which the desire to be mastered, to be taken over, was paramount. He had thought her superior, whereas in reality she was even less experienced than he was. And even his uncomplicated liaisons, his slender hoard of sexual knowledge, had made him aware of his status as a man, and of his responsibilities. While she, he thought, knew nothing, and was paying the price of knowing nothing, however desirable that ignorance may have been.

'I'm cold,' he said heavily. 'Let's have tea.' And seeing

her face again, however unwilling he was to meet it, he added, with an attempt at good cheer, 'I'll take you to Angelina. Have you ever been there?'

'What is Angelina?'

'It's a tea-room. My parents used to go there before the war. It used to be called Rumpelmayer. Come,' he said, taking her hand. 'It's only across the road.' Her hand in his was cold, unresponsive, but this time she did not withdraw it.

In the hot steamy clattering room, ignored by sharp-faced waitresses, they sat silently, while he tried to look about him, and failed. He was aware of a company of worldly women, and was repelled by their hammering conversation, the sharp descent of their forks into the masses of cream and chocolate on their plates. The air was thick with smells of sugar. Maud sat huddled in her wet raincoat, her head bent, making no attempt to drink her tea. Two tears slid down her face. With an effort she wiped them away, sat up straight, and composed herself. Watching her covertly, he was relieved to see something of her old resolution return. Yet he was aware that she hardly noticed his presence, and was surprised to discover how much this hurt him.

'Shall we go?' she asked.

'Where do you want to go?'

'Back to the flat. I'm tired. Aren't you tired? I think I'd like to lie down.'

But despite their fatigue, his now as well as hers, they walked back, up the Champs-Elysées, not speaking. At some point he was aware that more tears escaped her, that she wiped them away almost angrily. She took his arm, but he thought that was simply because she was tired. He was aware of her chill face, her hair beaded with moisture.

'You ought to have a hot bath,' he said, as he shut the door of the flat behind him.

'Yes. Yes, I think I will. What will you do? Will you go upstairs?'

'No, I'll wait down here for a bit.'

She disappeared. He sat in the salon, trying to ignore the damp patch his shoes had made on the yellow carpet. He wanted to summon help, but did not know whom he could ask. Tyler had been too clever to leave a telephone number. For Tyler he now felt an immense hatred. Perhaps he had always hated him. No, that was not true. He had liked him, been amused by him, though always aware he was not to be trusted. He would have continued to like him, to be amused by him, had this situation not arisen. For that, Maud was to blame as much as Tyler. He tried to hate Maud, and for a brief moment succeeded. Then he remembered her trembling figure beside him as he had manfully tackled his cake — and expected her to do the same — in the tea-room. So much for his treat, he thought, with a poor smile.

He badly wanted to leave all this and go home, but when Maud called to him from the bedroom he rose swiftly and went to her. She was naked, he could see, under the sheet. When she stretched out her arms to him he got down on one knee beside the bed and gathered her up. She pulled him to her, and he embraced her, awkwardly at first, then with rising excitement. When she kissed him, he kissed her back, feeling the tears on her face. His sadness did not surprise him. If he was aware of anything it was of descent into an even lonelier condition. He did not then, or for some time afterwards, identify this as love.

Gently, as gently as he could, he pushed her away, disengaged himself.

'You don't have to do this,' he said. 'I'll marry you.'

Later they lay very still, side by side. 'Did you know this would happen?' he asked. 'Did you intend it to happen?'

'I didn't know,' she replied, and he believed her, for was not ignorance an essential component of her behaviour?

He raised her up and looked at her, at her full and as yet unaltered body, her face so marked by pain. He fell in love with her then, or he supposed it was love, although it was for him a mournful moment, full of regret. He saw with relief that the colour had come back into her face, though there were lines round her mouth. He saw how she would look when she was older, as he supposed he would see her as time took charge of them.

'You'll telephone your mother?' he said, and then, as the tears started once more, 'Don't worry. I'll look after you.'

What united them at that moment was a sensation of unwanted maturity, of irrevocable and necessary compromise. They had reached a psychological watershed, in which love and even trust were irrelevant. He was aware of his crumpled shirt, she of her nakedness. She got back into the bed, feeling that she should cover herself. She did not quite understand what she had done, only that instinct had guided her. She felt like Eve after the Fall, remembering the stricken agonised figure in Masaccio's fresco, which Jean Bell, on one boring afternoon in Dijon, had excitedly explained to her, caressing the plate in her father's volume on Florence that she had been so glad to discover on Pierre-Yves's shelves. The book had lain unopened for years, since neither Maud nor her mother had been sufficiently interested to open it. Masaccio's Eve had seemed bent over in grief, her mouth apparently open in what could only be a howl. Maud understood, in the space of seconds, how one reacted to what was unalterable. The tears coursed silently down her face as she digested this knowledge. She was aware of Harrison standing silently beside the bed, looking at her. She was grateful to him for not speaking, for not insisting that her gaze meet his. Gradually she felt warmer, fell into a lethargy. As she slid into sleep one fact remained with her, a fact that would not be dismissed. When he had held her in his arms, and moved into her, she had felt nothing, even though she was aware of his arousal. That would be the way of it now. She had tried, and she had succeeded, somewhere along the line; she could not now remember whether she had willed

108

her actions or not. As sleep overcame her she realised that this was a matter she was genuinely incapable of deciding. If she had acted unwillingly, the fact remained that she had acted. She could reproach Harrison with nothing; he had been entirely honourable. It was not his fault that he was not Tyler: bodies are not interchangeable, nor are feelings. But she had felt nothing, and the only alternative to this realisation was the deeper unconsciousness to which she now surrendered herself.

When she awoke it was to find Harrison again standing by her bed — or had he been there all the time? He sat down beside her, and with an awkward hand smoothed her hair back from her face. She willed herself not to draw away. 'I made some coffee,' he said. 'Would you like some?'

She nodded and sat up, drawing the sheet around her to hide her nakedness. She drank down the coffee, felt its heat suffusing her face. This was almost a blush; she felt embarrassed. 'Talk to me,' she said.

'In a moment, when you've had your coffee, I'll telephone my mother. You'll love my mother, everybody does. And my father. And my sister. You'll love Bibi. You'll have to speak to them. Can you do that?'

'Not yet,' she said.

'But you'll have to meet them.'

'Of course. And I suppose you'll have to speak to my mother. You remember her — well, of course you do.'

'I remember her,' he said, with some distaste. He wondered what had prompted this sudden coldness.

She smiled faintly. 'You don't like her.'

'No, I don't, as a matter of fact. Though as we shall be living in London that hardly matters.'

'Tell me about your home.'

'Well, my real home is by the sea, where my family lives. I only have a rented flat in London. Though that can be changed. In fact, if you like I'll go on ahead and look for something bigger. Then you can join me. You'll have to go home to Dijon, you know. In fact when I've

109

telephoned my mother you'd better telephone yours. You know you must do that, don't you? After all, time enters into things now, doesn't it?'

'Yes,' she sighed.

'You'd better get dressed,' he said, gathering up the cups. He was absurdly sad. I am too young for this, he thought. I was never meant to be a married man. I was going to see the world, when I had summoned up the courage. But this has taken even more courage. At the same time he remembered Maud's body, and knew that he would never let her go. He knew that she did not love him, had known that she would never love him when he had watched her with Tyler. That had been love, blatant, shameless, the real thing. At the back of his mind, behind the sadness, was a small feeling that he was owed something. This he resolved to suppress for as long as he decently could. He would respect her; he would not act like Tyler, who took no heed of reluctance, or refusal, or any of the other reactions that indicated caution, hesitation. He had not inherited a violated woman. She had been all willingness, all eagerness. But not for him. He had not misread her hopelessness when he took her in his arms. But his mind was imprinted with the image of how she had looked when she had reached out to him, not loving, but longing. On that image he would hope to build.

Maud, washing up the cups in the kitchen, heard him on the telephone. 'Yes, it is very sudden, but I know you'll like her. Maud. Yes, it is unusual, isn't it?' She intuited excitement at the other end of the telephone, in that house by the sea. 'We'll have to get married in Dijon, of course. Oh, pretty soon, I should think. Tell Dad I'm counting on him. Oh, next week. I'll explain everything then. Lots of love. Goodbye.'

He judged it tactful to take her place in the kitchen while she telephoned her mother. After what he assumed to be the usual reproaches, he heard, quite clearly, the excited question, 'Tyler?' 'No, Mother,' said Maud tiredly. 'Edward . . . The other one.'

He did not wait to hear any more. Throwing down the dish towel he strode to the front door and opened it, incandescent with anger. He then strode back to confront her, only to be faced with more tears.

'I don't know why I'm crying,' she sobbed. 'I never cry.'

He could well believe it, had never seen her express any emotion other than ardour in Tyler's presence. He put a reluctant arm round her, feeling the softness of her breast against his hand. They sat together, wordless, in the dying afternoon, until she grew quiet. At last she heaved a long sigh. When he looked up Tyler, deeply tanned, stood in the doorway.

'Well, well,' said Tyler. 'You've been busy, I see.'

Harrison fished the key to his room out of his pocket. 'Go upstairs, Maud, and wait for me. Go on,' he said. 'I'll join you later.'

She looked at the key in her hand, looked at Tyler, waited for him to say something. Then, when he said nothing, she got up and went out of the door without a word.

'Indeed,' said Tyler, throwing his bag down on the bed. 'You didn't wait long, did you?'

'Maud and I are going to be married,' said Harrison.

A complicated expression, in which he could distinguish either anger or relief, passed over Tyler's face, and just as rapidly vanished.

'And then what will you do with her? Take her back to that shop of yours? How long will she put up with that, do you think?'

'Sod you, Tyler.'

'You know what this means, don't you? Jealousy, pure jealousy. You wanted what I've already had. Well, I doubt if you'll get it.'

'You never loved her. You've never loved anyone. I

III

doubt if you could love a woman to the extent of taking care of her.'

Anger, he decided. It had been anger. But there had been relief there too. Which argued that the stay in the Ardèche had been a tactical withdrawal. Nevertheless Tyler's face was pale, as Harrison had never seen it.

'We'll be leaving tomorrow.'

'Yes,' said Tyler, gazing out of the window. 'It's time to be moving on.'

'You will stay here. That will give you an opportunity to clear up this flat. The bed will have to be changed. And you might think about having the carpet shampooed. You'll have to ask your friend the concierge about that. Perhaps you could get her to give you a hand.'

Tyler smiled. 'This is really about you and me, isn't it, Noddy?'

'There's a laundry on the corner. I reckon a few thousand francs should cover your expenses. I'd be only too happy to let you have some money. If your journey to the Ardèche left you short.'

'You hate me, don't you?'

'I never want to see you again.'

'And I thought we were friends.'

'We were.'

That was the crux of the matter. In the dark room they gazed steadily at each other. Neither thought to switch on the light. In the street, beyond the window, the sounds of an ordinary day could be heard. Tyler's expression, which he could see clearly, despite the darkness, was rueful. Harrison had seen that rueful smile when Tyler was taking his leave, as he so often was, of a woman. He put his hand to his head and said, with some difficulty, 'I don't suppose we shall meet again. I'll go back, as you say, to my shop, and you'll no doubt have a flourishing career, in, what was it? Advertising? You should do well at that. Advertising is what you are particularly good at. After all, it's the others who have to deliver.'

'The clients,' said Tyler, with a smile.

'The clients. Who after all have the final say.'

'I never suspected you of this, you know.'

'That may have been your mistake.'

'Possibly. Though the story's not finished yet.'

'It is, as far as you're concerned.'

Tyler turned away, apparently unconcerned. 'Are you staying here tonight?'

'We'll go to a hotel. I hate this place anyway. Tomorrow I'll put Maud on a train to Dijon. Then I'll catch a plane to London. You can stay as long as you like.'

'Oh, I shan't stay. It's a pity we can't be friends.'

It was a pity, Harrison thought. He had loved the man, in a way, although he had disliked him. Now he looked at him blankly, aware that anger had deserted him. Tyler, head bent, appeared thoughtful, regretful. Yet even in this circumstance, Harrison saw, his physical splendour had not deserted him, saw also that Tyler knew it, was contrasting his long lean body with Harrison's shorter one, his finely shaped head with Harrison's unremarkable face, even his effortless elegance with Harrison's neat blazer. Harrison was aware that he was sweating, that he needed a bath. There was no question of that here. Slowly he straightened his back, summoned his suddenly depleted forces, gathered up Maud's things. 'That raincoat will have to go to the cleaner's,' he said.

'I'd better say goodbye to Maud, hadn't I?'

'Don't even think of it.'

'Perhaps she'd like to say goodbye to me, though.'

'Goodbye, Tyler.' On an impulse he stuck out his hand.

Tyler laughed. 'If you must,' he said, and shook it. 'Dear Noddy. If you could only see your face.'

'You've spoilt it,' said Harrison, and said it with genuine regret. 'Goodbye, then.' With that he was safely out of the door, but on the stairs was not surprised to find himself trembling.

On the following morning, in the noise and confusion

of the Gare de Lyon, he held Maud firmly by the arm, like a husband, if that was what husbands did. 'You'll be all right,' he said. 'You can have coffee on the train.' She looked at him as if she hardly remembered who he was. When the signal for departure sounded he had to push her into the train, then stood outside on the platform, grateful that there was no need to say any more. She leaned out, anxious, aware that he was leaving her on her own. As the train moved slowly off he saw her turn away, saw her back view retreating. Then she turned round, raised an uncertain arm. Before she vanished from his sight, he had time to hope that she would not be cold, in her thin blouse, without a coat.

9

Maud, in the train, recovered her composure to an extent which she would not have thought possible. Her present impassivity was achieved by a sort of willed regression, in which she was the age she was in reality but unencumbered by Harrison or even by Tyler, and all that she could contemplate was the sexless presence of some kindly companion who wore a passing resemblance to her cousin Xavier. As she sat, with her hands folded in her lap, her images of happiness were quite distinct: they were of herself engaged in some harmless or childish pursuit, eating ices, or sitting in the sun, or stretched out for sleep in her high narrow walnut bed in the rue des Dames Blanches. If the thought of her forthcoming marriage crossed her mind it was at a considerable degree of distance, as if it were someone else's fantasy. That fantasy was her mother's, and had relevance only as far as her mother had relevance in this strange translated state of mind. She was prepared to tolerate her mother as background, as guiding principle, as presiding genius of a certain domestic economy which should have prepared her for an entirely predictable destiny. As this destiny had been in some unforeseen way compromised, Maud did not see how her mother featured in the scenario in which she now had a leading part. She wished, in some dreamlike fashion, to be deprived of her mother as well as of her putative fiancé, whom she saw as mystically

115

allied: she wished to be alone, and single, and free, above all free, free to walk along a street and to know that no one was shadowing her movements, expecting her to return to an order which she had already renounced, free not to divulge her whereabouts, free not to telephone or converse even with friends, free if necessary to disappear.

If she were to disappear from her mother's vigilance she would have to go to London and marry Edward. If she were to disappear from Edward's life she would have to stay in Dijon and shelter behind her mother, who would defend her actions in so far as she considered Maud to be marrying the wrong man. Maud was quite aware of her mother's needs and desires. She knew that her marriage would put an end to an over-preparedness which they both found intolerable. How often had she winced to feel her mother's hand in the small of her back, propelling her forward to greet some man, any man, even the ancient family doctor, even Xavier (certainly Xavier), and to hear her mother's voice exaggerating her slender accomplishments. Yet she had also seen that mother's wry smile and downcast eyes in the presence of Tyler, and knew that she could have presented her mother with no greater prize than Tyler for a son-in-law. That chaste woman, with her long history of widowhood, had derived a speculative thrill from contemplation of Tyler's peculiar form of masculinity; the more dangerous, the more anarchic he appeared, the greater the satisfaction derived from what could only be an imaginative exercise, but one which was none the less thrilling for that very reason. And to have him in the family, to be able to rely on his presence from time to time, and above all to have abstracted him from Germaine's sphere of influence would have been a triumph which would have compensated for so many undeserved privations, not to speak of the timorous comforts which she envisaged for her old age.

But I cannot help you there, Mother, thought Maud; somehow it has all gone wrong. She watched as the train drew out of Sens and calculated that she was half-way home, a home she was by no means anxious to reach, since it would be dense with family implications, and her one desire at this moment was to be without ties of any kind. If she were free, which she was not, she would have gone to the rue des Dames Blanches, changed her clothes, and then gone out again immediately, perhaps to sit in a tea-room and eat cakes, or to wander round the streets, to look at the shops, never to have to give an account of herself again. Her mother she consigned to another place, some sunny retirement home in the south, perhaps, in which she would have no power. Days would pass idly; nothing would happen. This dream of irresponsibility was so beguiling that it brought a faint smile to the features which were already set in the impassive mask by which most people knew her. Paris retreated from her memory as though it had never been. It had betrayed her: that was her impression. She wanted nothing more do with it.

If she even fleetingly thought of her marriage it was as something provisional, something from which she could escape as naturally as she could wake up after a dream. As she saw it there would be little point in going to London, since she would not be staying there. The absolute inadmissibility of the situation she had subjected to a form of magical thinking which she found entirely reassuring. At the same time she was aware of the tenderness of her breasts, and of her stained and ruined shoes. She had no money, that was the fact of the matter. Even the previous night in a hotel, with Edward, was something she could not have managed on her own. Security was somehow mixed up with Edward, whom she thought must be quite rich, since he had paid for everything, and insecurity with her mother, whom she knew to be proud but needy. They had slept in the same room, but he had not touched her, and she had been grateful to him for that delicacy. After dinner she had felt so unwell that she would have been grateful to anyone who would let her go to bed and sleep, even to Tyler, had it been possible to imagine Tyler so quiescent. She had felt better in the morning, had even enjoyed the novelty of breakfast in their room, had appreciated Edward's discretion, although she was aware that he looked at her too fixedly, and once she was in the train had tried to forget him, and to a certain extent had succeeded.

But that image of insouciance which had initially proved so beguiling could not quite disguise the fact that she was in some physical discomfort, and had been for a few days past. Had she had any money she would have known what to do, or rather she would have asked Julie what to do and where to go. But then had she had any money she would not so promptly have fallen in with so many people's plans for her. She saw herself now as helpless, and wondered whether her dream of independence were entirely benign, or rather some kind of parody of her present situation. Before leaving the hotel she had wondered whether it would be possible for her to stay there, until what she thought of as her problem was resolved or had resolved itself. But she could not ask Edward for money, and she needed to get away from his anxious face, his regrettable expression of something that was not quite desire but more of a general concern, such as a seasoned husband might wear.

She knew that he had performed a brave action in declaring his intention to marry her, yet she was not able to appreciate that action for what it was. She was vaguely aware of this as an enormity on her part, an aberration of conduct, yet she realised that she was no longer able to think of herself as an honourable person, not because she had fallen in love with Tyler, but because she had not succeeded in making him love her. If she felt anything she felt shame in not bringing home Tyler as a prize for her mother. And the result of her love affair was this fleeting sensation of unreality. How had it been possible to feel so much then, and so little now? Her amorous life, her life as a woman, was apparently over, and the rest would be a simulacrum of a maturity she must soon assume. She would need a great deal of dignity and of self-control if this were to be possible. Yet all she wished for herself was a higher form of fecklessness, one which would obscure her duties and cancel all her obligations.

Her shoes, she calculated, would just get her home and must then be thrown away. The memory of those days spent walking with Edward was fading; only the shoes reminded her. If she thought of Paris at all it was in the grey damp of those latter days. The early heat of her nights in the rue Laugier, as well as the radiant sun which had bewitched them all at La Gaillarderie, had disappeared, vanquished by the colder certainties of the advancing autumn, which entirely mirrored her own situation. She saw the whole thing as an allegory, some mischief of the ancient gods who had painted the world in the beguiling colours of summer in order to tempt her, and had then abruptly switched their interest to some other mortal and left her with her broken shoes and her fallen state. They had no mercy, those deities, yet it was somehow appropriate to invoke them, since Tyler so beautifully conveyed the character of Apollo, whom she imagined as having the golden face surrounded by spiky rays of the clock in her mother's salon. Tyler was of course a mythical being, one who partook of that ancient company, and she knew that although her blood was now cool – cold, in fact – she would never blame Tyler for his legacy to her. The revelation of Tyler was such as to make her tolerant of her own weakness: if she were not now Tyler's partner it was because she had failed, and failed not for any mundane reason but because she was earthbound, obedient to more prosaic rhythms, because she was simply one of those whose destiny it was to be visited by a transcendent being, and then left alone to ponder her outcast state.

By the same token she knew that she had already enjoyed the best that there was to enjoy, and that she had, if she cared to use it, a knowledge of how to please, and to be pleased, in the act of love. She felt immeasurably older than any of her friends, than Julie, with her gossip and her parties, certainly older than Jean Bell, with her inscrutable enthusiasm for artefacts. The one person to whom she did not feel superior was her mother, whose amorous secrets had for so long been locked out of sight, and whom widowhood had restored to a semblance of virginity. To a memory of it, as well. To long unillumined and entirely predictable days, without that hint of spontaneous gladness which must once have quickened her step. Yet Maud understood that condition, understood what she had once unthinkingly accepted. Given a chance she would have hoped to return to a condition not unlike virginity herself. She had known love, or rather passion, and now she wished to regain her previous invulnerability, her physical integrity, which was so badly compromised. If she was to be the poor mortal, the unworthy recipient of her lover's transient attention, then she wished still to be in an allegory and to be restored supernaturally to that weightless state in which she had spent her previous existence and the very real years of her real life.

The one person who did not fit into this allegorical setting was Edward, with his one episode of quixotic kindness, and the covert expression, in itself unheroic, of which she felt she had already seen too much. Edward was the faithful shepherd in the *toile de Jouy* fabric that covered the walls of her usual bedroom at La Gaillarderie, always peering through undergrowth at the sleeping shepherdess, whose winsome smile is an eloquent indication of her recent activities. Those activities, repeated in ovals as far as the eye could see, never encompassed the shepherd, with his honest face and his clumsy breeches. In the same way Edward would love her, but she would never love him. His love would hardly touch her, since her thoughts would be given over entirely to other matters, principally to memory, which she saw as the appropriate repository of her desire – of her former desire – and to a loneliness which it would be heedless of her to ask him to share.

It was cold in Dijon, and leaves were already falling. As she reached the rue des Dames Blanches the sole of one shoe detached itself and slapped against the pavement. She longed now for cold water on her face and a change of clothes. As the door of the flat opened to reveal her mother, wearing a silk dress usually reserved for more formal occasions, she felt shabby, downcast, aware of her worn cotton skirt, the gooseflesh on her cold arms. Her mother, in contrast, looked formidable, two spots of colour burning in her cheeks. She had been to the hairdresser, Maud noted. She could have been preparing for a wedding. There was a smell of roasting chicken, which made her feel sick. She kissed Nadine, indicated her woebegone appearance, and hurried to the bathroom. Lavish applications of hot and cold water to her face did a little to restore her equilibrium, and a simple blue cotton dress her appearance. Nevertheless she took her seat at the table in a state of some apprehension.

'You are getting married, you said. Am I to believe this?' Nadine's tone was mildly coquettish; her fork hovered over her tomato salad.

'Certainly, Mother. I am going to marry Edward Harrison. You met him at La Gaillarderie.'

'When was this decided?'

'Oh, very suddenly.'

'I must confess I hardly noticed him.'

'He is very kind, Mother.'

'And that is enough? Kindness?'

'Yes.' She felt the beginning of tears.

'In one way I am relieved,' said Nadine, gently laying down her fork. 'There was a very unpleasant atmosphere after you left. Germaine asked what I was thinking of, letting you go off like that.'

'Really, Mother, this is 1971. I am not a child.'

'No well-brought-up girl – which I hope you are, Maud – would go off like that with two men she hardly knew.'

'Then why didn't you stop me?'

'I could see you were in love. We could all see that. That was what shocked Germaine. She thought you should have stayed with me, and let those two men go off on their own.'

'What difference does it make now?' asked Maud tiredly.

'It makes this difference. You may not know it but Germaine helps us out financially from time to time. We have never got on, but it has to be said that she plays her part. For her to disapprove of you, and therefore of me, is quite serious. We had a very considerable falling out after you left.'

'Then I can't understand why you both let me go.'

'We were at dinner, if you remember. Nobody argues at the dinner table.'

There was a silence. Nadine removed their plates, and brought in a platter of chicken.

'I should have done the same myself,' she said.

Maud looked at her in surprise. 'You would? Why?'

'My dear child, I am not a fool. I could see what had happened between Tyler and yourself. I was young too, remember. I am not old even now. I should certainly have followed a man like Tyler, if he had made it possible. So would Germaine, of course. One does not meet a Tyler very often in one's life.'

'You mean . . . ?'

'Tyler is a man who makes women love him, and to whom women forgive much. I hope you enjoyed him. I also hope you will manage to forget him. Life must become orderly again. Germaine was shocked that I could even entertain such thoughts, although she herself was mildly affected. We all were. Germaine is more conventional than I am, and therefore all the more insistent on good behaviour. Naturally, when I telephoned to tell her you were getting married she quietened down immediately.

Particularly when I said you were not marrying Tyler, but the other one.'

'His name is Edward, Mother.'

'I suppose I must get to know him. Why didn't he come back with you?'

'He said he wanted to go ahead and find a flat for us. I dare say he will telephone some time.'

'And do you want to marry him?'

'Of course. At least . . .'

'My dear, there is no at least about it. You owe it to us all. You have not behaved well. You put my life at risk, as well as your own.'

She thought back to the scene on the terrace, after the car had driven off. It was not a pleasant memory: two middle-aged women accusing each other of unseemly conduct, then of jealousy, while Xavier, embarrassed, tried to calm them down. Eventually he left them to it and wandered off, unhappy. He too had been shocked, she saw, but shocked at the abuse of hospitality, for she knew that he was aware of the lovemaking in the attic, as Germaine, fortunately, was not. Indeed, if she had known, Nadine's position would have been desperate. She saw Xavier's expression, bewildered at his mother's obtuseness, determined not to show it. She saw his disappointment, his disapproval. In a rare mood of enlightenment, brought on by this unaccustomed sharing of antagonisms, she saw that Xavier would have been only too happy to have accompanied Tyler to Paris on his own. When Xavier, with an expression of distaste, wandered off, she could see what was in his mind: horror at the spectacle of two women fighting, and fighting in effect over the same man.

She gave him credit for his feelings, but she could hardly know that he had most vividly at the forefront of his mind the scene which he had not witnessed, but in which he felt involved: Maud and Tyler making love, in the hot afternoon. She did not know that he pictured further scenes of lovemaking, although she did know that it was

Tyler's peculiar gift to make this voyeurism possible. Germaine had been affected by the atmosphere of sensuality, but because she was a very innocent woman she had not known that it was possible to move from speculation into action. Nadine had an image of her sister in bed at night, going over the day's events, or rather those she had witnessed, with a smile on her face. Nadine knew that Xavier did not like her, that he thought her an unworthy mother, sister, aunt. Yet there had been that irresistible desire for some kind of a victory over her sister's pretensions, since that sister left her with none of her own, and even at the risk of losing everything she had felt a savage pleasure, not for Maud, whose part she had so readily taken, but for herself.

'Germaine wanted to know the date of the wedding,' she said, wiping her lips, with the best linen napkins brought out for the occasion. 'I take it there is no hurry. We shall need a little time to send out the invitations. And I have already spoken to the Hôtel de la Cloche: they get booked up so early, you know.'

'We want to get married quietly, Mother.'

'Why?'

In that lightning glance across the table could be read her mother's suspicions, which she must at all costs do nothing to confirm. Maud ate the last of her chicken with application, although she now felt both tired and sick. The night in the hotel, the train journey, and now this conversation had exhausted her: she wished only to get away, out of the sound of her mother's voice. For a moment marriage seemed a very real possibility, more, a desirable outcome.

'We want to get married quickly and quietly. There is no need to go to any expense. Anyway, we can't afford it.'

'But didn't I tell you? Germaine has been quite generous. As I say she was reconciled when I told her you were marrying Mr Harrison.'

'Edward, Mother.'

'Edward. A simple white dress, I thought, and then a good suit for travelling in. You can't get married in under a month: October, fortunately, is usually fine. I'll get on to the hotel this afternoon, and let Germaine know. We owe it to her to let her be the first to know the date. You can make a list of the people you want to invite. You might as well do that this afternoon.'

'I'm awfully tired. I'd really like a rest. Or some air. I'd like a walk. I'll help you with these dishes first . . .'

'No. You can go. I'll take care of this. You don't look well, Maud. I can't see that your adventure has done you much good. If I had had a love affair I hope I should have looked better on it than you do.'

'But why did you let me go? You should have stopped me.'

Her mother put down the glass dish she was holding. 'I let you because . . . because I can't give you very much, not as much as girls of your age usually have, and because you are a good girl, and because you will get married and settle down, and we shall all live happily ever after. At least I hope we shall. I wanted you to have what I never had. Oh, I was happy enough being a wife, but I knew I had missed something. I married to get away from home, as you will, my dear – oh, yes, I know: you have always been docile, a good daughter. But Maud, when you get to my age you realise that being a good daughter isn't enough, or it shouldn't be. A woman should have an opportunity to be bad from time to time. I've shocked you, I see. Well, this is 1971, after all, as you so recently reminded me.'

'I think Tyler was rather wicked.'

'Of course he was. That was the whole point.'

'You shock me, Mother.'

'I'm not displeased to hear it. But listen to me, Maud. That is over now, do you hear? You have the chance to be respectable again. Not every woman is so lucky. You will settle down; we shall all settle down, and be as we were.

And next year you and your husband will spend the summer at La Gaillarderie, and . . .'

'Never.'

'Well, as you wish. I think it is the least you could do. But you will see Germaine at the wedding, of course. And now I think I shall make a few telephone calls. You had better tell me more about your fiancé. Everyone will be so interested. What does his father do?'

'Nothing. He is retired. His family lives by the sea, in Sussex.'

'Are they wealthy? Professional people?'

'I have no idea. Edward has his own business. He is a bookseller. He has a shop.'

'A shop?'

'It is in the heart of London, Mother. And I think he is quite well situated. At least he is buying a flat for us. He is very kind.'

At the memory of his kindness, and of what she had done to stimulate it, her heart sank. Nadine, looking at her daughter's woebegone face, said, 'You will get used to it. Every woman does. Men like Tyler don't last, and they don't marry either. At least not girls like you. You have had your love affair, and now you must put it behind you.' There was another swift glance. 'Are you quite well, Maud? There's nothing you want to tell me, is there?' In the face of Maud's silence she said, 'Is everything quite normal, Maud?'

'Everything is quite normal, Mother. There is nothing to worry about.'

She left the dining-room quickly, aware that this particular conversation was at an end, must never be repeated. She took a sweater from her cupboard, tied the sleeves round her shoulders, and left the flat, profoundly disturbed. She walked down the rue des Dames Blanches, conscious of a tenderness in her feet from all the recent walking. This then was the dilemma: not her own condition, though that was dilemma enough, but the fact that she had discovered a profound moral failing in her mother, and that she was about to commit a moral fault herself. Somehow the former served to make the latter unacceptable. She had thought to reinforce her mother's values by this marriage, only to be given to understand that her mother's values were more subversive than she had ever imagined. She would never have dreamt that her mother could countenance an irregular love affair, let alone promote one. She tried to persuade herself that the status of women had changed, that they were now permitted to voice their disappointment with their lot and with what they had to undergo at the hands of men. If her mother had urged celibacy, a life without men, she could not have been more shocked, but she would not have been surprised. Women urge their own behaviour on others all the time. But for her mother to have enjoyed vicariously conduct which she would never have permitted herself was too much. And then to accept without question this obviously hasty marriage in order simply to reinforce the status quo (essential after an aberration) was so cynical, in Maud's eyes, that her mother's fault quite eclipsed her own.

There was more at stake here than her own reason for this marriage, so nearly suspected, so deliberately undisclosed. There was her mother's security, even her future, for a start. With the whole of her meagre income supplemented by Germaine's contributions, about which Maud had not known, her mother could keep up a certain style, entertain, make new friends. The wedding alone, whatever it would cost, would be her introduction to society, for she would receive invitations in return. The wedding, in fact, would be for her mother's benefit, and how was she to be denied that pleasure? She would soon be alone, and winter was coming. Her gamble, for that was what it was, was the only one a decent woman of her class could make. Which made her recent remarks, her recent action, seem lewd in comparison. Despite the wisdom of the age, or rather the propaganda of the age,

Maud did not consider it seemly for a mother to countenance a daughter's love affair, particularly when that love affair was compounded by an abuse of hospitality on a grand scale. Maud was sufficiently aware of her convent education to know that a minor does not make love under a relative's roof. Her standards were those of the Fifties rather than of the recent Sixties, and among her friends she was thought old-fashioned. Her mother's impropriety, she thought, was in advance of her own, and therefore all the more disconcerting. She was left with the impression that, although she was alone responsible for her present dilemma, her mother was in some way to blame.

These reflections confirmed her earlier desire to revert to a form of prelapsarian integrity, if that were possible. She could not see herself as a mother. She doubted if she ever would want children, or even if she ever wanted to be married. Yet she knew that her mother's silk dress, the visit to the hairdresser, the heightened colour in her cheeks, all betokened some kind of wish fulfilled. The question now was whether she could fulfil her own wish: for freedom. She had once had a vague idea that she should train as an interpreter; her English was fluent, and she could teach herself Italian, had indeed planned to do so. She saw herself in a small flat in Geneva, working for some international organisation. Her present guilt she saw, more accurately, as a form of dismay. It amounted to this, she thought: she must get married and have a child in order to please her mother, yet at the same time she must not disclose the fact that she was pregnant. Of her own wishes no one had thought to enquire. Of Edward she thought with pity, perhaps a distant regard. Yet she knew that if, by some unimaginable feat, she managed to regain her freedom, she would not think much about him ever again.

When it was clear that there was no answer to any of this, she turned in the direction of home. She was irked by the greyness of the sky, the silently falling leaves, as if she had been tricked into this return. Chilled and uneasy, she planned to take a hot bath before dinner, and then beg an early night. She supposed that as a bride she would be allowed indulgences, one more instance of life's partiality towards the undeserving.

'Your fiancé telephoned,' said Nadine, hardly waiting for Maud to enter the living-room before giving rein to her newfound exuberance. 'He wanted to know that you got home safely. Very correct of him, I thought. And I got on to the hotel. They are booked up until the eighteenth of October, so I fixed the reception for twelve o'clock on the eighteenth. Just a simple meal, I thought, nothing too elaborate. Oh, and I've put something in your room for you.'

Maud found the dark pink silk kimono on her bed. The extravagant garment, with its fringed sash and its wide sleeves slashed at the armpit, fitted loosely over her cotton frock, changing her into a beauty. Instinctively she stood up straight, swept the silk skirts around her, saw herself objectively as a handsome woman, one who might in other circumstances have had a promising future.

'It's lovely,' she said. 'Where did it come from?'

'My mother's father brought it back from China. He had business connections there. That is Chinese silk, real silk. It was the only thing of my mother's that I kept. I wore it on my honeymoon. Then I packed it away. It suits you very well. Where are you going?'

'I'd like a hot bath: I've got a slight chill, I think. And thank you, Mother. I shall treasure it.'

She reckoned that the bleeding started even before she reached her bedroom and she hurried to remove the kimono before it got soiled. Her heart beating rapidly, her joy and shock vertiginously mingled, she ran to the bathroom, tore off her clothes, and lowered herself into the hot water, watching it turn red. Within a few moments she was alarmed by the volume of the loss. Faint, she wondered how she would ever disguise the evidence, wondered in fact how she would get back to her room.

She cleaned up as best she could, at last managed to accommodate the red tide. The buzzing in her ears gradually subsided, leaving behind a lightness of the heart which she could hardly remember.

That evening at dinner she ate voluptuously. Her mother watched her as she peeled a pear. 'You have got your appetite back, I see. Mind you don't put on weight.'

'I've come to a decision, Mother,' said Maud, patting her lips. 'I don't think I'm ready for this marriage. It was, after all, very sudden. And I am very young. So I think you'd better cancel the Hôtel de la Cloche. I think what I'd really like to do is study. I always wanted to be an interpreter anyway. Women marry much later these days, and it's not as if . . . '

Nadine's face was very pale. 'You were saying? It's not as if . . . ?'

'Oh, I didn't mean anything,' said Maud joyously. 'I'm just relieved at having come to a decision. I'm sorry, Mother. I hope you're not too disappointed. After all,' she added, as this last remark met with no response, 'I take it I'm allowed to please myself in this matter?'

'And how nearly were you not able to please yourself? And for how long do you suppose you are allowed to please yourself?'

'Surely I can decide . . . '

'You shock me, Maud. I hadn't realised . . . '

'Please, Mother, don't look like that.'

'I don't want you here, Maud. You had better make up your mind to that.'

'Yet it was you who let me go to Paris. What right have you to be shocked now?'

'Very little, no doubt. But it is not a question of rights. It is a question now of what is appropriate.'

Maud, shocked herself at her mother's sudden pallor, saw at a glance the obverse of her mother's boldness: a fear of consequences. A love affair was to be permitted only if it left the woman intact. Her mother's gift to her carried an important proviso: that a return to blamelessness be assured. And witnessed.

'I don't want you here,' Nadine repeated. 'And don't think you can please yourself. No woman can please herself indefinitely.'

'Now I am shocked.'

'Perhaps. I can't help that. I too want a life of my own.'

'At the expense of mine.'

'He is pleasant. You said yourself how kind he is.'

'Kinder than you, Mother.'

They stared at each other.

'Then you had better marry him.'

'Yes,' she said, getting up to clear the table. 'As you say, I had better marry him. Then you can be happy even if I can't.'

'Maud . . . '

'Goodnight, Mother.'

She saw her mother's head droop, saw her shade her eyes with her hand. She herself felt quite blank. But she had a sense of being no longer at home. She thought at last of Edward, who had gone to buy a flat, and she supposed she must live there, with him, and call it her home.

IO

As the plane began its descent Harrison celebrated his
return to England with a series of jaw-cracking yawns, as
if he had awoken after a particularly puzzling dream. He
was too tired to make much sense of his situation, or rather
he told himself that he was too tired: what he most actively
experienced was an onslaught of restless boredom. He felt
burdened, impatient, aware that he had wasted too much
time, spent too much money, and made a disastrous
decision about which he would rather not think. Somewhere, in some deep recess of consciousness, was a feeling
of hurt, as if he were suddenly friendless, doomed to make
his way in an adult world in which he had no place. The
previous night, in that dark hotel in the Boulevard Raspail,
he had dreamed of his sister again, and of that sunlit garden
which contained all of his banal but to him enchanted
childhood. He had woken with his usual sense of gladness,
only to hear Maud's breathing from the other bed. His
one instinctive thought, as he registered her presence, was
that somehow she must be inducted into this childhood
pattern, must become a part of his reverie, must love his
family, must love him; otherwise there was no hope for
either of them. He knew that he could not join her in her
sleeping fastness, that he would never become part of
her own dreams, would always to a certain extent have to
strive for her attention. For the present she was too distant

for him to reach. Her abstraction, the deeply preoccupied expression which she banished when he took her hand, hurt him, though he accepted them as inevitable. What affected him more deeply was the contrast between the effortless universe of his dream and the painful dark of the room in which he and Maud lay separated. He wanted to wipe her mind clear of the memory of recent events, to restore her to innocence, transparency, sinlessness, to be able to take her hand without that tiny moment of with-drawal which told him that she too looked back, but looked back only as far as that very recent summer. It was as if she had no childhood with which to endow him, as he hoped to endow her. What she brought to him was a kind of widowhood, the immense blankness of shock.

At the airport, after he had left her, he watched his fellow travellers and remembered his earlier ambitions to see the world, to be that courteous sophisticated character whom others would report seeing in Java or Goa or Kabul, whose freedom they would recognise with envy as being none of their portion. This he now saw as an entirely childish fantasy which belonged to and reflected his own woeful immaturity. He would never see the world; more to the point, he would never be free of a certain wistful longing to be cared for. Those weeks in Paris, which he had hoped would be a period of self-discovery, had in fact left him lonely. Had he not been so lonely he would not have been so glad to see Tyler, would not have fallen in so eagerly with his plans, would certainly not have accompanied Tyler and Maud on those terrible excursions, at which he now looked back with horror, would have seen what part he was expected to play ('the least you can do is be pleasant,' as Tyler had said), and have removed himself. In that way he would have reached home intact, rather than with this burden of feeling, in which regret and resentment struggled for pre-eminence, and which on reflection he identified as a sense of sheer loss.

Where he saw loss, he knew, others might see gain. His

mother's delighted reception of his news seemed to betoken a trouble-free introduction to the adult world, as if it were no more than a step on a clearly indicated path. He knew that his family would welcome Maud, rather in the spirit in which they had welcomed the friends he had brought home from school and later university; no awkward or intrusive questions would be asked. His parents believed so entirely in his own innocence that it would be impossible ever to tell them of the ache he felt when he thought of Maud, the responsibility that was to be his for making her smile, the longing that she might love him, the dread that she might not. He could never tell them that his mind was still imprinted with the image of her naked body in the Vermeulens' bed, and that his innocence had foundered on that occasion, not simply because he had made love to her with a passion that was not in his nature, but because in so doing he had imagined her making love to Tyler. This truth must never be known. The unwelcome revelation of that afternoon, and of the night that so chastely followed, was that side by side with this very ambiguous longing for her went something altogether more naked, more dolorous: a simple fearful hope that she might, spontaneously, and without any prompting on his part, continue to reach out to him, and if possible to spare him some love of her own.

He took the airport bus to Victoria, and reckoned that since he was so near he might as well go to the shop and see if Cook had made any progress in tidying up the place. Tidying up was the only activity he had envisaged: how to engage in commerce was utterly beyond him. He walked dejectedly to Denbigh Street, aware that sooner or later he must go back to his rented flat, that he must deal with the dirty washing in his bag, that he must decide how to make some money, that he must go to the bank and see the solicitor to decide what to do with Mr Sheed's investments, and that he must both go to Eastbourne and find a flat for himself and Maud to live in. This last seemed imperative in view of the fact that in the environs of Warwick Way Maud's image seemed to disappear. He could only remember her face now, its closed expression and its cautious smile; the rest of her seemed to have been mislaid in Paris, as if it had stayed there all the time. At least he could not mistake the reality of the shop, whose dim green façade proclaimed 'Sheed' for all the indifferent world to see.

'Cook?' he queried, throwing his bag in a corner. Here at least nothing had changed.

A thunder of footsteps down the stairs from the flat brought Cook down into the office at the back of the shop. Harrison held out his hand in gratitude at this evidence of continuity.

'Hello, Tom,' he said. 'It's Tom and Edward, by the way. How are you getting on?'

He thought it proper to ask how Tom was getting on, since he had done so little in the way of getting on himself, and since Tom, whom he did not know at all, had performed what amounted to an act of chivalry in not deserting him. The only sign that Tom had been present for the six weeks of his absence and had not just strolled through the door, a complete stranger, was that his hair had grown. This, and his apparently genuine expression of welcome, revealed him in an altogether more advantageous light than Harrison's impression, admittedly fleeting, had led him to expect. Cook he now saw as the sort of young man who would have been described as 'fair' in Elizabethan England, with a rosy anonymous face, a shy mouth, and steady eyes. He was cleanly dressed in a white T-shirt and black jeans, and there was about him an aura of soap. Harrison found his hand being warmly shaken. 'You've grown your hair,' was all he could think of saying.

'I'm going for a pony-tail,' said Cook. 'Coffee?'

As they stood drinking their coffee — stood, because books covered most of the available surfaces — Harrison felt a great need of renewal. The sight of the barred window at the back of the office re-awakened his sick feeling of imprisonment until he realised that in fact the shop was, or could be, a domain, a refuge. He had inherited the mantle of Mr Sheed, whose name he decided to retain on the façade, his own presence being as yet more insubstantial.

'First of all,' he said, helping himself to a biscuit, 'we must get the place cleaned up. Let me know how much you've laid out so far. And you've found a kettle, I see. First the window cleaner — that should be easy enough. Then a paint job. You said navy, didn't you? Why not? A navy blue façade and navy blue fittings in front.'

'Won't be too dark?'

'Not when the windows are cleaned. This stuff had better go downstairs for the time being. Then of course we'll have to decide what to do with it.'

'You could put it back on the shelves for a start. Make it look as if we're open for business.'

'Nobody's been in, I suppose?'

'Well, I've been closed, haven't I? Anyway I wouldn't have known what to charge, although some of the prices are marked. Not all of them, though. It seems sort of hit and miss to me. I found these ledgers in the basement, by the way; they might give us a clue. Can I help you, Sir?' he said in a glad voice, fairly springing into the shop in his alacrity to greet the stranger whom Harrison could only see as a solid black silhouette against the shop door.

'Good morning,' Edward said, with some apprehension. 'How can I help you?'

The visitor removed his hat to reveal a head of wavy grey hair. Close to he was seen to be fairly old, with a vaguely medical appearance, like a disreputable gynaecologist. He was formally dressed in a grey suit and highly polished black shoes, yet the hat, the gold-rimmed glasses, and the pouting childish lips seemed to indicate that he belonged in a place where the manners and customs were subtly different. When he spoke his accent was curious, part sibilant, part cockney. He gave an impression of a man of substance, just beginning to go to seed.

'Kroll,' he said. 'Max Kroll. I just wondered what had happened to old Ted's place. Only just heard of his death. Very sorry to hear about it. I always thought of him as the last of the innocents.'

'I'm beginning to think that's me,' said Harrison.

'And you are?'

'Edward Harrison. And this is Tom Cook. Mr Sheed left the shop to me.'

Max Kroll unfurled a fleshy white hand and presented it to Harrison and Cook in turn. 'Know the book trade, do you?' he enquired.

'I know nothing,' Edward said simply. 'Would you like some coffee?'

At a sign Cook retired to his flat and reappeared with coffee in a flowered cup and saucer, in contrast to the mugs which they had used earlier. More biscuits were fastidiously arranged on a glass plate.

'Do sit down,' Edward went on. 'I'm afraid there isn't much room. I was trying to decide what to do with the stock. I can't quite get the hang of it.'

'You've got a gold mine here,' said Kroll, helping himself to a couple of biscuits. 'Look at this,' he said, picking up a book and dusting it with a green silk handkerchief. 'First edition. Half the stock is first editions. You don't want to let this stuff walk out of the shop. This stuff goes to collectors.'

'How do I find them? I don't know any.'

'Well, you could advertise, for a start. Use the papers, the journals. "Books bought and sold. Enquiries welcome. Under new management." That sort of thing. But if I know Ted Sheed he's got a set of books somewhere.'

'Tom found these account books in the basement.'

'That'll be it, then.'

'But they're only about money. Sums received.'

'With names?'

'Yes, with names. But I don't know who the names belong to.'

'I found this address book,' said Tom. 'Would this help?'

'It would if you could match up the names with the sums received. This young man could do that.'

'Could you do that, Tom?'

'Then it'll have to go on some kind of collator. Got one of those? Ted wouldn't have one, I know.'

'I know about such things,' said Tom. 'I'd be glad to advise.'

'Advise! We haven't even thought about it yet.' He saw Tom's face grow dusky with repressed longing. 'Do you think you could buy one, then?' he said weakly. 'I suppose it's really necessary?'

'Essential,' said Mr Kroll. 'Any more of those biscuits? Or shall I take you both out to lunch? Yes, I think I'll do that. Nelly, that's my wife, says I eat too much. But you English don't eat enough! We'll go to Overton's. You like fish?'

'Yes, thank you,' they chorused, relieved to be taken in hand.

'It's very kind of you,' said Harrison. Kroll shrugged. 'I was going there anyway. If you take my advice, both of you, you'll have a good lunch. That way you'll keep going till six. You'll close at six, I suppose?'

'I dare say,' said Harrison, dodging in and out of the crowds, while keeping an eye on Kroll, who strode steadily ahead, his hands in his pockets.

'Mark you, most of your business will be done by post,' Kroll went on. 'Once you get your catalogues out. That's a job for you,' he said, poking a finger in Harrison's chest, oblivious to the traffic that was obliged to divide around them. 'Oysters, I think. You like oysters?'

Both shook their heads, lips firmly compressed.

'Then a nice sole. And over coffee I'll tell you about the book trade.'

'This is all very good of you,' said Harrison.

'Well, I'm retired, haven't much of anything to do with myself,' was the rather disappointing reply. He seated himself in the restaurant, motioned the two of them to sit facing him, and fell into a silent perusal of the menu. Waiters seemed to know him. Little was said until the oysters were placed before him. They watched, appalled, as he applied himself, then looked politely away, as if the sight should not be witnessed.

'Right,' he said, as the table was cleared. 'You want to know who I am and why I'm talking to you like this. It's very simple. I'm a bookseller, or was; that's how I knew Ted Sheed. I had a business in Long Acre. Sold it like a chump, because Nelly told me to. She worries about me, said I was doing too much. I always do what she wants, because I love her,' he said, eyeing the huge plate being set down in front of him. 'You got girlfriends?'

'Yes,' said Harrison, speaking, as he thought he should, for them both. Anything was simpler than an explanation.

'But I may have been wrong there. Not that I don't enjoy myself. I wander about, look in on friends. Not that there are many of them left. How old do you reckon I am?'

'Sixty?' queried Cook.

'Nearer seventy. I'm pre-war. My father owned a bookshop in Vienna. Now there was a bookseller! But he saw the light in 1933 and brought us all to London, me and my mother and Nelly, my second cousin, whom they'd more or less adopted. We stuck together, and then we married. We always knew we should. And then it was more like home. Well, it is home now.' He looked sad for a moment, older than seventy. 'No children, unfortunately. When we go there'll be nobody left. Eat up!' he said, rallying. 'Sometimes the time hangs a bit heavy,' he confessed, sombre again.

Stuffed, they could think of nothing to say, until Harrison finally managed, 'I don't know what we'd have done if you hadn't come in.'

'I haven't finished yet,' said Kroll. 'Just coffee, I think,' he said regretfully. 'You want to know about the book trade? I'll tell you. It's very simple. Identify your ideal readers and serve them faithfully. Give them what they want, or what you think they'll want. That stock of Ted's — that's fairly specialist stuff, although it may not look it. My feeling is that he catered for people who love a good story, whether it's old-fashioned or not. The English love a good story. What they don't like is showing off. And they are very nostalgic. Shall I tell you about my ideal reader?'

He lit a cigar and drew on it steadily. They watched him, sluggish now, and half hypnotised by the glowing tip.

'When I came to England I was heartbroken,' said Kroll. 'Safe, but heartbroken. London — we came to London — defeated me. Then gradually I got to know it, wandered around at weekends when it was quiet, got to appreciate little things, street corners, old girls out shopping, different-coloured front doors, flowers in the park. All the time I had this fantasy of England, of how we would live, Nelly and me. We'd be living in the country, or by the sea, and we'd be old, quite old. I'd be retired, and Nelly would be at home, in our house. I'd play a round of golf in the morning, and in the afternoon we'd take a walk or sit in the garden — because you must have a garden in England — and after tea we'd read. We'd read the classics, the English classics: the rest we'd read in Vienna. Only, if I were English, I'd also read J. B. Priestley, unpretentious honest stuff. Or Howard Spring. And Nelly'd be spoiled for choice with her Elizabeth Bowen and her Rosamond Lehmann and her Elizabeth Taylor. That's how I saw your English reader: not a satirist, not subversive. Bit out of date now, I suppose, but I'm willing to bet you'll find him in Ted Sheed's files, once you've straightened them out.'

'And did you really want to live like that?' asked Harrison, attentive now. 'Only I think my parents . . . '

Max Kroll had lost interest. Sighing, he pulled out his

wallet, extracted a number of notes. 'Live in the country, Nelly and me? Not a chance. We live in West End Lane, surrounded by Art Deco furniture. Nelly loves it. I leave it all to her. Nowadays I live in the past. I read what I read as a young man: Kafka, Colette, Thomas Mann. My day is done, I dare say. We're happy enough, we've got a bit of money behind us. But I miss the business, and that's the truth of the matter.'

'You're more than welcome to look in any time,' said Harrison.

'I'll do that,' said Kroll, extending his well-kept hand across the table to pick up the book-matches. Harrison noted his heavy ring, set with a dull red stone. A ring, he thought; I must buy Maud a ring.

'Now is there anything else you want to know?' enquired Kroll, as they emerged into the soft sunless afternoon. 'Compile your lists, get your correspondents straight, and start sending out catalogues. Advertise. You'll get some offers. I'll be happy to advise. How much are you paying this young man?'

By the time he had accompanied them back to Denbigh Street he had fixed the amount that Cook was to be paid, indicated a printer who might give them a discount on their stationery order, given them the name of a reliable shop-fitter, and told Harrison to buy a car ('You can't collect books by public transport'). He declined a further cup of coffee, and strolled off in the direction of Victoria, watched by Harrison and Cook as they stood on the threshold of the shop, unwilling to see him go but impatient now to put their own plans into execution.

'Will he come back, do you think?' asked Cook.

'Yes, I think so. He'll come back to see if we're doing what he told us to do. Do you want to get off and look at office supplies? Only don't spend too much. We're about to get through a lot of money. And I've got to buy a flat.' Indeed the thought of the future seemed suddenly so

141

foreign, so remote, that he wondered if it had been an illusion from the start.

'I'll get off then. What are you going to do?'

'I'm going to get married,' he heard himself say, and the doors to the future clanged shut in his face.

Again he experienced the doomed sensation of one who commits himself to a course of action utterly foreign to his nature and to which he has been led by either altruism or will-power. How much easier it would be to linger in contemplation of the day's events (surely unexpected) or to give a little uninterrupted time to a study of his equally unexpected associate Tom Cook. This gracile and accommodating youth, who, for some reason he could not hope to understand, had chosen to work for him, to espouse his interests, even to further them; yet he had been acquired effortlessly, and thus bore witness to the virtues of effortlessness as a strategy, or rather as a lack of strategy. Harrison knew that his happiest sensations, and even those rare decisions he had been forced to make, had come about by a process of almost magical passivity, which was in some way allied to the process of dreaming. Anything that involved hard adult ratiocination led invariably to a feeling of disappointment, as if he were being forced to act against his best interests, or even against nature. To be borne along on some wave of providence was his dearest wish, to be left in a state of reverie his most constant desire. He could even recapture his pleasure in surrendering his will to Tyler in those far off days of summer, which were in reality only six weeks distant. And the efficacy of this agreeable state was proved by the ease with which he had acquired Cook, simply by dint of not trying to acquire him, of choosing and accepting him almost absent mindedly, when his thoughts were fixed on some other matter, when he was impatient to buy his ticket to France and begin his journey in the wider world.

The irony was that, of that whole episode, only Cook remained. His illusion of escape had ended in greater imprisonment. He supposed he should count himself fortunate that he had not wasted more time on this fantasy, that it had only consumed a few weeks instead of a few years of his life. Yet how cold it was to come down to earth so young, before the world had been experienced! He knew himself now to be unalterably bound to home, to circumstances which until very recently had struck him as unbearably humdrum, to this shop which he had instinctively rejected, along with the enigmatic but surely home-haunting ghost of his benefactor. In a little while he would shut the shop and walk back to his rented flat, though that, he realised, would soon have to be relinquished, if he were to set himself the surely rather urgent task of finding a permanent home. A rented flat was only suitable for someone of an unpredictable way of life, suitable in fact for that traveller he could no longer emulate. Now he had to reconcile himself to a stay-at-home existence, the sort of existence he would never have contemplated during his years at university, when large and romantic ambitions were the norm. The view from his barred window did nothing to lighten his mood: through the smeared glass he saw patches of waste ground, a collection of builders' materials, and a pile of rubbish sacks. In the background he could hear the sound of suburban trains easing themselves into Victoria, stopping for twenty minutes or so, and then easing themselves out again.

Unbidden, there came into his mind the image of Tyler, as he had left him in the rue Laugier. The flat had seemed dark and unfriendly, filled with his own hostility, which had had time to mount while he was walking with the silent weeping Maud in the grey Tuileries. He could still see her raincoated back and her bent head as she contemplated the gravel of the path. He contrasted this with Tyler's sudden powerful reappearance, his even darker tan, his air of remoteness, of disengagement. It was a measure of his dominance that he had not responded to the insults rather hysterically offered to him but had appeared to think them

143

over, to test them for veracity, to ask himself if they were justified, and finally to accept them, not ruefully, not apologetically, but in a spirit of some amusement. Of course, thought Harrison belatedly, I gave him the ideal opportunity to free himself from the encumbrance of Maud, from the encumbrance, rather, of his responsibility for Maud's condition. Here he thought with some irritation of Maud herself. In fact in those last moments in the rue Laugier Maud had compared unfavourably with Tyler, although it was quite clear to anyone with any moral sense which one of them was to blame. But that was the painful fact of the matter, thought Harrison: effortlessness was always more attractive than guilt, even if it were attached to a line of conduct quite devoid of conscience. For this reason alone he would have found himself admiring Tyler, and indeed had done so during that tense last interview. That, after all, was why he had offered him his hand. If Tyler had chanced to walk in the door of the shop even now he would offer him his hand again. They were Steerforth and David Copperfield, he realised, with that poor girl between them. And there was no doubt in his mind that David had loved Steerforth, as Dickens had done, as the reader does, so great is the regenerative power of that unregenerate character, so profound the appeal of beauty and carelessness, and that somewhat unearthly aura of seduction.

Compared with Tyler, whom he could see possessed some of the characteristics of an older and more remorseless order, Maud, in her damp raincoat, had seemed to incarnate a sad Christian morality, in which destiny is dependent on some kind of Fall, whether personal or universal. Harrison's mind, which was free of any kind of religious conviction, as he suspected hers was, rejected this morality as distasteful, but because of his distaste felt or rather acknowledged her fears. It was as if a senseless superstition had suddenly been proved valid, and with it all the sad consequences of a fate once ridiculed. There was no difficulty in perceiving that Maud was in a fallen state, however little he wanted to see this. What then was the surge of feeling that prompted him to take care of her? Was it merely conscience, a sort of moral chivalry? Or was it more a fellow feeling, a sense of pathos, the quality that separated him from Tyler and his kind? He had fallen in love with her too precipitately, and that love was conditioned by the fact that she belonged to Tyler: he had felt passion for her when he made love to her, yet beyond his desire he had felt her loneliness calling forth some loneliness of his own. And during that sleepless night in the hotel, when they had both fearfully listened to each other's breathing, he had felt this sense of vulnerability connecting them and had felt it to be stronger than his own passion, stronger even than any desire he might feel for her again, in whatever life they were to manage together.

He had marvelled, when he made love to her, that Tyler had left no imprint on her body, as he had, again superstitiously, almost anticipated. Her beauty had surprised him, had inspired him to think and to act instinctively. She had not been passive, but he could sense that her thoughts were distant, not attentive to his. In the moments that followed had come the strong desire to attach her to himself, to make her love him, and there was even, if he were honest, a very slight antagonism in this impulse. But there was also ardour, mixed with disappointment, his own need to be loved, and that same sadness that united them both. He regretted being part of that fallen world, he regretted his awareness of duty and necessity, but there was nothing he could do to change matters. He could now hardly remember why he had offered to marry Maud, beyond the immediate cause. But perhaps he had been wiser than he knew. Perhaps there had been a moment of recognition, for him, if not for her. So that there was as little foundation in him for Tyler's moral freedom as there was for a life of unbridled adventure. For better or worse it was his fate to be obedient, to bow to necessity. Small wonder, then, that he yearned to be irresponsible.

On impulse he went up the stairs to Cook's flat, to see if he had managed to make himself comfortable. Although without curtains, the little living-room looked welcoming. There was a large and resplendent gas fire, installed by Mr Sheed for some previous tenant, or maybe for his own moments of withdrawal, and a capacious leather armchair, no doubt imported from some anterior home. Sheed himself, he remembered, had lived latterly at his club. Cook on the other hand showed signs of wanting to put down roots. He had rented a television set, ranged his paperbacks on the shelves. Harrison was touched to see that he had borrowed a couple of books from the shop: there was an Angela Thirkell beside the narrow bed, and an Edgar Wallace on the arm of the leather chair. In terms of decoration Cook's taste seemed to veer to the rococo: a complete tea-set in flowered gold-rimmed china — he recognised the cups from Max Kroll's coffee break — occupied the whole of one small kitchen cupboard, together with several glass plates of various sizes, suitable for the serving of gateaux. Harrison felt himself smile at this evidence of home-making, but he was also touched. When he caught sight of Cook's brand new wastepaper bin, complete with hunting scenes, he felt that if he stayed he would burst into tears.

Suddenly he could no longer bear the thought of his flat. The image of his mother's perfect domestic economy rose before his eyes, and he seized his bag and made for the station. In the train he fell into a doze which lasted until Polegate; he had just time to gather his wits about him, and decide to present the fact of his marriage as a delightful surprise, the kind of decision an impulsive young man might make, one at which his parents might marvel but could not question. It was late, later than he thought, no longer dusk but dark. He took the bus to Meads, alighted almost from memory, saw the house with lights shining from the downstairs windows, as if waiting for his return. In an instant he remembered the perfection of his mother's reign, and its material reflection in the sparkling windows, the glossy white paint, the smell of lavender polish, the promptly renewed cakes of scented soap in the bathrooms. In the garden, at this time of year, his father would be staking drowsy Michaelmas daisies, his cardigan worn, the seat of his corduroy trousers baggy, from use, or from age. His parents' ages: he preferred not to think about that. He rang the bell rather than use his key: he wanted to experience once again their lovely welcome. That was the essence of home to him: that sense of permanent joy at his return.

They crowded into the hall one after the other, laughing, embracing him. 'Give him something to eat, Polly,' said his father, trying imperfectly to control his broad smile. 'Come in, come in, but be quiet for ten minutes, there's a good fellow; we just want to see the end of this film.' Soon he was in a chair opposite the television set, a tray on his knees, an omelette and a sizeable piece of cold gooseberry pie in front of him, Bibi on her knees by his side, willing him to eat quickly and get on with telling them his news. But, 'That's that,' said his father, switching off the set. 'Rather an anticlimax, I thought. Now what's all this about getting married?'

He looked at them, saw himself reflected in three pairs of eager eyes, resolved not to disappoint them. 'Well, I told you. She's called Maud, and it was all very sudden . . . '

'How did you meet her?' asked Bibi.

'Through friends,' he said. That was true enough, anyway.

'And when do we get to meet her, dear?' That was his mother, eyes shining, tears not far away.

'I suppose she'd better come for the weekend, sometime before the wedding,' he said. This did now seem to be inevitable.

'And her mother too?'

'Oh, no.' The rejection was instinctive. 'You'll meet her mother at the wedding.'

When the two women carried off the tray to the kitchen, his father said, very quietly, 'Are you sure?'

'Almost.' He tried to make a joke of it.

'Only I don't want your mother upset.'

'She won't be. But what about you, Dad? Are you all right?'

'I'm always all right. A spot of indigestion, nothing to worry about.'

'I tell him he eats too quickly,' said his mother, coming back into the room. 'But he takes no notice. Here you are, dear, give this to your Maud.' She handed him a small faded box. This time there was no mistake: a tear was hastily wiped away.

He opened the box and found a heavy gold ring, set with a band of sapphires and diamonds, the sort of ring that might have been worn by a confident Edwardian matriarch. He smiled at the incongruity of this, bent forward and kissed his mother.

'Where did it come from?' he asked.

'A great-aunt on my mother's side. I've never worn it — well, a diamond always seemed more appropriate when girls of my age got engaged. But this old-fashioned stuff is coming back, so they tell me. But if she doesn't like it . . . '

'She'll love it,' he assured her. 'Mother, Dad, do you mind if I go to bed? I'm suddenly awfully tired.'

'Aren't you going to speak to Maud?'

'Tomorrow.'

'And you'll invite her over?'

'Of course.'

Somehow he got himself upstairs. But even here he was beset. Bibi lingered in the doorway of his bedroom. 'Is she beautiful?' she asked. He thought she was very slightly jealous.

'Yes, she is rather beautiful.' He longed to get rid of his beloved sister, though she dawdled in his room as

148

unselfconsciously as she had always done. 'Fair,' he said, making an effort. 'More of a dark gold. About your height.' He was suddenly dropping with fatigue. 'I shall need your help,' he forced himself to say. 'I'll need to find a flat. Will you come to London and help me?' He saw her face brighten. He decided he was too tired to take a bath. 'Goodnight,' he thought he said, and heard her switch off his light.

In the blissful dark he registered only the fact that he was home, and that he would soon have to leave. Strange how his thoughts were more direct at night than in the daytime, as if the hours of darkness were more authentic than the others. It was true that revelations came in sleep, and these always seemed more startling than those acquired laboriously through everyday experience. What he hoped for now was not a revelation, but some sort of confirmation or sanction that he was proceeding honourably. He was aware of fear, of shadows that seemed to body forth from the darkness. And suddenly of desire, so that he turned over abruptly in the bed. He could count on that, at least. But could he count on her? And what of the baby, of whom so little had been thought? But in the darkness, in the peace of his own room, the idea of the baby — of any baby — seemed too fantastical, so that even in the brief interval before sleep overcame him he contrived to think the poor baby entirely out of the way.

II

After the virtual defection of her mother, following so soon after what she dared not think of as the treachery of Tyler (for to do so would have deprived the world of its last vestige of morality), Maud resigned herself to a life of serious effort and genteel conformity. Her first taste of both of these endeavours came to her during her visit to Harrison's parents in Eastbourne during a sunny weekend in October. She had succeeded in getting her mother to postpone the wedding until the beginning of November. This had not been as difficult as she thought, for her mother, who spent much of her days now on the telephone, had succeeded in activating a circle of acquaintances, women who had hitherto found her both formidable and rather dull, but who were willing to appreciate her in this new mood of effervescence. And as the marriage of a daughter disarms most women, Nadine found herself invited out to tea rather more often than had been her lot in recent years. There was so much to discuss, so many addresses to be exchanged. She had the sense to ask advice, to seek her new friends' opinions; sometimes she brought sketches in her bag, samples of fabric. This was thought quite endearing, if mildly amusing. Something of the admiration previously felt for Nadine, whether sincerely or not, was now passed on to Maud, for her youth, her looks, and for the great feat of having secured a husband when she was barely out of school, filling in her time at the university, where, they assured her mother, her studies would have prepared her for her position as the wife of a man with an important bookshop in the heart of London.

Maud during this time detached herself as much as possible from her mother's new febrile condition, having won a reprieve in the matter of the wedding. This interval was important to her, not because she mistook it for liberty, which it was not, but because she needed to appreciate what she had so far taken for granted, the last of her youth. She had learnt all the lessons she was supposed to have learnt, knew that girls were no longer to be addressed as girls but as women, and thought briefly what a pity it was that in this new incarnation there was no opportunity to be inexperienced. Given the choice she would have welcomed a period of several years in which to discover what her tastes were, or whether she welcomed or rejected the feelings which came to her unbidden, even in the state of latency, almost of somnambulism, which accompanied her last days in Dijon. So unreal did these days seem that she almost welcomed Polly Harrison's invitation, placing more faith in the restorative possibilities of a holiday by the sea than in any more vital contact. Briefly she looked to Edward to provide the impetus, to introduce her, even to sponsor her, to plead her cause, something she felt unable to do for herself. This faintheartedness was due in part to the fact that she felt slightly unwell, and had done so ever since her return from Paris. Her mother, preoccupied, noticed nothing. There seemed no possibility of visiting a doctor. Besides, what could she tell a doctor, or a doctor tell her? She knew the answer: her body had undergone a change, and she herself was changed with it.

The day of her arrival at the Harrisons' house was well aspected: a mild golden October, the sea calm, leaves falling silently through the windless air. She wore her new blue suit, which she instantly recognised as being too formal, out of place, in a town where women habitually dressed in flat shoes and anoraks, clothes suitable for shopping, or for walking the dog. She had little time to admire the setting of the Harrisons' house before the door was opened on to their eager welcome. Soon she was seated in a bright drawing-room drinking coffee and trying to stem the enthusiasm that flowed so unstintingly in her direction. Within the first half-hour she could see that she had disappointed them. Her composure, her reticence unfitted her for what she saw as the childishness of this family, with the mother's easy tears (a handkerchief had appeared almost at once) and the sister's excitement. She suspected that they expressed emotion without difficulty, that they colluded in various homely rituals from which they derived a great deal of confidence, that they were good and well-meaning and utterly unacquainted with any form of doubt. She forced herself to praise the house, sensing that this was what was expected of her. The house did indeed seem to be charming, picturesque, as if inhabited by Snow White and the Seven Dwarfs. Finally she looked beseechingly at Edward, who was also downcast at the new reality with which he was faced. The ring, unfortunately, was found to be too big for Maud's thin finger. 'Never mind,' said Polly Harrison finally, 'I'm sure Edward will find you another one.' She spoke a little more stiffly than she had intended. Bibi came to the rescue, suggesting a walk while the weather was fine. 'I'll show you your room,' she said. 'Then if you want to change . . . '

'I only brought this suit,' said Maud helplessly. 'And a dress for the evening.'

'You were quite right. And you look lovely. But if you're going to Beachy Head you'd better borrow something of mine – a skirt and some thick shoes, at least. Don't mind Mother,' she added in a slightly lowered tone. 'She didn't know what to expect. I dare say she feels at a loss. She can see that you're rather more sophisticated than she is. She doesn't quite know what to say to you . . . '

152

'I hope she doesn't dislike me.'

Bibi looked horrorstruck. 'Of *course* she doesn't dislike you. How could she? You're so beautiful, so gracious. She's a little bit overawed, that's all.'

'Your father said nothing.'

'But he's very much in favour, I could see that. He's given Noddy, I mean Edward, a very generous cheque, you know. And we've found you a lovely flat, at least I think so. I do hope you'll like it.'

'I'm sure I shall,' said Maud bravely. Courage was called for now. 'And I hope you'll visit me often. I shall need your help, you know. I've never been married before.'

Bibi laughed dutifully, but looked at her in some perplexity. I am failing already, thought Maud, willing her features to give nothing away. And yet she felt as if she had already made a great effort. It was not in her nature to seek friendship. Such friends as she had were attracted to her without any effort being made on her part; her very abstraction counted in her favour, although a great part of it was informed by pride. She deplored the silliness of Julie and her like, while longing to be included in their gossip, their allusions. Indeed her longing was so great that she was at pains to suppress any sign of it. It was to be the same with this girl, she thought, so normal, so cheerful, and already so intimate that she could think of nothing to offer in exchange. Her politeness, which she sensed they found so disconcerting, was not the sort of currency that obtained here. Already she was out of her depth, but she did not think that they appreciated her dismay. Only Edward knew her; only he had met her as an equal. Whether his kindness extended to her in these new circumstances she did not know. Yet if he were not kind to her who else would or could be?

She changed into Bibi's clothes, thinking that these would somehow recommend her, and went timidly down to the drawing-room. There she found Edward and his father deep in conversation. She hesitated to interrupt them, but the father looked up and smiled. 'I see they've disguised you already,' he said cheerfully. 'Don't worry, Maud, we'll all get used to one another. And don't pay any attention to Polly. She's been in tears ever since we heard the news. Have a good walk, you two. I expect you've got lots to talk about.'

'You've been very kind,' she said, meaning to refer to the cheque. 'Very generous,' she added, seeing that in this house everything would have to be spelt out, every ounce of emotion offered for their gratification. She felt exhausted. Perhaps in London things would be easier. It could not be that she was meant to live in this way, among strangers. And yet it was no better at home, if Dijon were still to be thought of as home. She felt mortified by her mother, as she sped from one new-found friend to another, with scraps of fabric in her bag. Even her own friends looked at her expectantly, as if her new status should call forth new confidences, the sort of self-importance which they found so natural and which she had always despised. In a sense Edward was the only ally that remained to her. And yet she knew that real intimacy between them might take years to develop, might indeed have died at the outset. Neither of them, she knew, would find it easy to refer to that afternoon in the rue Laugier. Yet how she longed to be once again in that flat instead of in this bright house; how she wished to be in the Place des Ternes, late at night, her feet tender from having walked with Tyler through the darkening city, instead of in this placid sunshine which laid a patina of normality over encounters which she thought of as grotesque. Even now she could smell cooking from the back of the house, and hear the voices of Polly and Bibi Harrison in the kitchen. Aghast, she closed her eyes. 'Don't worry, dear,' she heard the father say, and opening her eyes again saw his kindly face close to hers. His hand stroked the hair back from her forehead. 'Such pretty hair,' he said. She reached out a hesitant hand and touched his arm. 'That's the way,' he said, and walked her to the front door, Edward behind them. 'Don't worry,' he repeated, and patted her hand.

Out on the pavement she took a deep breath and, quite as naturally as she had approached the father, linked her arm through that of Edward. She registered his look of pleasure, hoped her own fears did not show on her face. Arm in arm they strolled sedately along the promenade; air and light combined in a dazzle of midday sun to mitigate her dread. She quite liked the feel of her arm in his, appreciated once again his solicitude, gave him credit for his tact. All might be well, she thought, if he could continue to be tactful, and if she could continue to respect his good manners. He unlinked his arm from hers and they climbed to the top of the cliff. Few people were about. They stood side by side, staring down at the gently lapping waves below. After a while he said, 'I do love you, you know.'

'We are strangers,' she reminded him.

'Not quite. There was the rue Laugier, you remember.'

'I remember that you took care of me, in the hotel, at the station.'

'Is that all?'

She hesitated. 'I think so.'

'I expect you will need a lot of time. Well, we have time. We are young, remember. I'll try to make you happy. I know you're not happy now. But give me some credit, Maud. I'm not very happy myself at the moment.' He moved restlessly. 'I didn't think it would be such a strain.'

'It will be better in London,' she said. This was as far as she would or could go. Yet she thought him a pleasant enough companion, when he did not turn his brooding face towards her and she read ardour in his expression, all the more ludicrous for being restrained. His ardour would never touch her, that she knew; on the contrary, his kindness was a constant source of amazement. From no one else had she experienced such chivalry. That was her most resounding impression of the man she was to marry. To

155

the rest, she knew, she could never respond. But as she considered that part of her life to be over, she thought she would be the same with any man. She did not consider this state of quiescence to be abnormal.

'And the baby?' he said. 'I take it that's been arranged?'

'It was a mistake,' she said. 'I made a mistake. Nothing's been arranged.'

She knew he suspected her mother, at least of some sinister knowledge, of addresses, or recommendations.

'Even my mother didn't know,' she said, and took his arm for the homeward journey.

He did not quite believe her. He thought briefly of her dubious mother, and dismissed the thought. It occurred to him, but without much urgency, that the marriage need not now take place, that he might be free. But free for what? He needed a companion, since his new life was to be his own invention. Through the agency of Maud's presence he had become aware of subtle fissures in the fabric of his family life: he could no longer stay at home. By the same token he could hardly announce that the marriage was off while his own mother was telephoning her friends with the good news. He stole a glance at Maud and saw that she looked serious; she had looked serious ever since her arrival. He longed to cheer her up, to bring back her youth, which seemed to have deserted her. With this altruism, and not entirely divorced from it, went a desire to see her face turned to his in gratitude, in love. When she stood close to him, her arm in his, he experienced a tenderness that seemed to involve his entire nervous system. He put his hand over hers: she looked up at him with an expression in which he could see something of the gratitude he craved. He knew that he would marry her, had known it all along. Nevertheless he felt beleaguered, the full weight of the future on his shoulders.

For lunch there was fish pie and baked apples. All ate busily except Maud, who watched the others from under her lowered eyelids and responded gratefully when Arthur

Harrison aimed a general remark in her direction. She could not help but be aware that her stock was going down by the minute. The worst of it was that she knew exactly what sort of a girl they would have preferred: someone local whom they had known all their lives, who knew their ways, who was as healthy and as outgoing as they were themselves. That was it: they could only appreciate someone as near to identical to themselves as possible. Or if the unknown fiancée had to be French then let her be chic and flirtatious and entertaining, not grave and watchful like Maud. They suspected her of being sad, of not being properly appreciative of what they had to offer, and which they clearly thought should have been enough for any girl. In this context girls were girls and not women, whatever the feminists said. The irony was that Maud felt younger by the minute, unequal to these new challenges. She was even homesick for her mother's unyielding presence, and wondered what on earth she should do when the various parents and relatives met at the wedding. But then she reminded herself that she would not be called upon to do anything, for a bride is without responsibility on her wedding day.

Now more than ever it seemed that her course was laid out, that marriage was the only calling that would free her from dependency. Except on her husband. But she was now convinced of Edward's worth, although she thought his professions of love exaggerated, inappropriate. They were not marrying for love, whatever he might think. She had only to glance across the table and meet his unhappy smile to understand that. They were marrying because of one false step, one regrettable encounter, one shared shock; they were marrying because their lives were already going wrong, because they understood how and when they had gone wrong, because events that had taken place in the rue Laugier had bound them together, while at the same time making them incapable of explaining those events, and their prehistory, to a third party. They were marrying

157

out of a helpless sense of complicity, and because they could not go home again. Even Edward could not stay in this family for much longer, love them though he obviously did. There was a new restlessness about him, which they noted and deplored. Nothing was said; explanations would be avoided. Yet Maud knew that Polly Harrison felt an obscure sense of resentment, and that she would eventually – not quite yet – become its target.

After lunch she helped to dry the dishes. Then, because it seemed required of her, she acquiesced in their suggestion that she should take a rest. A rest, they implied, was necessary after the eating of such a lavish meal: she suspected that the house was under a strict ban of silence until later in the afternoon. In the pretty guest room, with its white walls and its flowered curtains and coverlet, she stepped thankfully out of her shoes and went to the window. She thought she could hear the sea, but in fact it was only a car hissing by in what had turned into a light shower of rain. This was symbolic, she felt; in the pale sunshine of this morning, standing arm in arm with Edward, it had been possible to speak the truth, to feel if not optimism then at least a calm determination. Now she was imprisoned again. She knew, without being told, that it would be regarded as highly irregular if she slipped out of the house and went for a walk on her own. Besides, she had no key, and it would be unthinkable to rouse them from their afternoon sleep by ringing the bell. She wondered where Edward was; then, looking down from the window, saw him getting into the car his father had given them as a wedding present. She would have gone with him, but evidently he wanted to be alone. Already the house was becalmed. She would have liked to have assured Edward of her continued good behaviour, on condition that he removed her from the bosom of his family. She did not think she could ever feel at home in this house. But there were two more nights to get through before they drove to London, and the time seemed very long to her.

Sad again, she removed her borrowed skirt and pullover and crept under the eiderdown. In the softness of the pillows – for everything in this house was soft, compared with the general rigidity of Dijon – she thought of Tyler as she hoped she would always see him, in the dusk of the Vermeulens' bedroom, looking down at her, his eyes watching her watching him, his desire made plain. Instinctively her body mobilised for the rush of feeling this image always called forth: she felt her cheeks flush, her breasts respond. She was lonely for Tyler, not merely because he would never again make love to her, but because he constituted her only emotional capital. He had accepted her, or had seemed to, just as she had accepted him; there was no question of her adapting her ways to his, or his to hers. It was still entirely natural to her to remember their long night walks, their last cup of coffee in the Place des Ternes, before turning in at last to the silent flat, where they would fall instantly asleep, only to wake entwined, making love silently and seriously, as girls dream of making love, love growing out of sleep, needing neither preparation nor consent. When they took their siesta the lovemaking was more deliberate: then the dusk was the afternoon dusk of drawn curtains and nudity explored with eyes and hands. Nor was there ever any regret. She did not even regret the fact that Tyler did not say he loved her. There was no mistaking the truth of their gestures, their embraces. It was that truth which helped her to tolerate all the rest. Even now it was her one certainty.

She thought that if Tyler had accepted her, as she had so fully accepted him, she could have played her part with confidence. She thought that if he had taken her home to meet his family she would somehow have become all that they would have wished. They were of a higher social class: that she knew. But she also knew that she had the requisite dignity to sustain whatever disparities there might have been. Somehow she knew that even her mother would have been found acceptable in the setting of Worcestershire or Chelsea; a hard-headed but not unsympathetic mutual appreciation would have ensued and would have left both parties satisfied. As for herself, she would have approached Tyler's parents with love and devotion, as the genitors of Tyler himself: she would have become the daughter she had never been, and they in turn would have been proud of her. Particularly when she produced a son. This fantasy had nothing to do with her recent upheaval, which she dismissed as the consequence of an all too brief sexual awakening. What had happened to her was not a baby, but an awkwardness of timing. Of this she was now certain. A baby would be produced when she was married to Tyler. She had no desire for a child produced in any other way. She was not particularly fond of children, did not warm to the few babies encountered when she and her mother pursued their unvarying progress through the streets of Dijon. Yet with Tyler everything would have fallen into place, and she would have matured effortlessly, instead of having maturity thrust on her in this alien place.

Yet she was mature enough even now to know that what Tyler had in fact offered her was only a brief liaison, not enough to build a life on. They had been lovers for only a few weeks: fate had seen to it that they were perfectly matched – that was all there was to it. He had not offered marriage or even continuity. It was Edward who offered both. If she could not accept him as a lover she had little difficulty in perceiving his qualities as a husband. He had stood by her; Tyler had not. Tyler had made no move to detain her when she had been told by Edward to leave the flat. Worse, she had seen on his face a fleeting expression of violent relief. It was that expression that had given her the courage, or the desperation, to construct her future. With Edward. Some primitive instinct, some archaic longing for security, had dictated all that had followed. And now she was left with this uncomfortable dichotomy: she could think either of Tyler's expression when he made love to her, or the expression that denoted a fundamental lifting of the spirits when he was sure that she was to be taken off his hands.

She must have slept, because she became slowly aware that Edward was in the room, and he had not been there before.

'I've brought you a cup of tea,' he said. 'I didn't think you'd want to go downstairs for a bit.' His eyes were on her naked shoulders and on the cleft between her breasts. She was wearing a pale pink lace-trimmed slip, part of her trousseau. She made no move to cover herself. Insignificant, perhaps, but this was in its way a meritorious act, for which he was grateful.

'I'm afraid I'm not what they expected,' she said, sipping the tea. They don't like me, was what she meant. That she did not say this was her own concession to the new proprieties.

'My father is entirely won over. Mother is simply reluctant to see me go. She's not a woman who can give words to what she feels. Be a little kinder to her. She thinks you're too sophisticated for us. Whereas I know that you're finding this very difficult.'

She digested this. 'And Bibi? I had hoped to have Bibi as a friend.'

He laughed. 'Bibi is jealous. We've always been very close, exceptionally close, perhaps. She doesn't want to let me go either.'

'How they must love you,' she said wonderingly.

'Yes, they do. They love me as they loved me when I was a child, and when they thought I'd never grow up. They loved me in the least helpful way, incuriously.'

'Yes, I see.'

'And now I bring home a beautiful girl, whom I've chosen without their assistance, and they don't quite know how to react. They would have been the same with anyone.'

'They don't find me lovable.'

'Of course not. Not yet.'

'You are very sensitive, Edward.'

'It's because I love you that I know what you're feeling.'

Not all of it, she thought, but reaching out her hand, she said, 'How on earth are we to manage?'

'By telling the truth, I think. Even when it hurts . . . For instance I know you don't love me.'

'Of course not. Not yet,' she said, echoing his words.

He smiled, recognising the allusion. 'And no doubt you find me very kind – I think you said so. I may not be kind all the time, Maud. I may have regrets too, you know.'

She looked at him, startled.

'I may quite seriously regret that you don't love me,' he said.

There was a silence.

'I will be good, Edward.'

'That's what Queen Victoria said to Prince Albert.'

'I know how she felt.' They both laughed briefly. 'Tell me about the flat.'

'It's rather pleasant, I think. You'll see it on Sunday. It looks out onto a little square, and it gets the morning sun. Bibi found it. She and Mother have already filled the place with towels and saucepans and things. Do you want to get up now? I'm afraid Mother's asked a few people in for drinks, to meet you and so on. Do you feel up to that?'

'I can hardly not be.'

'Quite. What will you wear?'

'Don't worry. I brought a silk dress; it's hanging in the cupboard.'

'Very nice,' he said, after inspecting it. 'And will you do something for me?'

'Yes?'

'Grow your hair. I'd like to see it longer.'

'Why not?' She was bored with this suggestion, which seemed to her inconsequential. It had never occurred to her to make herself beautiful for Edward. She had no seductive purpose in mind. Nevertheless she took care with her appearance, added a touch of colour, smoothed her bronze eyebrows, looked carefully in the mirror before leaving the room and going downstairs.

'And this is Maud,' said her future father-in-law, his arm round her waist.

She was introduced to eight people whom she would never see again, four husbands and four wives, the wives well built, combative, who gave the appearance of having put on all their jewellery for the occasion, the husbands shy, smelling already of whisky, two of them wearing blazers with an identical crest on the breast-pocket. She offered her hand, mustered a smile, and accepted a glass of white wine. She thought she would be subjected to scrutiny; instead she was ignored. It was Edward who was pressed for details. Her own part in the arrangements was reduced to her appearance, which was found to be adequate, more than adequate, to judge from the husbands' wavering glances, until sharply summoned to attention by their wives. She began to feel something more dangerous than irritation, went up to Edward, took his arm, smiled into his face, and began answering in his stead. Everyone relaxed: this was how brides were supposed to behave. A ghost of a smile remained on Edward's face as the guests took their leave. Polly Harrison was flushed and joyful. Her evening had been a success.

For dinner they had cold meat and salad; as a concession to her foreignness there was cheese to follow, but no wine to accompany it. The cheese was acceptable, thought Maud, but it called out for a good Fleurie, such as her aunt served. At home they drank an undistinguished but perfectly good Beaujolais. Wine would have provided the necessary tonic: she was still feeling rather angry.

'I expect your mother will miss you, won't she, Maud?'

'She will replace me with a television set,' said Maud.

Not knowing what to make of this, they chose to regard it as a witticism, and laughed immoderately.

163

The following morning Polly Harrison announced that she was going to do a 'big shop'. Maud offered to walk with her, anxious to see round the town. But they were to go by car, which Mrs Harrison drove decisively, wearing a special pair of gloves. In the supermarket she seized a trolley, which she loaded with unattractive items such as washing powder, a bag of green apples, a pair of rubber gloves, a bunch of bananas, a packet of bacon, and a box of soap-filled scouring pads. Maud did not see how the household was to subsist on this. At home shopping was brief and to the point: one shop for meat, another for salad leaves, a third for cheese. Twice a day Maud went out for bread; she always carried the wine. She had no idea where washing powder came from; in any event it entered the house discreetly, more discreetly than this. Mrs Harrison added two packets of digestive biscuits to her load and wheeled her purchases to the till. Maud was then allowed to carry the bags to the car. She suspected that this was something of a Saturday morning ritual. But why? These people lived well; they were even, compared to her mother and herself, in easy circumstances. Yet everything was turned into a chore. They needed hours of sleep to recover from eating a meal. They drew the curtains at nightfall, as if fearful of what they might see if they looked out. They lived by the sea, yet never seemed to leave the house. She could understand that Edward needed to leave home, had indeed already left. It was more for his sake than for hers, she supposed, that he had sought and found this flat. She would merely be a visitor. Because of this, and because of the boredom of the morning, she said to Mrs Harrison, 'You won't mind if I keep Edward to myself this afternoon, will you?'

'No, of course not, dear.' This line was obviously found to be appropriate.

'Get Edward to take you on one of his walks,' said Mr Harrison after lunch, his eyes already rosy. 'We shan't expect you back until teatime.'

But in fact she kept him out for longer than that, so that they had time for a drink when the pubs opened. Their high colour and shining eyes were remarked upon when they got home. They gave the appearance of happiness. In fact they had surrendered totally to the sound of the waves and had hardly exchanged a word. But there was something peaceful in their silence, so the afternoon was thought to be a success.

As they drove off on the following morning – the three Harrisons massing at the front door to wave – Maud felt so relieved that she was almost happy. They drove straight to London, where they had lunch in another pub: it was to be all pubs from now on, she thought. Yet when he ushered her into the flat she almost forgave him for everything. 'I could live here,' was her first impression, as she followed him into a room with coral-coloured walls and ceiling and a coral-coloured carpet on the floor. It was like entering a warm cave, from which the rest of life was excluded. 'This was all *in situ*,' said Edward, feeling the radiators, switching on the wall lights. 'I bought the carpet and the curtains as well.' He demonstrated the curtains by drawing them: they were in an expensive dark chintz, expertly made. She noted the black iron fireplace with the wooden overmantel, the sofa, armchair and *chaise-longue* upholstered in more chintz, and the two small tables covered with circular floor-length coral taffeta, to match the coral taffeta cushions. She saw herself at once on the *chaise-longue*, reading, dreaming.

'You mean all this was here?' she queried, incredulous.

'Yep. The owner went back to America, sold the lot.'

'So in fact you had nothing to buy?'

'Only the beds.'

He showed her into a pale green bedroom, with green and white linen curtains. The two twin beds were made up with new white sheets and pale green blankets.

'You can get around to organising bedspreads later, when we've settled in. I thought you'd prefer twin beds,' he said awkwardly. 'Actually I prefer them myself.' He thought wistfully of his dreams, which must now be consigned to the past, along with other fantasies. 'Do you like it?' he asked.

'I love it,' said Maud.

Which was more than she could offer in the way of assurance when she saw the shop. In the dark, with half the stock on the floor, the place looked what it was, a poor thing, a mess. She was handed a mug of tea by the youth who purported to be Edward's assistant: the three of them stood thoughtfully in the gloaming. It is lower class, she thought. He saw her expression, and his own tightened. It was as if at that moment she had measured the distance between them and their respective aspirations. He handed his mug back to Cook; he was obscurely glad that the gold-rimmed cups had not been produced. 'Come along,' he said quietly, and to Cook, 'We're staying at the flat tonight, if you want us. Otherwise I'll see you tomorrow, after I've taken Maud to Heathrow.'

'Goodbye,' she said, holding out her hand to Cook. She did not think she would ever have to see him again: another face to be consigned to limbo.

They made love that night, as Edward intended. Her response was polite, and might have been convincing to anyone who was half asleep, as they were not. The morning was a rush, and there was no time to discuss this, nor were they ready to do so. Maud knew that she would never be able to be open with him on this matter. In the plane despair descended again, as she reflected that this part of her life was over, and over before it had begun. It was of Tyler that she thought, not in the act of making love with Edward, an act from which she removed herself, willing her mind to remain dead, but walking with her through the night-time city, during which time she had been so attuned to him that all other thoughts were absent. As they were now. In a brief and unwelcome moment of lucidity she thought how ironic it was that the balance of her life had been destroyed by so banal an episode; then something strangely resembling her conscience told her that what might appear to others to be no more than an episode was to her an experience so seamless that she might well spend the rest of her life contemplating the memory of it. It was unfortunate that that particular memory should have set up such a barrier to what was to be her married life. For all its difficulties marriage now seemed inevitable. Despite her indifference she could not disappoint Edward, who, in his calmer moments, was or might be a genuine friend. She supposed that many women marry in just such a spirit. And she was tired, tired of keeping her thoughts to herself, tired of living up to her mother's pretensions, tired of having no home to return to – for the flat in the rue des Dames Blanches, filled as it was with preparations for her departure, was no longer home — tired of life without Tyler. Deprived of Tyler she could think of nothing better to do than to marry Edward. If this was mercenary she did not care. She would make it up to him, would be a good wife, would be dutiful, as she had always been dutiful. Only in one respect might she fail him, yet she thought that men did not retain a memory of lovemaking as women do. That morning, drinking his coffee, he had borne her no grudge, had expressed no disappointment, had even seemed indifferent. She knew that these matters did not affect men so profoundly. That Tyler might have been less profoundly affected than herself was a thought that had occurred to her but been dismissed. There was a perfection about the whole encounter that no amount of objective thinking could destroy. She knew that if ever Tyler entered her life again she would forsake everything and go to him.

Nevertheless she crossed Paris fearfully. Now that summer had gone and the weather was chill and misty the city seemed closed to her, even hostile. She endured the train journey, lulled by a repetition that would soon no longer be familiar. At the station her mother was waiting to take her into custody. Incurious, she listened to the news being given to her in her mother's new animated voice. Avid for details of the flat, Nadine was at least satisfied on that score. 'And the parents?' To Maud, in Dijon, the memory of that weekend was almost parodic; she longed to serve it up for her mother's amusement; she longed to give her mother an easy victory. But she found to her surprise that loyalty to Edward forbade this. 'Very pleasant,' she replied to her mother's questions. 'Very kind. You will see for yourself at the wedding.'

To the wedding itself she was indifferent, though Nadine seemed to luxuriate in every day of preparation. In order fully to enjoy the various consultations that seemed to be called for – with the dressmaker, with the chef at the Hôtel de la Cloche, with those friends to whom, did she but know it, her assiduity after years of independence came as a surprise – she required to be alone, not hampered by a silent daughter whose pace was so much slower than her own. Maud left the flat on the pretext of visiting friends and then took refuge in the museum, where no one would think of looking for her. In these last days before her wedding she accorded herself a treat: tea in a tea-room, among women spending an inconsequential afternoon gossiping, before going home. Yet the treat failed to match her expectations, and she was reduced to going home herself. In her room a mysterious swathed white garment hung on the outside of her wardrobe.

Edward telephoned every evening. She listened to his voice with a mild pleasure, though he had little to say, until the evening when he told her that his father had had a mild heart attack and that his parents would not be able to come to the wedding. She was genuinely sorry; she had liked the man, even loved him, had glimpsed through his kindness to her how her life might have been had her own father lived. Then Bibi came on the phone sounding tearful. 'I am so sorry about the wedding, Maud. I hope it won't spoil it for you.'

'But you will be there, Bibi. And I shall look forward to seeing you again.'

Finally the day arrived, and Maud Lucie Simone Gonthier was pronounced the wife of Edward Harding Harrison. The brief civil ceremony was a mere formality; everyone knew that the real celebration was the wedding breakfast. There were thirty guests, Nadine having found it impossible to muster a greater number. Even so, many of those invited were surprised to be remembered. The bride, in her white silk tunic and short white silk skirt, was judged to be well dressed for the occasion, though her expression was rather glum, as was that of the bridegroom, preoccupied no doubt by the state of his father's health. The bride's mother's outfit – peacock blue jacket over a multicoloured silk skirt – was thought a success; she at least seemed to be enjoying herself, though as course followed course (too elaborate, they decided: a buffet would have been more appropriate) her colour mounted dangerously; between her flushed cheeks and her peacock blue hat her fine eyes issued a challenge and an invitation to the husbands of all her new-found friends. Bibi, looking very pretty, was seated next to Xavier. They appeared to be getting on extremely well, until Germaine put a stop to that. How she managed to do so, subjecting Bibi to a flow of bewilderingly charming conversation, Bibi never knew. Maud and Edward exchanged a sour wry smile at this performance. They might have been married for years.

They spent the night in Paris, at a pompous hotel that Edward thought she might enjoy. They soon realised that he had been too ambitious, forsook the restaurant, and ordered chicken sandwiches from room service. She felt sorry for him, for having spent so much money, and for aiming so wide of the mark. They were both exhausted, they told themselves and each other; they would have an early night. It seemed better not to attempt an embrace. In the morning they flew to London and their new home.

A mild sun pierced the cold mist. It seemed impossible not to accept this as an omen.

12

Of the two of them, it was Harrison who found married life difficult and who sometimes gave vent to unjustified irritation. He was particularly irritated by Maud's cooking, which he judged to be too ambitious, too far removed from the comforting platefuls to which his mother had accustomed him.

'What's this?' he might ask, poking with a suspicious fork.

'It's fish. You like fish.'

'What's this stuff on it?'

'Sauce mousseline. Don't you like it?'

'I like plain food. Anyway I don't want a heavy meal in the evening. I'd rather have something simple. Tea, fruit, that sort of thing.'

Later she would find him sitting at the kitchen table with a book, an open packet of biscuits to hand. So she got used to preparing a fruit salad for him, and a pot of Earl Grey tea. Shortbread biscuits, of which he never tired, were arranged on a flowered plate. He would inspect this modest supper to see if she had added anything out of the way, then when he was satisfied that all was in order would eat with every appearance of enjoyment. After a while, tired of seeing her dishes neglected, she joined him in this simple meal. Both ate lunch separately, Maud in the flat, Harrison more often than not at Overton's, with any visitor to the shop who seemed inclined to stay and talk. On Fridays he took Cook out and stood him a good meal, after which they both spent a somnolent afternoon going over the books and waiting to shut for the weekend. Maud made painstaking vegetable soups for herself, and meat dishes which she put in the freezer. She ate her lunch calmly, laying a place in the dining-room for herself, drinking a glass of wine. Very occasionally, when Bibi came up for the day, or when Jean Bell was over from Pittsburgh, where she was doing postgraduate research, she went out to wine bars, bistros, restaurants in department stores, but was always happy to get back to the quiet of the flat, to whatever book she was reading, and to the unchanging landscape, becalmed in the winter afternoon, beyond her window. As darkness fell she would get up to switch on the lights, go into her bedroom to draw the curtains, briefly inspect her face, and prepare for Edward's homecoming.

She was always relieved to see him, standing in the doorway with an aura of cold night air surrounding him. She never failed to kiss him, anxious for his approval, conscious of the slight constraint between them. If she felt apologetic it was because she sensed an unhappiness greater than her own. Indeed she was not altogether unhappy, having found a setting and a line of duty in which her peaceful temperament felt at home. She knew that all was not well between them, knew that, in ways she refused to examine, the past impinged on the present. She knew that she was more pragmatic than her husband, had settled unadventurously into what had been offered, submitted to her husband's embraces not unenthusiastically but always with a slight timidity, as if fearful of awakening ghosts, willed herself to be passive so that he could be all the more uninhibited. She discovered something she had not expected, a slight savagery in his lovemaking which she learned to accommodate.

It seemed to her daily that she knew him less and less,

and that she had married a stranger whose kindness was not entirely to be relied upon. Yet she looked forward to his homecoming every evening, conscious, after the long silent day, of loneliness, conscious of the black leafless trees outside her window, and the sad sound of footsteps in the quiet street, where no cars passed all the long afternoon, so that she sometimes had the impression that she was the only person alive in this permanent winter. Combing her hair at her dressing-table, adding perhaps a necklace, she tried to summon up a sense of anticipation. But there was little to anticipate, apart from the mild kiss, the modest meal, the peace and comfort of an uneventful evening. Frequently she would say to him, 'I'm going to bed now. I'll read for a while. You won't disturb me.' She did this as much for his sake as for hers, knowing how he savoured his solitude, once he had satisfied himself that she was at home, waiting for him. She sensed in him an immense disappointment that he had failed to bring her to life, failed in fact to bring them both to life. Sometimes, when she looked across to him in his chair, she would see his expression as brooding, thoughtful, even yearning, but yearning not for her presence, which he had, but for some promise which she had failed to fulfil. She had seen that look before, in the rue Laugier, when he had offered to marry her. Because that sad look of yearning was unbearable to her she would close her book, bid him goodnight, and go to bed. She longed for darkness and for sleep, but stayed awake until Harrison joined her in the bedroom: it seemed only good manners to exchange a few last remarks with him. Their final 'Goodnight' released them both from the day's obligations. She slid into sleep easily, gratefully; he, his hands behind his head, stared for some time into the darkness, his memory more active in those night hours than it was in the daytime, when he was agreeably besieged by preoccupations of a more practical nature, distracted by decisions and conversations. In the daytime he would think gratefully of Maud, of her fastidious quietness. At night he

173

would feel a certain familiar sadness when he listened to her steady breathing from the other bed.

She was amazed at her lack of unhappiness, while he was eternally surprised at his sense of loss. In the first three years that followed their marriage they gave the appearance of a well-matched couple. Neighbours who saw them out walking on a Sunday afternoon thought them exemplary, their silence if anything a forceful indication of their inner harmony. Max and Nelly Kroll, dining with them once a month, were charmed by Maud's ceremonious preparations, her meticulous menus, her poached salmon or her lamb with flageolet beans, her apple tart or her lemon soufflé. Nelly Kroll, a sparkling seventy-five-year-old, exclaimed at Maud's beauty, and privately thought how greatly she would be improved by a little animation. Max, happy with his cigar, his brandy, and the chocolates that Maud always bought for him, thought how much he would have appreciated her had she been his daughter. But there were no children. The Krolls had made their peace with this long ago, their disappointment faded into a comfortable resignation. Nelly Kroll, in the kitchen, had broached the subject with Maud, relying on an old woman's privilege to examine this most delicate of matters.

'No,' said Maud. 'It's not that Edward doesn't like children. It's just that I seem unable to have them.'

'Have you tried?' said Nelly.

Maud turned away. 'Of course,' she replied, her voice as calm as she could make it. 'But I don't seem able to proceed beyond a few weeks. I'm sorry for Edward's sake. For myself I've more or less come to terms.'

'Have you seen a doctor?'

'There's no need. I'm perfectly well. Shall we join the others? You prefer camomile tea to coffee, don't you?'

And Nelly Kroll, convinced that Maud's sadness, and Edward's too, was the result of this simple incapacity — or were they mismatched? — told herself there were no more questions she could decently ask and returned with relief to her husband's side. Absentmindedly he took her hand. He had noticed, as she had, that the Harrisons rarely touched each other. He would have liked to have known more, but his tact was superior to that of his wife.

Besides, there were more interesting matters to discuss, such as the current state of Edward's business, and — to judge from the lavishness of Maud's appointments, the comfort of this room and the excellent meals they always ate — the extremely gratifying state of prosperity which he had already attained and which he looked, if anything, to increase in the years ahead, if he had the good sense to rely on Max's advice.

For the shop was a success. Since his marriage Harrison had discovered that he had it in himself to be an excellent businessman. Truth to tell, the shop was a refuge from a home life which he could not help but think of as unhappy, though he was careful not to probe too deeply into the causes of that unhappiness. With his lists of subscribers and correspondents, many of them American, brought up to date, he found himself writing to them as if they were old friends. His advertisements had brought him a few regular visitors for whom his unusual stock, now carefully augmented, was a constant joy. It was Maud who suggested that he carry more classics, preferably in good editions, a suggestion for which he was grateful. Further advertisements in literary journals brought in enquiries from retiring dons, or the widows of defunct dons, on the verge of moving to smaller houses, and only too willing to surrender a complete set of Balzac, or George Eliot, or Zola. Out of a delicate feeling for his wife, the feeling that subsisted when all others seemed stale and crude, he concentrated on French books, putting on one side for her books with the names of women, *La Cousine Bette*, or *La Petite Fadette*, or *Germinie Lacerteux*, books he thought suitable to her frail composure, having forgotten what quiet horrors such titles concealed, and in any event immersed, as always, in Dickens. He allowed Cook a little sideline of his own: review copies collected from critics and journalists, and sold on at the book fairs he occasionally attended at the weekends. Cook too had his own list of subscribers, and was becoming increasingly familiar with contemporary fiction. In the afternoons, if there were no visitors, a calm settled on the shop: both read, as if reading were the reason for their being there at all. Customers were impressed. Their reputation was excellent.

It was when he set out to walk home, in the winter dark, his hands in his pockets, that doubts began once more to assail him. He was oddly reluctant to join his wife, while at the same time feeling an intense relief at the sight of the lights shining from the windows of the flat. This image of home beguiled him every evening, though he knew it was illusory. But it was a necessary illusion. The warmth, the light, Maud's greeting, and the exchange of what little news they had to impart to each other, soothed him into a feeling of normality, behind which he was aware of serious discrepancies. Their union, he knew, was weak, lacking in solidarity. There were no children, virtually no parents, no significant elders to guide them. After Arthur Harrison's death Maud declined to accompany him to Eastbourne. 'You go,' she would say. 'Your mother would rather see you on her own. And Bibi is coming up next week — we shall have plenty to talk about.' He on his side manifested a violent antipathy to Maud's family, particularly to her mother and her aunt, whom he saw as corrupt and infinitely corruptible. This feeling was largely retrospective, since he in his turn failed to accompany her to Dijon, and was in fact instrumental in dissuading her from going there on her own, with the result that Maud got into the habit of speaking to her mother on the telephone, conversations which both found sufficient for their requirements. Maud and her husband existed in a limbo which had its attractions, most notably in that moment of recognition at the end of the working day, when they would emerge from their respective silences to greet each other with something like joy, only to relapse again, and all too soon, into another silence, the silence which continued to subsist between them, and which neither of them could break.

Then, as if in acknowledgment of this, Maud would go early to bed, and he with a sigh would eventually join her, only to stay awake, staring into the darkness, long after he could hear her quiet breathing. Yet in the morning, with their blue breakfast cups filled with excellent coffee, and the honey and the marmalade in their pottery dishes, they found it impossible not to feel mildly optimistic again. When Maud put his boiled egg in front of him, remembering that he liked the eggcup with the cockerel painted on it, it seemed to Edward that he was like every other married man, with no more than an average man's wants and needs, and those largely satisfied. The pristine newspaper, the cheerful buttery smells, the consciousness that he was leaving his home in the hands of an excellent housekeeper, all contrived to make a nonsense of his night-time fears. Even when he heard her sigh he knew that she would never be indiscreet enough to burst into tears, or indulge in public soul-searching, or reproach him with an occasional silence. He knew that he could trust her good breeding. He had little contact with women, had no idea what they did all day. Like most men he preferred to think of Maud devoting her solitary hours to considerations of his ease and comfort. He would not have been surprised to hear that she spent the whole day shopping for his food, preparing his meal. That logic might have told him that these activities took no more than an hour at the most made no difference. In his heart he knew that he could rely on her excellent care. What she did with the rest of her time did not concern him.

In fact she walked a lot, mostly in the mornings, mostly round the neighbourhood. She prepared her soups and purchased her breads and her cheeses largely before midday. In the afternoon she might visit a gallery, even if Jean Bell were not in town, or go round the shops with Bibi: this she found disheartening, but warmed as always to Bibi's bright eyes and ingenuous conversation. She was out every day, but particularly appreciated the days when she was left entirely on her own. Solitude did not alarm her, nor did silence. Once she had greeted her downstairs neighbour, a fierce elderly woman with a little dog, whom she encountered at the entrance at the same time every morning, she was fully prepared not to utter a word until her husband came home. She found it natural to keep her thoughts to herself, to be studious, to commune with the characters in a picture or in a book. Every day, after her cup of tea, she would settle down with her book for a couple of hours, rather like Max Kroll's ideal reader, until with a sigh she would realise that her day, her own particular day, was over, would go into the bedroom, would put on her lapis necklace, brush her hair, and prepare for Edward's return. She even found herself impatient for him; she thought he felt the same for her. Yet, their sight of each other satisfied, both lapsed into a silence. Paradoxically, it was only the sight of the other that made the silence bearable.

'A letter from Dijon,' she said one morning at breakfast. 'Two pieces of news. Mother has broken her ankle, and Xavier is getting married.'

'To one of those awful girls?'

She consulted the letter. 'To a Pascale Lacombe. I don't know her, neither does Mother. Germaine is very pleased, apparently. I shall have to go to France, Edward. I must go and see Mother and I shall have to go to the wedding. She says that she can't move, and I must represent her. That's what she says, not what I say. Can you do without me for a few days? Or do you want to come?'

'No, I don't. You'll be all right on your own, won't you?'

'I shouldn't be more than four or five days. If I go straight to Dijon . . .'

'Where is the wedding?'

She consulted the letter again. 'Paris. Saint-Philippe du Roule. I could catch a late plane back.'

'I don't want you travelling at night. You'd better stay in a hotel and take an early flight the next morning. You'd better go to the Washington.' It was where they had spent the one night of their honeymoon. 'Can you book it yourself, or do you want me to do it?'

'I'll do it.'

'And you'd better have a new suit, or dress, whatever.' No wife of his was going to appear less than perfect.

'Thank you, Edward.'

She went to the dressmaker that morning, and together they devised a dark red suit with a mandarin-collared jacket, and a small hat in the same dark red ribbed silk. She described this outfit with some enthusiasm to Edward, who only half listened. He liked her in any case in her usual clothes, the silk shirts and the tweed or tartan skirts she had learned to wear. He thought, when he saw her off the following week, that she looked cold, as she so often did, and wondered whether she would like a fur coat. He dismissed the idea after a few minutes, knowing how modest her tastes were. Nevertheless he noticed that she was wearing a different scent, not one he knew. She kissed him at the airport, as if fearful of seeing him go. When he looked back he saw her staring at him fixedly. He waved, she waved back. Then she turned to go.

In Dijon she found her mother sitting comfortably, with her bandaged ankle on a footstool. Keeping her company was the concierge, Mme Fernandez, now referred to as Clarita. On a table by her mother's side was a slightly dog-eared pile of women's magazines, of no great pretension. It was clear that the hoped-for re-entry into society had not taken place, and that Mme Fernandez was Nadine's constant visitor. It was also clear, after a slightly embarrassed half-hour, that Nadine had found a certain satisfaction in letting things slide, and herself with them. Maud noticed sadly that her mother's hair was largely grey, that there was a new pair of spectacles on a cord round her neck, that her lipstick was worn away to the corners of her mouth. Yet despite this negligence she was fairly vividly made up, as if following the tips in those magazines which were now her favoured reading. Her eyelids were green, and a wavering pencil had accentuated her fading eyebrows. She gave a small smile in perceiving Maud's worried expression. She was completely aware of the process by which she had been overtaken, but after a lifetime of unremitting effort had succumbed without protest. 'You see', she said, with a resigned gesture, indicating the far from immaculate room, 'why I can't go to the wedding.' The gesture explained more than the broken ankle. 'Germaine is on the telephone every evening. The girl is rich, apparently. They are pulling out all the stops.'

Maud reflected that she would never have used so vulgar an expression in the old days. 'But who looks after you?' she asked. 'Do you want me to stay?'

'Clarita looks in every day. We underestimated her, Maud. She really is a very interesting woman. Sometimes we go to the cinema together. You should have asked her to stay. It was not nice of you to be so high-handed, thanking her in that dismissive way.'

'I'm sorry. I didn't realise she was your friend.'

'You'd better have a word with her when you go down-stairs. Make yourself agreeable. How long are you staying?'

'I don't know.'

But after a night in her old room, now cold and dusty, she decided to leave the following day. It was clear that she was no longer wanted.

In the hotel in Paris she telephoned Edward, unpacked her bag, hung up her red suit, and laid the pink silk kimono on the bed. The weather was misty, wintry. She went out, walked down the Champs-Elysées, then, defeated, walked back again. All around her light streamed out from shops, cafés; crowds sauntered in the pre-Christmas euphoria. She felt isolated, conspicuous. She went into a bookshop and chose the current bestseller, knowing that she would not read it, then returned to the hotel. She ate in her room, feeling unequal to the restaurant, any restaurant. The next two days were spent in the same manner: the same walk, the same reclusive meals. She missed her flat and her peaceful habits. A slight feeling of horror dogged her footsteps on her solitary perambulations. She wondered whether she would have the courage ever to speak to anyone again. It was with a feeling of relief, as well as of extreme nervousness, that she woke on the morning of the wedding. The nervousness was of the wedding itself, the relief at the realisation that she could soon go home.

In the church the first person she saw was Tyler, in a grey morning suit, looking far more resplendent than the bridegroom, whose best man he was to be. Of course, she thought, I knew this all along. Even his back, which was all that she could see of him, looked expensive. She hardly noticed Xavier, or the pale pretty little bride, or Germaine, whose colour was high and whose expression was triumphant. She sat through the service unthinking, and drifted in the wake of the exclamatory crowd to the cars waiting to take them to the reception at the Crillon. There, her colour as high as that of Germaine, who was mercifully too busy to pay her any attention, she took a glass of champagne and waited for Tyler to cross the room to her. She had no doubt that he would do this. Even if he made her wait, she had every faith in their inevitable encounter.

One or two of the guests attempted to speak to her but soon gave up as she gazed at them without, it was obvious, responding to their presence or listening to their words. At one point Germaine, noticing her at last, insisted on introducing her to the bride's mother, a tall vaguely smiling woman who shook her hand with a polite lack of interest. Maud went back to her place by the buffet, where she was determined Tyler should see her. She suspected that he had already seen her, had made a note of her presence, was reserving her for later. Either that or he had decided to treat her as just another wedding guest. She drank a third glass of champagne, willing him to join her; her eyes never left him. She saw once again his superiority to every other man in the room, saw the glances of women, saw a speculative look cross several faces: hands caught at his arm, attempts were made on all sides to detain him. It was not merely that he was handsome, absurdly so, or that he was performing his duties with a great deal of charm. It was that he aroused, in that largely middle-aged assembly, old atavistic longings for the perfect son, the perfect brother, the perfect lover, the archetypal man who would take care of a woman's desire not only for love but for protection. It was quite clear that many women among the guests felt a languor at his approach, longed to reach out to him, oblivious to what faults of character he might display. Those faults were automatically forgiven, or if not forgiven, excused. The aura of his great glamour was made available to all. It was largely owing to Tyler, thought Xavier, suddenly depressed, that his wedding was such a success.

At last, his eyes steady, his mouth rueful, he stood in front of Maud.

'Well, Maud. Do you remember me?'

'Of course I remember you, Tyler.'

'You're looking splendid. Your hair is longer. At least I think it is; I can't see under the hat. How's married life?'

She ignored this. 'And you? Are you married?'

'Engaged,' he said briefly. Then with a smile, 'Well, what did you expect? Since you wouldn't wait for me, Maud.'

She registered this without flinching. 'And will you marry her, this girl of yours.'

'Probably not. Where are you staying?' he said, in a lower voice.

She told him.

'I should be free about seven. Wait for me there.'

He drifted away. Composed, she fought her way through

to Xavier and wished him every happiness. Then she embraced her aunt, who looked surprised.

'Lovely to see you, Maud, and looking so well. How long are you in Paris? We must have a talk about Nadine. I am not at all happy about her. How did you find her?'

'I am leaving tomorrow, Aunt. And I'm sure Mother will be perfectly fine. I know you will make it your business to keep an eye on her.'

She thought how easy it was to assert herself after all the years of being submissive, how even arrogance excites a certain respect, while modesty brings few rewards, calls forth few tributes. Having delegated her aunt to look after her mother, she felt free of all old ties, her life her own at last, her wishes paramount. Escaping from the heat and noise of the Crillon into the starry dark of the Place de la Concorde, she felt inside herself a steadily beating pulse that signified intent. Too impatient to wait for a cab she walked up the Champs-Elysées, anxious now for the hot scented bath she would take. After that she was not quite sure. She only knew that they had met, that they would at last have that conversation that should have taken place long before. She looked back on the quiet years of her marriage with incredulity. How could she so have scaled down her life? She had denied herself, or had been denied, the play of instinct, and instinct was now what was awake in her. She could imagine herself pulling Tyler down with her on to the bed, could imagine it vividly, even scabrously, yet at the same time she knew that that was not what she wanted. All these years she had been over-prepared for her eventual meeting with Tyler. Now she knew that she desired him only as he had appeared to her that summer, and later in the dusk of that room, naked, his head lowered, his desire made plain. The prestigious charmer in the grey morning suit had irritated her, and the irritation had increased her own new feeling of self-worth. Above all she thought that her excitement had less to do with arousal than with anger. She wanted to attack Tyler, to ravish him, but knew that in doing so she would destroy the perfect memory of his own desire that was her most precious possession.

She had changed, and was brushing her hair when the telephone call came from the reception desk informing her that a gentleman was asking for her.

'Please ask him to come up,' she said carelessly, and also knew, from the tone of her voice, that she was behaving out of character, and that if by any chance he remembered her it would not be like this, in this clichéd setting for a seduction. In that moment she knew she would deny herself her dearest wish, and in that way keep her image distinct in his mind, so that if possible it might stay that way through all the receding summers of his life.

He had changed into an open-necked shirt and pullover: his overcoat, the collar turned up, brought with it all the cold of the December evening.

'Are we going to bed?' he asked, eyeing the pink silk kimono spread out on the coverlet, which the maid had already turned down for the night.

'No,' she replied. 'We are going for a walk. Do you remember how we used to walk, Tyler?'

'I remember.'

'Come then.' She held open the door for him, took her key, left the light on.

'Are we coming back?'

'No. We're not coming back.'

Silent, they walked down the Champs-Elysées. She did not take his arm, nor did they instinctively find their rhythm; both were aware of this, although they were hardly aware of the crowds separating them, or the jolt from a careless shopper. Once past the Rond Point they were in darkness. Few walkers, except those with a purpose, lingered in those stony gardens at nightfall.

'There's a bit in Proust about this part of the Champs-Elysées,' he said finally. 'About children, and falling in love as children.'

'I must read it,' she said. 'We should have fallen in love as children, Tyler. That way we should have known each other so much better.'

'I always felt I knew you, Maud.'

'But you didn't really, did you? You didn't want to know how I felt.'

He made a gesture of impatience. 'Oh, women's feelings! The fuss made over them! Besides, I did know how you felt. You said you loved me.'

'But you are used to hearing that.'

He glanced at her in surprise. 'Don't be cruel, Maud.'

They walked on again in silence.

'The trouble was', she said, 'that I never felt I knew you. Even when we were making love I felt that you denied me a certain intimacy, a certain knowledge.'

'Look, can't we sit down? I'm actually feeling rather tired. I've been on my feet nearly all day, may I remind you. And I don't know whether I'm up to the sort of conversation we seem to be having. My suggestion was much better.'

'You'd probably have fallen asleep, if you're so tired.'

'Probably,' he agreed.

'I want to cross the river,' she said. 'Then you can sit down if you must. I'm tired too, now that I come to think of it. The champagne has worn off. I never thought I'd have this conversation with you, Tyler. And in a way it's too late. I feel too grown up to be talking about myself in this way.'

'You never did talk about yourself. That was part of your charm.'

They drifted across the Pont des Arts, their steps matching now, and stopped instinctively to lean on the parapet and stare into the water. A crushing feeling of anticlimax descended on her; she felt foolish and ashamed. As if sensing this, he put his arm around her, a gesture familiar to her only from her husband. It seemed out of place, homely, comforting, whereas she was used to Tyler merely taking what he wanted. Which was how he should remain, she thought. He belonged to others now, although those others might change and be replaced; she lacked, as always, or so she reasoned, some final persuasiveness. She had said all she had to say, and as usual had captured only a fragment of his attention. They straightened up and walked on, again in silence, everything having been said, the longed-for response once more in abeyance.

He brightened once they were seated in the Deux Magots; the noise and bustle added to his assurance.

'Where's Noddy?' he asked. 'Minding the shop?'

'I like you better when you don't speak,' she told him. 'I remember those walks we used to take, far into the night. We hardly spoke then. Do you remember?'

'I remember,' he said, finishing his coffee and signalling the waiter for the bill.

'I wanted those walks to go on for ever. I wanted us to walk like that this evening.'

'It's winter, Maud,' he said gently. 'It's no longer that summer. Not for you, not for me. It's all in the past now.'

'I loved you,' she said shakily. 'I think I still do. At least, I remember you all the time, even when I'm doing something quite mundane, like peeling vegetables, or making beds. I only ever wanted to be with you, Tyler. It hardly mattered that you didn't love me . . . '

'I worshipped you,' he said.

'Too late,' she said, the tears slipping down her face. 'I wanted to marry you. And now I'm married to Edward.'

'Oh, you'd have had a terrible time with me.' His tone was light now, unconcerned. She could no longer believe that he had meant a word of what had gone before. She wanted to be alone now, so that she could remember his — what was it? His avowal, his confession? She wanted quite urgently to take the memory home, so that she could keep it safe.

'I'm tired now,' she said. Her voice was dull, her colour gone.

He looked at her, faintly shocked by her appearance. 'A taxi, I think. Or rather two taxis.'

In the street he took her arm again, and to her infinite surprise she sensed that he was aroused. Even her piteous face had aroused him, restored his predator's instinct. 'How long are you staying?' he asked. 'There's nothing to say we can't spend tomorrow together, is there? And no walking this time. Just your hotel. Unless you change your mind about tonight?'

'I'm too tired,' she said, meaning too tired for you, too sad, not as you remember me.

He kissed her. 'I'll ring you in the morning,' he said. 'Now don't rush off anywhere.'

But in those words, she thought, he had told her what she must do, simply because he no longer really expected her to wait for him, because, with his lightning changes of mood, he no longer wanted her to. To wait for him would be to test the limits of his desire, and she knew, obscurely but insistently, that those limits had already been reached. She had known him when his desire was limitless: how could she now sit in a hotel room, waiting for him to call? And even when he did, for she had no doubt that he would, their lovemaking, the real purpose of this further meeting, would be deliberate, self-conscious, and not what either of them cared to remember.

In bed that night she felt anguish, not at the thought of losing him — he was already lost — but at not having realised earlier how many risks it was legitimate to take. And she had settled for safety, not for freedom; she had been fearful of giving offence, and yet had managed to inflict damage. She might be thought to have acted in a worldly and self-serving manner, whereas in fact she had been frightened. And all the time Tyler might have loved her . . . But he had not loved her enough, had not over-ruled her, was finally not convinced that his response to her was stronger than his response to all the other women who crossed his path, cajoled him, seduced him, protested their love for him . . .

She had derived from this meeting both more and less than she had hoped. With their admission of love came a certain regret that this had not been made in due time. She had done what she never wanted to do, to make Tyler feel mildly ashamed of himself. She did not want him repentant, in falsely humble mode; she still wanted him to triumph. With the knowledge that he had almost certainly meant what he said went the conviction that she had imagined it so much better, so many scores of times more. Reality was an insufficient record; as if in proof of this the dawn brought no comfort. She felt pity for them both, even embarrassment. Had they made love, she knew, they might no longer have been in accord.

She had no need for the little travelling alarm clock that Edward had given her. She had to wait until seven before she could order her breakfast and ask the reception desk to prepare her bill. It was barely light when she left the hotel and stepped into the taxi which was to take her to the airport. She shivered in her coat, was impatient to reach home, to take another bath, to begin an ordinary day. Her mind was calm, even blank; the events of the previous evening were put aside for future contemplation. Yet even now she knew that they would not yield much. There was no disappointment in the fact that she had not waited for Tyler, nor did she think that he would be disappointed, or even surprised. He would telephone, to be told that she had left; he would shrug his shoulders, and leave in his turn. She would never see him again.

In the flat, which felt cold and empty, as if her presence had been removed for ever, she took a bath, dressed in warm clothes, and went out again. She walked to the shop, where Edward and Cook expressed some surprise at seeing her. 'Have we got a Proust?' she asked.

'Over there,' said Edward. 'The Pléiade edition.'

Disheartened, she rifled through the thin pages. 'It's like the Bible,' she said.

'To some people it is the Bible,' said her husband. 'It will keep you going for some time. Are you going back? If so, I could give you a lift. I've got to pick up some books in Wimbledon.'

'No,' she said. 'I'll walk. I need some shopping.'

'You had a good time?'

'Oh, yes, very good. I'll tell you about it this evening. Goodbye, Tom. Nice to see you.'

She walked through the blank streets, suddenly violently missing Paris, where the crowds had seemed so indifferent. She thought at last of Tyler, of the walk of the previous evening. 'I worshipped you,' Tyler had said, but his voice was flat. Their steps had been ill matched. She was left with a conviction of defeat, and was almost sure that he must feel the same.

In the flat she made a leek and potato soup, ate lunch, then settled down to read. '*Longtemps, je me suis couché de bonne heure*,' stated the first sentence. She looked up, marvelling. The early dusk found her still reading, her tasks ignored. When she got up to switch on the lights she had to shade her eyes, so immersed had she been in that other summer, in which a small child waits anxiously for his mother to come and kiss him, waits for the guest to leave, for the gate to click shut, and for the sound of her steps on the stairs. Steady now, as if she had found an occupation for the dark days of winter, she went into her bedroom, brushed her hair, and put on the pearl necklace her mother had given her for her wedding. When Harrison came home he found her quite composed, as it was his joy and his torment to find her.

It was not until they were seated at the table, and he was drinking his tea, that a monstrous realisation exploded in his mind.

'Was Tyler there?' he asked.

'Oh, yes, Tyler was there.'

'Did you know he was going to be there?'

'No, of course not. How could I? He was the best man,' she added.

'He always was, wasn't he? The best man?'

'Don't be foolish, Edward.' He looked at her in some surprise; she had never criticised him before.

'And did everyone fall for him?'

'I have no idea,' she said calmly.

'Everyone falls for Tyler, don't they? Everyone is in love with Tyler.'

Even you, she thought; but managed to say nothing.

'We went for a walk,' she said, still calm. 'We needed the air.'

'And then you went back to the hotel,' he said, his expression excited and furious.

'I did. I don't know where Tyler went. I don't know what he did. I didn't see him again. More tea?'

That night she went to bed earlier than usual, hoping that she might be asleep before Edward came in. But he chose to be early too. They lay in the dark, listening to each other's breathing.

'Don't leave me, Maud,' said Edward suddenly.

She was aware of blackness, of silence, of days and nights of winter before the sun could break through and bring them back to life.

'Maud? Did you hear me?'

'Of course I heard you. And of course I won't leave you.' She took a deep steadying breath. 'You are my life now.'

13

Their daughter, Mary Françoise, soon shortened to Maffy, was born in the ninth year of their marriage, when hope had been given up on all sides. There seemed to be no particular reason why a child should have been conceived at this time. There had been no noticeable increase or decrease in affection, no heightening or lowering of the emotional temperature, no jealousy on the one hand or longing on the other. They were successful partners, but partners rather than husband and wife: they tended each other's needs and respected each other's wishes. The flat was warm, welcoming, but always appeared empty if one walked into it unexpectedly; the food was lavish and inventive, but they ate little of it, reserving it for the dinner that was served to Max and Nelly Kroll, or the lunches that Maud occasionally gave for Jean Bell and Bibi, both of whom, slightly irritated by her passivity, urged on her the qualities which they thought desirable in the modern woman and to which she seemed such a stranger.

It was true that she was quiet, and dependent on her privacy; she was even more dependent on her husband, who preferred her to exhibit a slightly invalidish calm. His strength, it was felt, increased as hers declined; if anything he would have preferred her more passive, confined if possible to a *chaise-longue*, Elizabeth Barrett to his Robert Browning, with the promise of their flight indefinitely postponed. He was born, he thought, to cherish, though all the while he realised that his attentions were received absentmindedly, as if Maud were engaged in some deep mental process which would eventually make sense of her life and set her free. Since, at some heavenly tribunal, she would have been prepared to defend her actions, both irrational and rational, she would have been at pains, if questioned, to explain why this process took up so much of her time and her attention. But she was not in the habit of explaining, moved easily and equably through her life, performed her domestic duties admirably, and gave no cause for complaint.

Her mother-in-law and her sister-in-law, however, found her deeply abnormal. Polly Harrison, who had never taken to her, now disliked her more than she knew; Bibi, sent on reconnaissance missions to Tedworth Square, brought back stories of how she, with or without Jean Bell, had made helpful suggestions about voluntary work at the local hospital, or courses at the City Literary Institute (or a lover, thought Jean Bell), but had met with no response.

'I asked her what she did with herself all day, and she said "I read," ' Bibi reported to her mother.

'Well, I read, we all read,' riposted Polly Harrison. 'There's no need to advertise the fact. Did you see Edward?'

'I went past the shop, yes.'

'Did he seem worried about her?'

'No, why should he be? She's all right. Just a bit odd, really.'

'I'm afraid she has been a disappointment,' said Polly Harrison, no more than echoing Maud's first impression of her prospective mother-in-law. It occurred to neither Polly nor Bibi Harrison that Maud might have felt some disappointment on her own account. The Harrisons might even have appreciated some kind of argument or confrontation, as irrational people not infrequently do. But no one could fault Maud's good breeding, an additional cause of irritation. Mrs Harrison thought Maud's habitual calm 'put on', but was slightly afraid of her. For this reason her visits to London were announced with a full accompaniment of nervous symptoms, which were only allayed by a long tête-à-tête with her son over lunch, so that too little time was left for a visit to Tedworth Square. She would consent to drink a cup of tea with Maud, her eyes roving round the flat for signs of neglect. When she could find none she would return Maud's polite enquiries with an aggressive account of how well liked she was by her friends and neighbours.

'They often ask after you, Maud: we don't see you, do we? That has caused some surprise, I must say. Still, I'm not one to interfere. I thought Edward was looking rather thin, by the way. I worry,' she added, in a tone which adroitly matched concern for her son with regard for her own sensitivity. Maud said nothing, remembering how easily Polly Harrison was moved to tears. Even now the handkerchief was coming out. 'I don't say I'm lonely, Maud; I've got too many friends for that. It's just that I'm a worrier; it's my nature. I wish Edward lived nearer. If something goes wrong in the house it's not very nice for a woman on her own to ask for help. Only the other day I had to ask one of Bibi's friends to replace a washer in the kitchen.' The voice was now heartbroken. 'I think she's going to get engaged, by the way. Not that I'm keen on seeing her go. I shall be all on my own then. Well, I'd better be on my way, I suppose. Tell Edward to give me a ring tonight, would you?'

'You know I don't have to tell him.'

'Yes, well, I'm glad he still remembers his mother.'

When she had gone, leaving behind a disturbed scent of dislike and unease, which managed to penetrate the superficial layer of *Arpège* which they had given her the previous Christmas, Maud walked to her window and once again surveyed the leafless trees in the square, noted that her downstairs neighbour, the woman with the dog, was on her third outing of the day, and saw the sun struggling through the ever present mist only as a source of cold, for all its briefly combustible appearance in the lightless sky. She reflected, as she always did, that not once during their meeting had any enquiry been made as to her own well-being. This was now standard procedure, the manner in which Polly Harrison chose to convey her resentment. Maud's feelings were no longer hurt. She acknowledged the fact that she had failed to give satisfaction, but she also acknowledged the fact that to give satisfaction was to surrender her own life and allow herself to be remade in Polly Harrison's image. This she had never had any intention of doing. There was a slight additional loneliness in her increasing isolation from everyone but her husband, but her own calm good sense was there to remind her that she was not at home, that she had never expected to be at home, and that those who did not rely on their inner resources, as she had been obliged to do, were forever condemned to weep in other women's drawing-rooms, or to complain into the ears of friends who might not be displeased at this evidence of dissatisfaction.

Maud presented no surface which was permeable to her mother-in-law's attacks, to Bibi's well-meaning exasperation. Her solution to her very great sadness, which was never apparent, was, as always, to read. Here Edward was of very great help to her, continuing to find her books with women's names as their titles. In this way she read not only *Anna Karenina* and *Mme Bovary*, once the subject of her half-forgotten studies, but *Manon Lescaut, Effi Briest* . . . What she read confirmed her in her knowledge that love was a vital and terrible thing, that men and women die for it, that it is the lack of love that makes a woman desperate, but that the partners on whom she pins her hopes will not always meet her needs. Why should they? How could they? How could the conformist Vronsky take on a woman who had left her husband and child, or the seedy Rodolphe, who had never read a book in his life, understand Emma Bovary, whose notions of chivalry proceeded from a mind stuffed with romantic novels? The appalling lack of suitability in these pairings oppressed Maud, who wondered if all women suffered from this imbalance between their hopes and the reality they were forced to endure. It was all very well for Jean Bell to urge her to attend the lectures at the National Gallery ('You might meet someone'), she knew, as if she had been unalterably programmed to do so, that it was her destiny to live with the reality of her situation and to keep a closely guarded secret the fact that she had once defied reality, that she knew the difference between acceptance and danger, and that even as she went about her ordinary everyday tasks she would be filled from time to time with the incandescence of a certain memory, and the momentary conviction — or was it merely hope? — that that memory was shared.

Therefore the realisation that she was pregnant was something of an irony, although the version of reality that the situation proposed was certainly an improvement. Edward's delight, the welling of tears in his eyes, when she told him the news of her visit to the doctor, she privately dismissed as sentimental. She did not intend to be a sentimental mother; indeed the pregnancy made her think more kindly of her own mother and less kindly of Polly Harrison, who, she suspected, would have preferred her to be barren, as she had for so long suspected she might be. It was immediately and mutually decided that they must move to a bigger flat. Edward made enquiries in the modern building on the other side of the square, saw what he wanted, and bought it immediately, without even a telephone call to Maud. Prospective fatherhood had given him an authority that had not been there before; to his wife he appeared bigger, weightier, more able to make decisions. Again they were lucky: the previous owner wanted to sell everything, so that they moved into what was virtually a furnished flat, bigger and more spacious than the flat they were leaving, with higher ceilings, taller windows, built-in bookshelves on either side of a marble fireplace. To Maud it did not appear to be comfortable; she regretted her *chaise-longue*, left behind because there was no room for it, and made her way instinctively to the sofa, flanked by two brass-stemmed lamps, which she thought would give a good light for reading.

There was one change: a very large double bed in the spacious and formal bedroom. Since the bed was weighty and had been obviously expensive, and since it came fully furnished with a white padded rococo headboard and a white quilted counterpane, they accepted their altered state and settled down together quite naturally. Edward thought he had never been happier, although, waking in the night and feeling Maud's increasingly bulky body beside him, it did occur to him to regret the fact that his freedom was now truly gone, as were his dreams, that he would never again enjoy the sunlight in that remembered childhood garden, nor would he plan to travel the world, only to realise that he lacked the requisite courage. Now he too could look back selectively, recasting in his mind his solitary days in Paris, before the encounters which in their mysterious way had brought him to this bed. In his mind's eye he saw himself peering into a glass case in the Louvre at tiny secretive figures, saw the expression on his face as he gazed. He deplored his innocence at that time, but regretted it now that it had gone. Then Maud, who slept badly at this time, would turn over and lodge against him, and he would think how grateful he would have been for such an intimacy in the early days of their relationship, and how time occasionally respects one's wishes, but always with a significant alteration in what it delivers.

After the birth, which was perfectly normal, Maud was ill, with an unspecified illness which lasted for some months and which left her significantly weakened for a long time after that. A nurse had to be engaged to look after the little girl, at whose sight Maud often wept, the irruption of strong feeling proving too much for her. The nurse, a girl called Eve, proved a godsend, not only to the child but to Maud as well, and indeed to Edward; the presence of a third person relieved them of their preoccupations and proved useful at dealing with the child's respective grandmothers, who, on one fateful weekend, arrived simultaneously and gave conflicting orders. Polly Harrison was persuaded, with rather more tact than Maud could have managed, to retire, while Nadine was allowed to stay, but under strict supervision. This, oddly enough, she did not appear to mind, as long as she was allowed to watch, if not to touch, the baby. 'Ah,' she sighed, as she contemplated the dark head in the crook of Edward's arm, 'Ah.' Eve judged her superior to Polly Harrison, whose dislike of Maud spilled over into dissatisfaction with the baby, whom she found too thin, too dark (though the darkness was Edward's) and too placid. They could see that she did not know how to deal with these feelings, that her strongest desire was to distance herself from the whole event, and to blame Maud for the languid state into which she had fallen, thereby laying up any future condemnation of the child's behaviour at the mother's door. 'I don't think your mother's good for Maud,' said Eve to Edward, and he was obliged to agree. His own mother-in-law, whom he had never liked, now appeared to him in a far more favourable light, as she sat, humble and attentive, in the bedroom they had made into a nursery. Maud deduced that throughout her own childhood, which she remembered as austere, all that her mother had lacked was a language. She lacked a language for endearments even now, but there was no mistaking the love in her eyes, or the eloquence of her sighs.

'So that's where you get the habit of sighing from,' said Edward to Maud.

'I never heard her sigh before,' Maud replied. 'But then I never saw her so moved.'

Nadine alone addressed the child as Françoise: to her parents she was always Maffy. She was a calm competent child who seemed to have her own development well in hand. Under Eve's expert guidance she presented no difficulties in eating or sleeping: indeed she rapidly adapted to adult food, though she continued to have her meals in the room they designated as a playroom, although she was not much given to play, being of a staid disposition which took more readily to sensible walks, and eventually to school, which she attended early. Edward, in the strange awkward fits of exuberance which overcame him when his love for her could find no easy outlet, would sweep her into his arms and dance her round the room, singing, 'You're the tops, you're the Coliseum,' only to be immeasurably cast down when she wriggled free and stood within the protective circle of her mother's arms, judging him with eyes that were disconcertingly like Maud's own. Faced with what was palpably a rejection (or so it seemed to him) Edward tended to lose his head and accuse his wife of an infidelity which was more imagined than real, but none the less powerful for that. And Maud said nothing to rebut his accusations, perhaps judging them well deserved, but more often so atrophied by her strange illness that she no longer knew whether or not she had truly merited them. Her thoughts these days were more on the level of dreams, reveries: she left Maffy to Eve, read her Proust, took her walks. Sometimes, when she turned the corner of Tedworth Square and met Eve and the child coming home from school, an inexpressible pang of joy overtook her and she would run forward, her arms wide open. And the little girl would run to her with equal joy, although quick to disengage herself and run back to Eve, to continue the conversation to which Maud was only occasionally admitted. Nevertheless, as they proceeded home to tea, she would consent to hold their hands, and be quite content with them both.

Maud persisted in her state of languor, which the doctor

qualified as depression, for two or three years, although presenting few signs of illness. She performed her household duties as scrupulously as ever, providing excellent meals for the four of them, though she ate little herself. They were glad to keep Eve on as a safeguard, mainly to protect Maffy from her mother's dreaminess, although the child accepted this as entirely natural, and would sometimes lean against her mother's knee and turn the pages of her book, as if reading were her mother's true and only occupation.

'Depressed? What's she got to be depressed about?' Mrs Harrison would demand indignantly of her son. Privately she considered Maud to be mad. 'After all, she never fitted in,' she would say to those sympathetic friends of hers, for whom she now provided an agreeable serial story of her daughter-in-law's inadequacies. 'Pregnancy sometimes does that to a woman,' they assured her, unwilling to let the delightful subject drop. 'The hormones, you know. Has she seen a gynaecologist?'

'She only sees her own doctor. Not that he's done any good.'

'And I suppose the little girl will be coming down here for her holidays?'

'Oh, yes,' said Mrs Harrison unenthusiastically. To her own considerable shame she disliked the child. 'But I shan't have much time for her, now that I've got Bibi's wedding to prepare.' For Bibi was to marry a local dentist. Her wedding was the last occasion on which Maud accompanied her husband to Eastbourne. She wore a long flowered dress, which was judged inadequate, although her mother had sent it from France, and it became her wonderfully. To critical eyes, which had not seen her recently, she appeared neither older nor younger, and certainly not ill. It was when she escaped to the garden that lips were pursed and knowing glances were exchanged.

'You'd better go after her,' said Polly Harrison to her son.

'Why? She's fine. She's only got a bit of a headache.

Why don't you sit down, Mother? You're looking very flushed.'

His attitude to his wife at this time was one of helpless yearning, knowing himself to be incapable of piercing her armour of loneliness. One part of him rejoiced to see her so dependent on him, felt an uneasy pang of desire as he watched her drooping head, which straightened immediately when she felt his eyes on her. He made love to her ferociously these days, but the response he sought was not physical but emotional. Physically, she responded uncomplainingly, even with pleasure, but she said nothing, and he knew that her response was automatic, engendered only by nearness, and the dark, and the sleeping state from which he had roused her. He was rougher than he intended to be, longing for a cry, an endearment, a loving hand. But although, over the years, he had undoubtedly made her his wife, he felt that she remained distant, and that that distance was consciously or unconsciously maintained. None of his dissatisfaction was of the same order as his mother's: his own disappointments were more primitive, more secret, could be traced back to the rue Laugier and all that had transpired there. Nor did he ever stoop so low as to accuse her of seeing Tyler, in some fantasy concocted by himself and dependent for its strength on the fact that it too was a closely guarded secret. Indeed Tyler seemed to have vanished off the face of the earth. Sometimes, when the afternoons at the shop were particularly quiet, and Cook was out collecting review copies, Edward contemplated telephoning Tyler's advertising agency and suggesting a drink, only to draw back at the last minute. One day, a Friday, he actually made the call, to be told that Tyler worked in the New York office and had done so for the past two years. Was there any prospect of his coming back to London, he asked. They thought not; in any event he could be contacted direct on such and such a number. He made a note of it, then put the envelope on which the number was written into a drawer. Although he did not destroy it, he knew that he would never use it. He had learned what he had wanted to learn, that there were no meetings between Tyler and his wife. This was to him a source of both reassurance and regret.

In public, as they always were outside the bedroom, they behaved well. They entertained far more frequently than before, many of Edward's customers having become valued friends. Max and Nelly Kroll still came once a month, and now it was their turn to provide the chocolates and the candies to which they felt that all children were entitled. Maud, with her quiet ways and her high standards, was appreciated in this circle. She served excellent meals, and she was, despite her illness, or supposed illness (for they could see no trace of it), a beautiful woman. Her calm eyes looked across the candle flames at her husband with every appearance of deference; she intercepted his wordless questions gracefully, turned the conversation when it needed turning, overlooked no aspect of the fine and unobtrusive management which made these evenings such a success. Only Edward knew how dreadfully they tired her, as if she had undergone some form of necessary sacrifice. In the bedroom she would unclasp her pearls as if she were already in a dream, and would sit on the bed unprotesting while he loosened her dress. She would sink into sleep as readily as she had always done, and when he woke her in the night would adapt her body easily to his. At such moments he dreaded to hear her sigh. But her sighs were only for the daytime.

She accepted her strange condition, which threatened to become permanent, as an accurate reflection of her state of mind, which she saw as one of endless rumination, quite divorced from any thought of action. For this reason there were few outward manifestations of an abnormal state, no tears, no tantrums, no untoward appetites, only an immense fatigue, which she disguised with a half smile, thinking any allusion to it vulgar and unnecessary. She managed the formal part of her life successfully, so that none of Edward's business friends suspected her of anything more grave than a constitutional delicacy. If her mother had doubts about a hereditary illness she was strong-minded enough to keep them to herself, encouraged by the fact that Maud had never until now suffered any alteration in her health. With Eve in the background the household ran successfully: the little girl went to school, made friends, was encouraged to invite them home, and did so. It was not thought unusual to be given tea by the nanny. Since there was little for Eve to do as the child grew older Maud encouraged her to begin a fashion course, and afternoons would be spent in the calm of an otherwise empty flat, an emptiness which Maud, reclining on her sofa, did little to disturb.

Maffy grew used to her mother's quietness, less so to her father's love, which she sensed was both diffident and excessive. By the time Eve left, regretfully, she was largely able to take care of herself. She had inherited her mother's sense of order, was tidy, calm, and studious, although in looks she resembled her father, with her father's dark hair and slender build, and only her steady gaze unnervingly like her mother's. At the age of ten she was judged competent to spend her holidays alone at Eastbourne, although they telephoned her anxiously every evening to see whether she was happy. They were both relieved and puzzled by what they judged to be her stoicism, not realising that she felt nothing more potent than boredom. She was driven every morning to Bibi's house and instructed to play with Bibi's son William, aged three. She did not dislike William, or Bibi, or Polly Harrison, but she found them rather restricting. She looked forward to spending future holidays in Dijon with her other grandmother, whom her parents had taken her to visit, in Nadine's new flat in the rue Alphonse Ballu. Both the move and the family visit were an unexpected success. Nadine's former taciturnity had yielded to her new-found status as a family member: once she had satisfied herself that Maud was not physically ill, that Edward was prosperous, and that her granddaughter was apparently fond of her, she surrendered to an unusual sense of well-being.

At fourteen, at fifteen, Maffy thought it entirely natural to sit in the garden of the Château d'Eau with her grandmother, who passed her sections of the newspaper when she had finished with them and congratulated her on her French accent. On the way home there would be cakes in a tea-room. Grandmotherly status had restored Nadine to her former dignity. Her hair was now grey, her face innocent of the colours with which she had formerly enlivened it, and the gaze which fell on Maffy was attentive, no more, or so she liked to think. When she saw Maffy off on the train at the end of her summer holiday she felt a pain in her heart which was not merely organic (although there had been warnings, which she chose to ignore). She mentioned to Edward, with whom she was now on excellent terms, that it might be convenient for Maffy to go to university in Dijon.

'I couldn't bear to lose her for so long,' he confessed. But he did agree to letting her spend part of her year off with her grandmother.

'I only suggest it because good French is such an advantage,' said Nadine negligently.

Edward smiled. He had seen that noble face crumple when, as a small child, Maffy had fallen over and hurt herself. He did not begrudge Nadine her hunger, knowing how admirably she would always control it. And Maffy was no longer a small child, could return affection in such a way as to appease her grandmother's unknowable heart. Cautiously he began to consider whether his fears had not been exaggerated. His feelings were quite another matter. These, he knew, would never fall quite within the recognised boundaries. This knowledge too he managed to keep to himself.

14

So, seamlessly, their lives continued, at least to a less than observant eye. Maud's strange languor gradually improved. Edward, meanwhile, kept concealed certain changes taking place in himself. He did this out of a love fast threatening to turn to helplessness. He set himself the task of holding on until his daughter was old enough to leave home, by which time Maud and he would cling together, their frailties combined, with a sense of duties discharged. Privately, each had a warning of endings. Maud, still intermittently weakened by lassitude, sought and sometimes found solace in her books, her ordered empty life, although she would start up as if in fear when the silence of the afternoon threatened to overwhelm her, would go to the window to see if she could catch a glimpse of an absent sun, would will her daughter away from this sad place and out into the world and another life. She had no fears for her, knew that their communion was close, but longed to set her free. So might her own mother once have felt, she reflected, but to reflect on her own case was unwise: better by far to rejoice in Maffy's untroubled passage through adolescence, her wholly agreeable acceptance of adulthood. She had never expected to feel so confident, so detached, in the presence of so great a love. The experience was so astonishing to her that it merited all her spare moments of reflection. She tried to restrain her expressions of that love, and was successful: she saw where Edward blundered, and felt sorry for him. She had always felt sorry for him. This too was not a matter on which it was wise to reflect. She valued him, appreciated him, and even loved him, though not, she knew, in any way that would make him happy. She had reached an accommodation with her feelings, was not anxious to examine them, deliberately kept them out of sight. Her one success, she thought, was her daughter, their daughter. As for her husband, she hoped that she was mistaken in her perception of him as unhappy. She thought he seemed angry, despairing; Maffy's forthcoming absence would leave him desolate. He was if anything desolate already. There was a desolation in him which she could not reach. She wondered when it had begun to overtake him, wondered whether to blame herself, thought on the whole that this was not appropriate.

'Are you comfortable, Edward? You are frowning.'

'I'm fine, fine,' he would say, his eyes preoccupied. 'Where's Maffy?'

'At Sophie's house. She won't be late.'

'I don't want her to be late.'

'You will have to get used to it. Don't worry,' she would say, more and more often. 'It will be all right. She will only be in Dijon.'

'And then at Cambridge.'

'Did you think you could keep her here for ever?'

'I wanted to.'

'Come, Edward.'

'Oh, I know. I think I'll go out for a walk. You don't mind, do you? I've got a bit of a headache.'

'I don't mind, of course not.' She was bewildered. 'Won't you take something for it?'

'I just need some air. It's too hot in here.'

'Then open a window.'

'Leave it, Maud. I shan't be long. You go to bed. Yes, that's it. You go to bed.'

She watched with anxious eyes as he wound his scarf

round his throat and jerked his arms into his raincoat. She thought his movements hasty, exaggerated. She put a hand on his arm.

'She will love us more if we let her go,' she said. 'Whatever you feel — and I feel — is irrelevant, irrelevant to her, that is. You must not grieve for her, Edward. She'll come back, but only if you let her go . . . '

He pulled his arm away. 'Goodnight, Maud.'

She heard the front door shut, felt the first whisper of alarm. Then she slowly put the room to rights and went to bed. Thus she was not aware of his strange behaviour in the street, his uncertain walk, his shaking of his head as if to clear his vision, his hands clasping and unclasping in his pockets. She stayed awake until he returned, which was late. She heard him listen outside Maffy's door, then come to bed.

'She came home half an hour ago,' she reassured him. 'Did you enjoy your walk?'

'Yes, thank you.'

'Goodnight, then, Edward.'

'What? Oh, goodnight, Maud.'

In the dark he put up no resistance to what he thought of despairingly as his night thoughts. He loved his daughter as extravagantly as he loved his wife, and with, he knew, the same lack of success. The impossibility of being loved as he had hoped, as he had dreamed of being loved, began to play on his mind. Sleep deserted him; his headaches increased. He accepted that his daughter was as undemonstrative as her mother, whom she so closely resembled; what he could not accept was the fact that she felt for him only a steady affection, and not the rapture that he longed to inspire. If he searched his mind and his memory, as he so often did these days, when he felt so strange, he discovered yet again those images which seemed to have accompanied him for as long as he could remember. First among these was an impression of light and heat; then came a garden; then a spray of droplets iridescent in the summer sun. In the background was always the loved figure of his sister as a baby, and his urge to cherish and protect her. But now that his sister was older, she was somehow less lovable. She had married rather late, and had immediately taken on the caretaking properties of advanced wifemanship. 'I'm afraid my husband can't eat anything fried,' she might say, or 'Tim! I've warned you about going out without a jacket,' as if her husband, a moderately successful dentist, were incapable of thinking or answering for himself. It occurred to him now that the reason why he went to the Louvre every day, during that fateful sojourn in Paris, was to gaze at the Egyptian brother and sister, small, rigid, smiling through eternity, in the glass case that everyone passed by on their way to the Winged Victory. Those two small tense but contented figures, married to each other, appeared to have no fear of this world, or the next.

And that was what had escaped him: lack of fear. There was no need of complicated explanations. It was the look of calm-eyed plenitude on the Egyptian faces that had moved him. He himself could not recapture that original wholeness, first experienced in the garden of his childhood and restored to him in dreams, so that he remembered waking with a feeling of bliss. He had tried to read some spiritual message into those waking moments; for a time he had firmly believed in Wordsworth's clouds of glory. But now there was no choice; he had to experience those shades of the prison house by which he felt more and more constricted. It was not merely the headache that descended on him for most of every day. It was more likely to be the fact that he had tried, and failed, to strike an answering spark from both his wife and his daughter, who continued to be all that his rational mind could desire them to be, but who, he thought, could quite well live without him. If he should die unexpectedly soon (and he had secretly taken out additional insurance policies), he thought that they would not greatly notice his absence.

He envied his wife her apparent wholeness, thinking

her without guile. What she concealed from him was so little concealed; his imagination had always supplied what her words had never conveyed. Out of a sort of modesty they never referred to the past: his outburst, when he heard that Tyler had been present at Xavier's wedding, had been heated, certainly, but his feeling of jealousy related to the remote past rather than to the few days of her absence. He knew that she had not been unfaithful to him, that she would never deceive him. What doubt remained attached itself to a matter which he could not bring himself to discuss: her enjoyment of Tyler as a lover. And here his own dolorous excitement entered into the equation: that was why the matter could never be discussed. The proof that it was he who was at fault lay in his present state of doubt and disorder, as if both had grown throughout the years of a marriage which most would judge to be successful. And his wife, who was the principal victim of that original hurt, had matured into an apparent calmness which was denied to him. The very fact that it could find no place in his life put him on edge, caused him to grind his teeth. She would look at him wide-eyed, as if distressed for him, but, he could see, quite uncomprehending. He longed to shout at her, 'What do you feel? What did you feel? What did he do to you? How do we compare?' but would never do so. Thus he prolonged his own strange torment, which again he tried to infuse with some spiritual meaning. Was it loss of innocence? And was all innocence doomed to be lost? Apparently not, for Maud had not lost hers, and this was puzzling, for hers was the first defection, while he had been conscious of behaving 'well'. He remembered his brief glow of satisfaction in the rue Laugier: 'I have behaved well,' he had told himself. And yet that good behaviour had led to this despair, as if bad behaviour might have yielded better results.

But all this was in the past: the present was a wife whom he loved more hopelessly with every year that passed, and a daughter made in her mother's image, as if she had been immaculately conceived, only her dark colouring a polite acknowledgment of his paternity. As a child he had hoped to drown her with love, only to see her back away, frightened by his exuberance. Her attitude now was one of respect: she questioned him about the shop, about Cambridge, where she was due to read Modern Languages, but seemed uninterested in him as a person, whereas he had heard her ask her mother, 'Did you do this when you were young?' He thought that when she was older — and she was already extremely self-possessed — she would resemble the French side of the family completely, and he would be excluded all over again. His mother, who had made the connection long before he had, was now more open in her dislike, which overflowed onto Maffy herself. Polly Harrison, being a simpler, cruder character, had already made her adjustments: Bibi's son William received all her love, William's father having been judged sufficiently malleable to be entirely satisfactory. Every time Edward contemplated his nephew, during his increasingly rare visits to Eastbourne, he was convinced of the beauty and superiority of his own child. Something of the same conviction might have struck Bibi: her contact with Maud was now more intermittent than before.

'You were restless in the night,' Maud said to him. 'Should you see the doctor?'

'I don't need a doctor.'

'Nelly thought you were looking unwell. She thought you were pale. Are you pale, Edward?'

'I'm quite well. You're supposed to be the one who isn't well.'

'But I'm better,' she said, with some surprise. 'I hadn't noticed. I was so used to feeling odd, under a cloud, almost behind a pane of glass. That feeling seems to have vanished, quite suddenly. What do you think it was?'

'That doctor of yours called it depression. Depression is a form of anger, or so I've read.'

'I'm not angry.' She looked at him wonderingly. 'Why on earth should I be angry?'

'Maybe you were angry without knowing it. Maybe anger is merely undigested experience.'

She looked at him with her calm eyes, as if judging him to be a danger not to her but to himself. She went to the window and opened it wide. 'Look, the sun! It seems to be spring. Somehow we've managed to get through the winter. Maybe that's why I feel better.'

'If you say so.'

'Don't let us be on bad terms, Edward. We've always managed to be on good terms, haven't we? And now that Maffy is no longer at home so much it is even more important for us to be on good terms. Do you miss her so terribly?'

'Appallingly.'

'I can see that. I think I can bear it better than you, partly because we are so alike that I know what she is thinking. Now that she is with Mother in Dijon I have only to look back to know where she is going and what she is doing. When she is at Cambridge I shall truly feel that I have lost her. She will be closer to you then.'

'I doubt it. I've lost her already.'

'Don't say that. Can't you see how she looks up to you?'

'I wanted more than that.'

'But it is wrong for a father to want too much feeling from a daughter. Do you remember my friend Julie? Her father was always kissing and hugging her, and she hated it. It was all quite innocent: he was such a nice man. But he loved her too much. In the end she couldn't return his love. It was awfully sad.'

'Am I like that with Maffy?'

'No, of course not. You are impeccable. She is quite proud of you, you know.'

'But you are the one she wants to be with.'

'But of course. I'm her mother.'

'You say that with such pride.'

'I am proud,' she said quietly. 'I am proud because you have allowed me to be. My prospects were not good. I had none of the advantages that my mother thought indispensable for a girl who wanted to attract a husband. I can remember being a poor relation. Yet thanks to you I married and had a daughter who will never know any of this, and who has grown up beautiful and clever and good. Why shouldn't I be proud? And grateful to you.'

'Grateful!'

'What is wrong with gratitude? Why aren't you grateful? We are comfortably off, we have a handsome home (though strangely enough I preferred the other flat: perhaps we should move again?), a healthy child, and no worries that can't be dealt with. If only you could relax, Edward, stop grinding your teeth. It is grinding your teeth that gives you those headaches. Or used to. You've been better lately, haven't you?'

'Much better,' he lied.

'All you need is a mild sleeping pill. And Maffy will do well at Cambridge, and you can go and visit her, and take her out. You know it so well. I thought it a cold place. Beautiful, but cold. You will know her life as well as I know it now. It will be your life all over again.'

'I don't want my life all over again.'

'Then you had better make the most of this one. There are muffins for breakfast, and some of that apricot jam that you like.'

'You are feeling better, aren't you?'

'Yes, I am. I want to go out. I want to go for a long walk.'

'Walk with me to the shop.'

'That's not far enough. I want to go to the park.'

Her improved health removed her somewhat from his sphere of protection, and although he was pleased to see her active once more, he could not help regretting the fact that she was increasingly independent of him. She did indeed seem to have found a new faith in herself, and with it a new dignity, as if the ghosts of the past had left her undisturbed. He was glad that her doctor was old-fashioned enough to rely on bromides rather than to recommend any form of analysis: that, he knew, might have threatened her fragile unity, put her again in touch with more primitive impulses, with promptings now buried deep. He had reason to be grateful for her restored health, now that his own was under threat. When Maffy departed once again, this time to Cambridge, it was Maud who was the more competent, Maud who found him sitting on the bed in an attitude of utter dejection, and who talked him round into some sort of acquiescence.

'What will you do when she marries?' she asked, thinking to bring a smile to his face.

He looked at her bleakly, but said nothing, thinking, I shall not be here.

Gradually she took control, became the guiding partner. One year, two years passed, and they both survived. Maffy did not always come home in the vacations, and they tried not to mind. She had a lot of new friends; men found her attractive. Her lithe figure and her splendid eyes had earned her many admirers, and she was not averse to taking them seriously. Maud, who had some inkling of this, encouraged her to pursue her affairs away from home. The less Edward knew of them the better. She merely distracted him, with more dinner parties, more long walks. She saw to it that they took holidays, though neither of them really enjoyed them. She watched him covertly, but could see no dramatic change in him, being used by now to his unpredictable moods. He looked older, of course, complained of his back, as old people do. She herself was older, and the thought of making love was now faintly embarrassing. She went back to Proust, thinking she had been cast all along for a quiet life. Sitting on the sofa, at the end of a calm afternoon, when winter came round again, she too would think back to the past. A bad sign, she had always heard. Yet what she saw was herself sitting in the garden of the

Château d'Eau with her mother, the sun hazy. She could no longer imagine the sun as anything but hazy, all other suns having vanished without a trace, just as that prime mover had vanished. She no longer thought of him, at least not consciously. Nevertheless she wished that she could recapture something of that first splendour, which she remembered as part of her youth. When she looked in the mirror now, at the end of the day, she saw a handsome dignified woman, one whose youth it seemed impossible to imagine.

When Cook brought Edward home one evening, he merely said, 'He fainted,' but his eyes held hers in warning over Edward's drooping head.

'Edward,' she said, kneeling on the couch on which they had laid him. He made no response beyond straining to look at her, his eyelids heavy.

Perplexed, she turned to Cook. 'Has this happened before?'

'Once or twice.'

'Why didn't he tell me? Edward, why didn't you tell me?'

'I think he may have had a stroke of some kind.'

'But he is too young! Edward, can you tell me what happened? Could you ring the doctor, Tom? The number is on the pad.'

She turned back to her husband, held his hand, did not hear Cook on the telephone explaining to the doctor that Edward had been staggering a lot in the shop, knocking things over. 'He's been having headaches,' he added, not making known his own suspicions.

'I see. How's the wife taking it?'

'She doesn't know what's happening.'

But at last she did. When he tried to reach out a hand to her hair, and failed, when she saw his upper lip drawn back from his splendid teeth, and those teeth dulled by a gummy saliva, she clutched his hand, held it tight. 'Don't leave me, Edward. I can't live without you. Stay with me.'

She kept begging him to stay with her until she felt the doctor's hand on her shoulder. Cook, in the shadows, seemed uncertain as to whether he should remain there. Yet it was Cook who closed Edward's eyes.

'Brain tumour, by the sound of it,' said the doctor. 'Not that he consulted me about it. I'd have known what to do. Did he see anyone else, do you know?'

'I don't know,' lied Cook.

'I'll send someone round. There'll have to be a post mortem, I'm afraid. You'll stay with her?'

But she sent him away, and sat down on the sofa, in the space next to Edward's body. When that was removed, she continued to sit there, spending the night there, and the next day, and part of every day after that. When Maffy telephoned to say that she was thinking of becoming engaged, she merely said, 'Yes, do, darling. He would have been so pleased,' knowing that the opposite was true. It seemed important to her now to keep Edward's secrets, to keep faith with Edward. Gradually she began to neglect herself, summoning the strength only to assure her mother, who telephoned every evening, that she was well. She was, she thought, well enough. It was simply that she no longer wanted to eat, to go out. Sometimes, in the evening, she arranged some fruit on a plate, as she had done so many times for Edward. But mostly she read, and slept. Sleep continued to be her main resource, and her deliverance. She no longer minded being alone in the big bed. In those moments before sleep came, her mind was completely blank. 'Longtemps, je me suis couché de bonne heure,' she would repeat to herself, and when she slept it was deeply, and without dreams.

15

In the year following my father's death I both left Cambridge and broke off my engagement. (I am Maffy, called Mary by my friends.) I went home to be with my mother, although it was doubtful whether she found my presence a help. She was quite calm, but her air of inwardness, of preoccupation, increased. She remained tender but reticent, and when she urged me to find a flat of my own I could see that what she really wanted was a life without interference or communication. Although this worried me at first I thought her wishes should be respected. She never struck me as being in any sort of danger, and I knew that she had a strong character; I never saw her in tears or out of temper. I found a flat quite nearby, so it was easy for me to keep an eye on her, although as far as I could see she was not in need. She missed my father, of course, and she grew very thin, but I could see no immediate cause for concern. Her mind was as lucid as ever. Later on her reticence became more noticeable, so that in my presence she was polite but absent-minded. Again I did not attempt to distract her, merely sat with her, asked her what she was reading. Very occasionally her hand would steal out and take mine.

I believe that certain deaths are a form of suicide. That is how I explain my father's neglect of his illness, and my mother's slow descent into sleep, or into a state almost indistinguishable from sleep. My father's death was the greater shock, although my relations with him were not altogether straightforward. I loved him, but I was aware that he loved me more, and that embarrassed me. He felt the same way towards my mother, from whom I must have inherited my attitude. Sometimes he must have felt unhappy: in fact I am sure that he did. In a way it was a blessing that he died first, for without my mother I think he would have found it difficult to carry on with his life. I always got the impression that this life was something of a burden to him, and that, although he was devoted to my mother, he had no confidence that his devotion made her happy. Let us say that he had a romantic disposition. I have noticed that this preserves one; my father always struck me as a young man, but of course he was still quite young when he died, in his early fifties. I mean that he looked young, with his hair still dark, and also that he was impulsive and brooding, in strong contrast to my mother, who was always equable.

Her death, which overtook her by almost imperceptible stages, was caused by inanition. She ate little, went out less, then finally not at all. I let myself in with my key one Sunday morning, and found her on the sofa, her reading lamp still on. She looked very peaceful, so peaceful that it did not occur to me to grieve for her. When the formalities had been completed I telephoned my grandmother in Dijon (my other grandmother was in a nursing home on the south coast: Parkinson's Disease). She urged me to go to her in France, meaning to live with her permanently. But when I replied that I could not leave the shop, which I took over when my father died, she made me promise to spend my summer holidays with her and I agreed. I am very fond of her, and I know that she is lonely. Her grief over my mother's death has been protracted, and has aged her considerably. I think she feels something like guilt, although as far as I know my mother was always on good terms with her. It was not an effusive relationship: in fact there was a great deal of formality, but also a certain respect, exactly what I felt for my own mother, and what I hope my children, if I ever have any, will feel for me.

I sold the flat, my parents' flat, exactly as it stood, with the contents. I found that my mother had already disposed of my father's clothes, and indeed of most of her own. Her few pieces of jewellery, her birth and marriage certificates, a silk kimono, and a tiny notebook I put into a suitcase, which went into the back of one of my cupboards. I did not open the notebook until some time later, when I could bear to dispose of the pitiful relics she had left behind. What was particularly pitiful about the notebook was that all the pages except the first were empty, as if there were nothing to record. Only those few notations — 'Dames Blanches. La Gaillarderie. Place des Ternes. Sang. Edward' — around which I have constructed this fantasy, wishing to give my mother more substance than she left behind.

And it is a fantasy: I have no idea what any of it means. I recognise La Gaillarderie, because I have stayed there with my grandmother: a pretty house, resounding with the noise of Xavier's grandchildren. The two old ladies sit on the terrace, reconciled at last, while I walk and read. There is nothing mysterious about the place, no ghosts, no emanations. 'Dames Blanches' is particularly baffling. When I went to stay with my grandmother she was living in the rue Alphonse Ballu. If there is a rue des Dames Blanches in Dijon I have never found it. 'Dames Blanches' might also refer to a convent, which is more likely. My Larousse states that a Dame Blanche, in the singular, is a sort of diligence. Dame Blanche is also a comic opera by Boieldieu, and an order of chivalry 'pour la défense des dames et des demoiselles nobles', founded in 1399. On the other hand I have it in mind that a Dame Blanche is an ice cream confection, which would fit well enough; my mother had a sweet tooth, and might have remembered such a treat from her girlhood, if this is indeed a record of her life.

'Edward' is of course my father. All I know about the

Place des Ternes is that it is in Paris, in the seventeenth *arrondissement*. And '*Sang*' quite defeats me. It is my own perversity, and not only perversity, a desire to bring my dead back to life, that has made me link them together. All life is good, even if it is fictitious. And the lives of those we love must hold some meaning for us, and if that meaning is withheld, who can blame the survivor for his or her curiosity, even if that curiosity holds as much mourning as celebration?

I may sell the shop next year, when Cook retires. He is still quite young, but he says he wants to go round the world while he is fit and active. He will be quite comfortably off: I have seen to that. He tells me that my father always wanted to travel, although he never did; the circumstances were never quite right. If I sell the shop I may travel myself, or I might move out of London and start again. But in fact I shall go to Dijon and keep my grandmother company until she dies, and not decide until then. Women now are so free that it seems ungrateful not to enjoy that freedom. In my bag I keep my mother's notebook, with its mystifying code. Codes are meant to conceal secret information, of course. I think it entirely fitting that my mother, who may or may not have had secrets, should have declined to explain herself. There is no virtue in confession, although it is said to be good for the soul. I am inclined to favour indirection, which has its own power. If I labour the point it is because I am still in search of that hidden life, those hidden lives. The past, as Proust makes clear, and at considerable length, is always with us. In that sense nothing is lost.

But it is also true that most lives are incomplete, that death precludes explanations. How then can one not be intrigued by the unfinished story? I too read the obituaries in the *Figaro* these days, and find myself nodding in agreement with the pious platitudes and humble evocations. 'Le soir venu, Jésus leur dit, "Passons sur l'autre rive." ' I too like to think of the dead as being comforted. For my own part I am fairly tough. But that notebook serves as a reminder. Its lesson — that any notation, any record, is better than none — tells me that life is brief, and also that it is memorable, that the trace it leaves behind is indelible. And if the trace is inscrutable, this too may be appropriate. The dead, perhaps even more than the living, have a right to their mysteries. And who knows? We, the survivors, may be called upon to explain them, if only to ourselves.